Totally Bound Publishing books by
Catherine Curzon & Eleanor Harkstead

Single Books
The Colour of Mermaids
The Man in Room 423

The de Chastelaine Chronicles
The Ghost Garden
The Glass Demon

The de Chastelaine Chronicles

THE GLASS DEMON

CATHERINE CURZON &
ELEANOR HARKSTEAD

The Glass Demon
ISBN # 978-1-83943-994-0
©Copyright Catherine Curzon & Eleanor Harkstead 2021
Cover Art by Erin Dameron-Hill ©Copyright June 2021
Interior text design by Claire Siemaszkiewicz
Totally Bound Publishing

THE
GLASS DEMON

Dedication

CC & EH — We're raising a glass to all our readers, whether demons or not.

Chapter One

They'd been travelling since early that morning, and Cecily had wrapped herself up in a blanket to keep warm in Raf's rattly Austin 7. A frost was silvering the landscape when they had set off but once the sun had pushed above the hills and its light had strengthened, the earth had emerged from under its icy crust.

Cecily had never been to Yorkshire before, and certainly never to Acaster Garrow. It almost seemed like a fable whenever Raf mentioned it, and their journey from Devon had been such a long one that Cecily had been half-convinced they'd never arrive.

But eventually Cecily noticed a change. Seagulls swooped overhead and the air took on a briny tang. And once they'd crested a hill, Acaster Garrow was laid out before them, as vivid as a drawing in a child's book.

Beyond the clustered white cottages and little fishing port and the pointed spire of the church was the wide-open expanse of the sea, gentle waves lapping over its surface and washing against the edge of the sandy beaches. Fishing boats bobbed on the horizon, a little welcoming committee for the returning hero and his new companion. This was her home now, a place where she would love and be loved.

"Smell that fresh air," Raf declared with a merry smile, drawing in a deep breath. Trapped in the school that had been her prison, Cecily had never seen anyone actually look happy to be home, but she knew that she was seeing it now. "And there's the sea!"

Cecily gasped. "It's beautiful. It's so beautiful, I've never seen *anything* so beautiful before! Where's your house, Raf? Can we see it from here? Will you show me? Show me *everything!*"

The car puttered to a halt and Raf peered out through the windscreen. When he turned his glittering gaze on Cecily, she felt once more that almost overwhelming surge of love for him that had become her balm and blanket, her comfort when she had thought all hope was gone. They had saved each other in so many ways.

"Right, Miss Sissy Pincombe," he said. "We can see my house plain as the nose on my admittedly handsome face. But which one could it be? What's your guess?"

Cecily sat forwards on her seat, her nose almost pressed up against the windscreen. She squinted, and as she did so her vision blurred and the village turned into a daub of colour — the many greens of the trees and grass, the grey stone and the darker grey sea. And —

Cecily shot back in her seat in surprise. She opened her eyes and pointed down into the valley below them. "There — isn't *that* your house? All those flowers, all those reds and purples and yellows!"

A blossoming garden in the creeping autumn cool. It can only be Raf's house.

"That's it! Our little nest. The de Chastelaine family pile!"

Little? Hardly.

Set a short way outside the village, with its kaleidoscope of a garden ending in the cliff edge, Cecily could see a large, rambling stone house. It was just as she had seen it in her mind when Raf had asked her to use her powers as a sensitive to picture it. It had huge chimneys and a long tree-lined drive, and although it was not more than three storeys high it was wide, which gave it an open, welcoming aspect. The curl of smoke rising from one of the chimneys put her in mind of a cosy fire and she shivered with anticipation. She was coming home.

No wonder I thought it was a hotel when I pictured it.

And all those flowers, and — *surely it can't be blossom, not at this time of year* — but from where Cecily sat, she was certain Raf's garden boasted fruit trees covered in white and pink fluff. *A very particular sort of fruit tree*, Cecily decided.

And in that garden she'd plant the lavender cutting she'd brought from Devon, though it would seem a paltry little thing next to all those flowering giants.

"What do you think?" Raf asked, his voice filled with the same excitement that Cecily felt at the sheer sight of the place. "It's missing a bit of southwest lavender and a gorgeous chatelaine called Sissy, but apart from that it's a nice old place."

"I'm in love with it already!" Cecily put her arm around Raf and rested her chin on his shoulder. "You're such a clever gardener. How do you get your garden to look like that in the autumn?"

"Transylvanian magic!" *That's probably true.* Raf turned his head and kissed Cecily's nose. "Ready to go home?"

"Yes!" Cecily clapped her hands. Then she bit her lip, suddenly shy. "Sorry, darling... I don't mean to carry on like an irritating child..."

"Is that a joke? That'd better be a joke." He reached up his hand and rested it on Cecily's cheek. "You've got years and years of fun and silly and being loved to make up for. I love you, Sissy. You can be as excited as you like!"

"As long as you're sure you don't mind?" Even if she and Raf were in love, Cecily had spent so long with a husband who had been indifferent to her at best that she still wavered. Sometimes she forgot she could be herself now, beholden to no one.

Raf shook his head. Then he grinned, showing those sharp canines that were a clue to his rather unusual heritage. "You're free. And you're now one half of Britain's foremost *spiritual operative* team. You're a woman to be reckoned with!"

Cecily sat up straighter in her seat, but she was still a little unsure. It was such a welcoming scene yet she still felt trepidation. She shouldn't, but she could only think her unease stemmed from the prospect of being around new people in an entirely different environment from what she had known before. "And the people in Acaster Garrow, they won't mind you've brought me home?"

"You're joking? They'll probably throw a party!" With that, Raf's car set off down the hill and they continued on the final leg of what had been a monumental journey. With Raf's sprawling home in sight Cecily felt nothing but a wonderful sense of homecoming, of belonging in a place she had never even seen except in her mind's eye. The few people they passed welcomed Raf with a wave or a cry of greeting or, in the case of an elderly man on a bicycle and a younger man fitting a gate to a pasture, a signal that clearly meant they were due a catch-up in the pub.

"How will I ever meet everyone? And remember their names?" Cecily laughed awkwardly. "Is there a fête? Maybe I could win them over with my biscuits."

"Don't worry about winning folk over. We're a nice bunch," he assured her as the car rolled to a halt before a pair of tall and elaborate wrought-iron gates. In them she saw flowers and leaves, intricate boughs on which birds perched and—Cecily smiled—from which slumbering bats hung by their toes. "If you want a fête, we'll have a fête. Anything for my lass."

Cecily stared at the gates. Their home lay beyond. "Do you ever have garden parties? Perhaps we could throw one? I'd love to meet the people in your village."

"I love a party!" Raf climbed from the car and opened the unlocked gates before joining her again. "Shall we have a *Welcome Sissy* party?"

"Maybe!" Cecily grinned. Up ahead she could see the roofs of Raf's house. *Their* house, she reminded herself. *Their vast house*, in fact. Though autumn had by now taken hold of the land, the lawns on either side of the driveway were verdant and the flowers still blossomed in every colour of the rainbow. The house could have been imposing but instead it already felt homely, as welcoming as Raf's arms.

As Raf piloted them up the sweeping driveway and the house grew nearer through the trees, she was surprised she had thought it could have been a hotel when she'd first spied it from the hill above the village—it was a happy home, she could sense it.

"Home at last!" The car drew to a halt and Raf finally turned the engine off. Cecily's attention was drawn to the large door, dominated by an ornate door knocker in the shape of a single monstrous, reptilian eye. "Shall we get the kettle on?"

"*Please*, I'm gasping!" Cecily turned to Raf with a beaming smile. Then she paused. "Is there tea? And is there anything in for dinner? I can rustle up something from tins, and maybe if you have a vegetable patch too I can pick some potatoes or carrots, and perhaps—"

Cecily stopped herself. She didn't need to be nervous about going into her own home. And she was no longer shackled to a husband who pilloried her for the tiniest housekeeping mistake.

"There's tea and there's probably something to eat. If there isn't we'll nip down the pub and see what's cooking. There's always at least a pie," Raf told her. This was life now, a world where there was nipping to the pub and holding parties and not worrying about every speck of dust. Raf helped Cecily from the car but this time he handed her what looked like an ancient key. "I'll grab the bags in a bit. Captain, would you do the honours and unlock your home?"

Cecily gladly took the key. When she closed her eyes a multitude of faces whirled by her as if they were on a fiendishly quick carousel, men and women, in bonnets, ruffs, cravats, tricorns and hoods, leaving their mark through the centuries. People who had once held that very same key and, like Cecily, called this house their home.

She went up the low stone steps to the front door, and with one last look around her—at the large windows and the abundant garden—she put the key in the lock and turned. The old, heavy door creaked open and as it swung wide Cecily blinked at the sight of her new home.

And the door knocker blinked back.

Of course it didn't. How could it?

But it did.

"Welcome to your new nest," Raf announced. "I hope you'll love it here."

"I already do, I—" Cecily glanced back at the knocker. It was unmoving, but somehow she sensed it watching her. "Where *did* you find that?"

"Do you like him? Great-granddad a few times over got him from John Dee in a card game." Raf closed the door. "He keeps an eye on the place."

"As long as he's friendly!"

Cecily sighed happily and leaned back against the front door, not quite able to believe that they were finally here. And almost in one piece. She glanced around the hall, unsure what to look at first. The place was bursting at the seams with what she assumed was Raf's collection of artifacts and bric-a-brac gathered on his journeys around the world and brought back to assume a space beside the ephemera his family had left in the house before him.

"You certainly have a lot of…*things*."

"That's true." He laughed. "Lots and lots of things!"

"Is the whole of your house like this?" Cecily stared at an antique taxidermied owl inside a glass dome which stared back at her. Although unlike the eye on the door, it didn't blink.

"Not all of it." Raf slipped his arms around Cecily's waist. "Some of it's cluttered!"

The parts of the wall that Cecily could see were wood-panelled, peeping out from behind a suit of armour, what looked like flags or sailcloth, decorated shields, umbrellas, netting, scattered footwear, a brass elephant, half-unpacked tea crates, a tennis racket in need of restringing, framed portraits and landscapes in oils and watercolours, spears, a dented violin, a small Egyptian casket and objects that Cecily had never seen before in her life. Just what purpose did that ornately carved and clearly ancient stone disc have, with its square-featured face at its centre, its tongue poked out as if it didn't appreciate her staring? Just how many generations of de Chastelaines had contributed to the array of random items in the house?

Cecily planted a kiss on Raf's cheek. "I can't tell you how glad I am to see such a mess — it's brilliant!"

"Honest?" He widened his eyes, teasing her. "You're not going to produce a duster and tell me to get tidying? It's spotless though, that much I can say for sure."

"It doesn't feel dusty, that's true." Cecily peered into the knight's visor, then stepped away. This was the sort of house where someone might peer back.

"That's because of the lovely lady who takes care of me and *might* still be here but might've tactfully gone home even though she's desperate to get a look at you." He spun Cecily across the floor in an impromptu dance. "The house likes you!"

"It *feels* happy here!" Cecily laughed. "And I can't wait to meet your housekeeper either! Now, let's see...kitchen this way? There's a lot of joy in the kitchen, I think..."

But Raf was standing very still, his nose twitching as he turned his head this way and that. For a moment Cecily's heart leapt with trepidation, then he gave a little smile and whispered, "I smell...carbolic soap. So Mrs Hodge is here. And beer and perfume and — " He wrinkled his nose and fanned his hand in front of it. "The trawlermen've been gutting fish! But even *I* shouldn't be able to smell that — What do you sense?"

"A crowd." Cecily reached for Raf's hand. "Is your house *very* haunted? Only...there's so many of them!"

"Those aren't ghosts!" Raf entwined his fingers with Cecily's and together they approached a closed door. He kissed her cheek then threw the door wide open with a cry of delighted excitement.

Cecily tottered back in surprise because there in front of her was a room crammed with people. Complete strangers, all cheering, waving a home-painted banner on a sheet of canvas that said *WELCOME HOME!!*

"Erm..."

Cecily grabbed Raf's arm and tried to hide behind him, but being a few inches taller than him, she knew she must only have made herself look absurd.

"Look at you, you daft whatsits!" Raf laughed as he looked at the assembled faces. "I've missed the lot of you!"

But every gaze was on Cecily. And in those gazes she saw such happiness, such joy, that it tugged at her heart. They weren't judging her or sizing her up—this gathering was a welcome for her as much as for their returning hero.

Cecily gave the crowd a tentative wave. There were women in their housecoats, fishermen in their smocks, one or two ladies in coats with fur collars and one or two gents in pinstripes, the milkman, and men in their battered best clothes, children balanced on hips and—last but not least—a vicar.

Cecily stood self-consciously on the old, uneven flagstones in her new heeled shoes, trying her best not to look as gawky and awkward as she felt. "Hello, everyone," she said.

"This is Miss Cecily Pincombe," Raf told them. "My business partner. And my sweetheart, in case any of you saucy Yorkshiremen are plotting a wooing!"

Raf was met with laughter from some quarters and knowing looks from others.

"Pleased to meet you." Cecily executed a careful curtsey and someone cooed an *awww*.

As she straightened up a woman stepped forwards and gave a little curtsey of her own. As plump as a pudding and even shorter than Raf, the lady wore a coat and neat hat upon which a rather fancy collection of fruit was perched.

Fresh fruit, Cecily realised.

"Mrs Hodge!" Raf threw his arm around the lady. "Sissy, this is Mrs H, the world's finest housekeeper. Mrs H, this is Sissy, the de Chastelaine chatelaine!"

"I've heard so much about you, Mrs Hodge." Cecily tried to still her nervous tremble as she held out her hand to Raf's housekeeper. But she didn't sense any animosity in Mrs Hodge, just warm kindness.

"Call me June," Mrs Hodge said in rather proper tones, as though she were addressing a senior member of the royal family. "And don't listen to anything that one tells you about me, he's full of mischief."

"I had noticed!" Cecily grinned at Raf. "I do hope you won't change anything with me being here — I would hate to spoil your routine. I like to bake but I won't get in your way, and I'm very tidy. I always clear up after myself, I promise."

"Ha! Good luck with tidy and Rafael in the house!" But the look on her face was nothing but affectionate indulgence and she shook her head. "Well, you're welcome here, love. You don't worry about my routine, I'll fit in with you. The larder's stocked with enough to feed an army — or one Rafael. And if he's told you he's no good in the kitchen, he's not lying. Happen it's time you had a few lessons, young man, Miss Pincombe hasn't come here to wait on you!"

"Dad said this would happen. Ladies gang up, he told me!" Raf laughed, earning a supportive nod from the men in the room. "I see it all now!"

"Well, I'm glad to see you back, lad, and with such a lovely girl on your arm," Mrs Hodge replied, having clearly forgotten her theatrical voice in favour of a rather more natural Yorkshire one. "We've all been wondering about the pair of you!"

"Raf's been looking after me," Cecily told her. "And he had a scrape, but—all's well. All's *very* well."

"And your father's written this very morning," Mrs Hodge said. "He's in Morocco of all places, says to tell you he'll be home after Christmas and he'll call in to meet his lovely new daughter-in-law to be."

Cecily heard someone clear his throat close beside her and she glanced up to see the vicar. Now he had approached and beyond his dog collar, she could see he bore a striking resemblance to Raf. He had the same bright blue eyes and dark hair, the same small stature. But unlike Raf, Michael's hair was tidied and pomaded, and there was something of the cloisters about him, as if he rarely went outside.

"Reverend Michael!"

He nodded. "Welcome to the village, Miss Pincombe. And my dear brother, home again!"

Michael clasped Raf in a tight hug and a stream of quick Romanian filled the air. As they parted Raf took his brother's face in his hands and kissed him once on either cheek. A look passed between them, as though Michael was checking that his brother really *was* safely returned to him. He alone knew the full story of what had happened on that last night at Whitmore Hall, of the vines and the devil who had lurked among them. Cecily knew that Michael alone shared the secrets of the Hall because she had taken down Raf's letter for him, saving him the struggle with penmanship that his word blindness presented.

"Home at last," Raf told him with a beaming smile. "And in one piece."

"My prayers have been answered," Michael said, his accent devoid of Raf's Romanian twang. He sounded like some of the teachers Cecily had known at Whitmore Hall. "You look well after that long journey of yours, both of you."

"We travelled the scenic route," Raf admitted. It had been a scenic route that included a good many cosy inns and comfortable beds. "Sissy, *this* is Mike! I know you know that, but I'm doing things sort of properly."

"Welcome to the family." Michael gave Cecily an assessing glance. Then he whispered something to Raf.

'What a lovely lass.'

"Lass? I'm a lass?" Cecily chuckled. She'd picked up Raf's thoughts again, like hearing a distant voice through static on the wireless.

Michael glanced at Raf, surprised and somewhat flustered. "Erm… That is to say, a lovely lady…"

"*My* lass. With…*serious* hearing skills. You don't even have to speak and she hears it." Raf put his arm around Cecily's waist, but she knew there was nothing but love in his tease. Her late husband had believed her to be his possession. To Rafael de Chastelaine, the dhampir with Transylvanian and Yorkshire blood in his veins, she was an equal. "Where's Mim?"

"Mim? She's elbow-deep in her Women's Institute jam-making," Michael said. He clasped his hands together, a pious gesture which Cecily supposed came second nature to him, given his calling. "She sends her best, and she'll be over to say hello later. And bring some jam, too. She makes excellent jam, Miss Pincombe."

"Please call me Cecily."

Michael nodded. "Then I will—Cecily."

"Give her our best." Raf grinned and Cecily realised that his brother didn't have *the* teeth. Only normal teeth. "I'm sure you'll be nipping up to sample her jam!"

"I shall indeed, but—now look, will I be reading the banns on Sunday? Mim has been talking about doing your wedding flowers, but you haven't mentioned a date..." Michael's hands were still clasped, his voice still gentle, but his knuckles had whitened. He raised an expectant eyebrow and glanced back and forth between Cecily and Raf.

"Just like a vicar!" laughed a tall, wiry man with a luxuriant black beard as he slapped his hand on the reverend's shoulder. He looked like a fisherman, Cecily decided, in his cap and sweater. "Let's have a party first and talk weddings later!"

A cheer went up around the kitchen and Raf told his brother, "Don't you fret, vicar, we'll be good!"

As drinks were poured and cake sliced, Cecily smiled and said hello and tried to remember everyone's names, but she heard Michael's voice through the hubbub as he said to Raf, "And you'll come to the church as soon as you can? I don't mean for a wedding. It's just that there's *something* I need you to see."

"Is it an important something?" Raf took a sip from his bottle of dark brown ale. "A tomorrow something or a today something?"

Michael leaned closer to Raf and whispered, rather loudly, "*Today.* I had no wish to worry you during your convalescence, but...there's something rather bad, I fear, in my church, and that'll never do."

Raf glanced back at Cecily and smiled, but she knew him well enough to know that he would go. And she would love him all the more for it. "Then I'll come over later. What time will you be there?"

Michael took his watch from his waistcoat pocket and tapped the face. "Six o'clock."

"Whatever it is, we'll sort it," Raf promised him. He patted Michael's arm. "Don't worry."

Michael spoke to him in Romanian again, a farewell, Cecily supposed. He waved to her as he hurried out of the kitchen and was gone. Before Cecily could say anything to Raf, she had a glass in one hand and a plate of cake in the other and Mrs Hodge was introducing her to everyone. Raf was never far away from her in the kitchen, just as he had stayed close as they journeyed from the south-west to the far-flung North Yorkshire coast. Not watching and policing, but simply being near. They had become bound to each other in the most wonderful way, lovers, *in* love, dipping into shops and restaurants, hotels and guest houses on their adventure, not so much learning to be a couple as discovering that it was simply an instinct.

And sometimes, when Cecily was least expecting it, a little bat would swoop down and sit on her shoulder.

Chapter Two

Just before six o'clock, Cecily and Raf headed for St Anastasia's, Acaster Garrow's ancient parish church. The tower, with a spire as pointy as a witch's hat, poked up above the old, gloomy trees surrounding it. As soon as they drew near enough for the lychgate and the tombs in the churchyard to be seen in the glow from a solitary streetlight, Cecily's breath was almost stolen from her.

Not in awe at the sight of a magnificent old building, although the church seemed far too big for a village the size of Acaster Garrow, but because something was very wrong. She felt it like a cold breath at the back of her neck, spreading through her veins like ice.

She hadn't experienced such a sensation since she'd been at Whitmore Hall. Evil thrummed through the atmosphere even in this quiet, rural place, a malevolence as heavy as lead that seemed to make the air shiver with rancour.

And as they came through the gate she heard it, beating against her skull, rattling her teeth — a dull thud sounding over and over, on and on and on.

"Can you hear that?" Cecily whispered to Raf.

He paused and cocked his head to one side as Cecily waited for him to tell her that yes, of course he could. He could hardly *fail* to hear the incessant thump, thump, thump — little wonder that Michael wanted to speak to him about it.

Raf shook his head. "What can you hear?"

"That thudding noise, over and over and over again." Cecily shivered. The cold night and the uneasiness around them made her turn up the collar of her new velvet coat. "Like someone hammering in a post — or someone knocking on a door and not giving up when there's no answer."

"A thudding noise." He listened again, but Cecily already knew that he wouldn't hear it. And that wasn't a good sign. "How fast would you say? How loud?"

"Like this…" Cecily rapped against the wooden upright of the lychgate. *Tap-tap-tap-tap. Tap-tap-tap-tap.* "Like that. It's not giving up. It isn't terribly loud, it isn't making the ground shake, but — *tap-tap-tap-tap…*"

Raf took a deep breath. He slipped his arm through Cecily's and asked, "Got your *cocosul?*"

"Of course, it's right here." Cecily patted her chest where the protective charm bearing the cockerel rested. Raf had made it as a child, painting on the cockerel's bright feathers with his mother, and Cecily always wore it.

He kissed her cheek, the rasp of his evening stubble ticklish against her skin. It was one of the sensations she would always associate with him now, and it usually accompanied a kiss or several.

"Let's go in and see if we can find the thumper," Raf said. "The sooner we do, the sooner I can show you our bedroom!"

Cecily ruffled his hair. She shouldn't fixate on the malicious presence here, not when they were celebrating their first night in their home. "Oh, Raf, you saucy fellow—Mrs Hodge told me she's made a room up for me. Though I must admit, I don't intend to sleep in it!"

Above them the clocked chimed the hour.

"She knows that, but she also knows that a lady should be treated like one." He kissed the tip of Cecily's nose and she saw the moonlight glittering in his eyes. "Even if she's living over the brush with a sometime-bat."

As they headed up the path to the church door, the malevolence growing stronger at each step she took, Cecily distracted herself. What would she find in their bedroom back at the house? A tiny bat-perch by the bed? Or did Raf, when not living in the masters' accommodation of a school or staying in a hotel, sleep in a velvet-lined coffin?

And were there such things as doubles?

The door creaked open as if it had done so of its own accord, and all thought of bedrooms fled her mind.

Cecily stepped back in alarm but Michael stuck his head around the door and beckoned them in.

"I do appreciate this, Raf—and Cecily. Do come in. I know it isn't usual for you to carry on consultancy work for the family, but I haven't a clue what can be done."

"Mike, can you hear thumping?" Raf stood back to let Cecily enter ahead of him, ever the gentleman even now. "Sissy can hear it but she's got a talent that I lack.

Well, lots of them. But this one's for hearing things that other people don't."

"*Thumping?*" Michael shook his head. He gestured them to follow him. "No, I don't know about that. But it might explain why when I put water in the font it ripples and upsets the babies. *And* why there's a terrible draught."

And the thumping had grown louder now that they were in the church. Cecily forced herself not to clap her hands over her ears. It would make no difference if she did—she would still hear it deep inside herself.

She took in the neat ranks of pews, the abundant floral arrangements, the memorial plaques on the walls and the colourful coats of arms on the high wooden ceiling. There was even a Byzantine icon of the Madonna and child above the votive candles, which was unusual for an Anglican church, but fitting for a vicar who was half-Romanian. It was a cosy church, not an austere, unfriendly place at all, and certainly didn't seem to be the natural home for that insistent, dogged thumping. But there was definitely a draught, a chill which skittered and moved as if it were a live thing, and it seemed out of place at St Anastasia's.

"Yes, thumping, like this—" Cecily beat the tattoo against the back of the nearest pew. "It's louder inside than out."

Even for the hour, the church seemed oddly dark and as Cecily turned on her newly shod heel, she saw why. Above the altar, dwarfing it with its sheer size, a heavy crimson curtain covered the east window. It was a vast thing, falling like a velvet fog to skim the floor, shrouding the church in shadows.

And the banging was coming from behind it.

"Bloody hell!" Raf touched his fingertips to his lips and gave an impish shrug of apology. "Sorry, vicar.

Sorry, God! What's that bloody curtain doing here? It looks like a knocking shop!"

Michael sagged, looking suddenly tired. "I should not be surprised, I suppose, that the views of a humble parson are ignored by a bishop. Quite how the Archbishop of Exeter can hold sway *here* over the Archbishop of York I do not know, but...I now have a curtain that looks like something from a malodorous side street because behind it is a brand-new window. Well, new to us, at least." Michael clasped his hands, pious once more. "You will have heard of the cathedral of Kwaalveld?"

Cecily slowly shook her head. The thumping and the oppressive atmosphere were giving her a headache, and in desperation she gave in and put her hand over one ear, hoping it would silence the thudding. But still it went on, dull and muffled.

"It's in Belgium," Michael replied. "Famous for its windows. But when war came the windows were all taken out from their settings, every last one, and were packed away until peace came. And as a gift to the nation from our Belgian friends, St Anastasia's has been chosen to receive one of the windows." Michael paused and waved his arm towards the curtain. In a quiet voice, almost as if he were talking to himself, he said, "Yet I did not want the window here, although no one listens to a parson... It is an extraordinary piece of art, and I am told I should be exceptionally grateful to have it here, but there's something about it that I really do not like at all."

"Can we see it?" Raf thrust his hand into the pocket of his jacket and wandered up the aisle towards the curtain, escorting Cecily along beside him. "When I was over in Belgium, I had a flit about when they were whipping the windows out. Seemed like a queer business but I'm not Belgian, so I'm not one to judge."

Michael hurried after him, almost skidding over on the well-kept carpet. "Please, Raf—no, you mustn't. The curtain can't be opened, there's no way to open it until the big day. The dedication ceremony will be a grand reveal. Exeter doesn't want any Acaster locals taking a peek in advance of the ecclesiastical nobs he's invited."

"What about outside then? What've they done, boarded it up?" Raf peered up at the shroud of velvet and Cecily knew that he was keener than ever. "And it'll be too close and too dark to see from behind the curtain. Because I know you've tried, Mike."

"It *is* boarded up outside. No one can see it—there's only a gap at the top where one might peek, and...and..." Michael clasped his hands, a blush illuminating his pale cheeks. "One would need the power of flight for that."

As Raf quirked one eyebrow, Cecily had no doubt that he wouldn't be convinced out of his desire to see the window now. And she'd quite like to see it too, though there was no *power of flight* for her.

"And not be a massive, showy big bat." Raf cocked his head to one side and looked at his brother. "You'd need a little wee bat for that job. The sort of little wee bat that used to get teased by his big brother."

"You *are* a very tiny bat, Raf. You laughed at *me* for being so *big*," Michael said. He stretched out his arms and gave a reluctant flap. "And I'm a clumsy flier— dash it, but I broke another teapot at home the other week."

Raf looked at Cecily, who was already wondering when living with a sometime-bat had become so marvellously normal. But it was, because he was just

Raf to her. He said nothing, but she knew he was waiting for the go-ahead.

Cecily took Raf's hand. "Raf's ever such a nimble bat. He could have a look. And he might discover whatever's making this hellish noise."

"As long as no one will know — I'm very uneasy about it." Michael shuddered. "Do you feel that draught? Perhaps one of the panes is loose and it's nothing more sinister than that. After all, it is a rather old window. Only...only the flowers on the altar wilt and a terrible pong rises up from them, like something old and rotten..." Michael trailed off. He looked pained for a moment as if wrestling with something intense. Then he apparently overruled it as he said, "Oh, do fly up there, Raf! We're under the auspices of York, not Exeter. But do try not to be too *naked* when you turn back. This *is* a house of God!"

"He won't mind!" Raf assured them. "Where should I change? Right here's fine by me, but you're the vicar..."

Michael glanced down the aisle to the door of the church, then up at the enormous, louche curtain. "Mim's already been in for organ practice — I'm not expecting anyone else this evening. You may as well do it here as anywhere else, although I do hope Cecily won't be too shocked. We are, however, made in the Lord's image, so he oughtn't to complain."

"Nothing he hasn't seen before, I reckon. And nothing he won't see again." Raf lifted the tangle of charms he wore from around his neck and held them out to Cecily, the leather thongs and metal chains from which they hung clutched in his fist. "Look after my luck, Captain?"

Cecily took them and held them tight. "Will do, Raf!"

Raf kissed her cheek and a moment after his lips brushed her, his clothes crumpled into a pile on the flags of the church floor. The tiny bat that fluttered out of them was almost lost in the shadowy church, but in his new form Raf circled the altar until Cecily was able to pick him out in the gloom.

"Do be careful, Raf!" Michael called. He gave Cecily an embarrassed smile. "He's my little brother—I always worry."

But Cecily had worried enough for one lifetime. She had fretted and hidden for too long and now, watching her lover ascend against the crimson velvet, she felt nothing but wonder and affection. The tiny bat flitted back and forth along the heavy wooden pole to which the curtain was affixed, then disappeared behind it and out of sight.

Tap-tap-tap-tap. Tap. Tap.

Why had the thudding slowed? Cecily stepped forwards, past the altar rails, past the choir stalls. She watched the curtain for any signs of Raf behind it, a little fast-moving bump under the velvet. But she couldn't see anything.

Her heartbeat grew faster with every second that passed. Then the bat flitted out from above the curtain and flew the length of the pole. As Cecily watched Raf settled atop it, his head moving in a series of little movements. This went on for a minute or so until the immense swathe of velvet sagged, then plummeted to the ground below with a sound like a thunderclap breaking overhead.

"Oh heavens, the curtain!" Michael exclaimed. But he didn't move from where he was standing, and neither did Cecily, because in front of them was the most extraordinary window she'd ever seen.

The thumping was louder than ever, filled with a new violence. This time, though, Cecily didn't feel as if they were being watched. She was sure of it.

"There's something inside the window," Cecily said.

But where could she start? The mediaeval glass was exquisitely detailed—it was an incredible sight even boarded up. What it would look like with sunlight pouring through it, Cecily could only guess.

Across the top was what looked like a jester ringing a handbell, with a huge crowd of people apparently gathered to watch him pass. The jester appeared again in a panel across the bottom, this time wearing a crown and an ermine-trimmed robe with a procession following behind. And the biggest panel of all was at the window's centre, depicting Christ's temptation in the desert, accompanied by Satan.

"It's beautiful, but at the same time"—Cecily tried to take in the huge amount of detail the window contained—"my word, there's something ugly in it."

Raf passed over their heads as she and Mike studied the window, its vivid colours rendered dull by the boarded-up exterior. A second later Raf said, "Naked dhampir behind you, Mike, don't turn round."

Michael covered his face but Cecily turned her head to see Raf standing completely naked in a church. She winked at him, then turned back to look at the window. In case Michael noticed where she'd been looking.

There was no loose pane in that window, nothing flapping loose in the breeze. But for all its beauty it was terrifying, and the hair on Cecily's neck stood up.

"Sorry about the curtain." Raf took his place between them, dressed in his rumpled shirt and trousers, his feet bare against the cold floor. He took the charms back from Cecily with another peck to her cheek. "That's not right for us, Mike. We liked our old window!"

"The old window was very special." Michael sighed, defeated. He told Cecily, "It was a de Chastelaine window, you know, with our family devices picked out in it, apostles and prophets all over the place. It even had some bats in one corner! But Exeter insisted, because Exeter does, and…this is what we have. Mediaeval, and rare, and my *word*, what a nasty-looking Satan!"

Raf approached the window slowly. As the shadow of the cross that stood on the altar fell across him, he gave a howl and threw his hand to his face as he flinched back, snarling and bestial. Then he opened one eye and the furious grimace turned into a grin as he told Cecily, "I thought I'd give you a bit of vampire!"

Cecily laughed. Even in this place, with such a horrible atmosphere, she was so glad that her Raf could make her happy. "You're so naughty, Raf!"

"Sorry, Rev." Raf smiled. He put the charms around his neck and looked up at the monumental window. There could scarcely have been a more delicate depiction of Christ, and the detail the artist had achieved was breathtaking. It was an image of peace and strength, of kindness and determination. But it wasn't that figure that Cecily couldn't tear her eyes from, it was Satan.

There was something bestial in the slight figure of the tempter. This was no dashing, charismatic fallen angel, not even the easy-to-miss serpent in the garden. It was a creature of dirty dark red, like old blood that had long since seeped into a stain, its spidery limbs and distended belly like something that would melt into the day from a nightmare, its wings engulfing and veined. Two clawed hands were pressed against the glass with such exquisite artistry that one might imagine the demon was really there, standing on the other side of the window, its contorted face turned downwards to watch the congregation through pale yellow eyes.

Except there was no congregation. There were only three here to be watched tonight.

"He's an ugly bugger!" said Raf.

"And he's watching us," Cecily whispered, pressing her hand to her forehead.

Thud. Thud.

It was louder and louder with each passing moment.

"He's—" Raf turned back to them as the devil looked down at him. "Mike, we've had this foisted on us because of Beatrice, haven't we? Beatrice the Builder?"

Cecily had never heard of her before. She looked back up at the window as if it would offer a clue, but other than the colourful roofs depicted in the background of the window's scenes, there was no woman armed with a set-square or a trowel.

"We have, yes." Michael nodded. "So Exeter says. *Beatrice worshipped here, the window should be at St Anastasia's.* I said we were perfectly happy with the existing east window but it's been torn out and some of our family window broke when they moved it, Raf. They wouldn't let me see this thing being installed—it was always hidden during services too. It's been so oppressive, having the window blocked off, and I complained, but…no one listened. Exeter was very cross and said I was bordering on the blasphemous when I wrote and said, *Begone with the curtain and let there be light!* And even with it hidden behind that dashed curtain, I had an uneasy feeling about it. That something wasn't quite right."

"Sissy?" Raf took Cecily's hand in his own, the touch instantly comforting. "Do you want to leave?"

"Yes, please." Cecily clasped Raf's hand. "I — I don't like it at all. My head... It's pounding so loudly."

"I'm terribly sorry, on your first day back too," Michael said. "But with the dedication tomorrow, and all those grand people — I had to ask you to see it, Raf. I wasn't sure anyone else would believe me and you, with all your knowledge of those sorts of things, you'd know at once if I was right to be nervous of it."

Raf smiled and told him, "You did right. It's a bloody ugly thing. There's something off with it." He glanced back at the window and Cecily half expected the scene to have changed but of course it hadn't. *How could it?* "And there's nothing York can do?"

"He told me I should be proud that St Anastasia's was chosen. An honour, he said." Michael shook his head. "Oh, I am not so sure... That curtain's not going back up there, is it? Impossible, I'd say, without scaffolding. Never mind." Michael seemed to brighten then as he said, "My small act of rebellion after being forced into having the dratted window! The curtain is gone!"

Cecily grinned at him. She knew all about small acts of rebellion.

"I'll be here for the show tomorrow," Raf promised his brother, just as Cecily would have guessed that he might. He never shirked from helping, or just standing beside someone when they needed it. "What time's the kick-off?"

"At ten o'clock tomorrow morning. They want to hold it near sunrise, you see." Michael picked up his coat and hat from the back of one of the pews. "Thank you so much for agreeing to come. I will feel a lot happier with you here tomorrow."

As Raf stepped into his shoes he told Cecily gently, "You don't have to come, Sis, I don't expect that. Even spiritual operatives have to get used to the job."

Cecily looked back at the window. The devil was still watching them, its eyes wide and almost glowing, though Cecily knew they could not.

"I want to," she said. "I didn't shy away from evil before, and I shan't now."

Raf stooped to pick up his jacket from the floor, his gaze never leaving her. As he slid his arms into the sleeves he said, "Then *we* will be here. Ready for trouble but hoping there isn't any. I'll bid you goodnight, brother of mine, because I've got a lady to escort safely home."

"Of course, of course. Safe journey—I will see you tomorrow, both of you." Michael ushered them out of the church and locked the door behind them.

As they headed out towards the lane, Cecily turned back one last time. The thudding was even more determined now, and she was glad they were walking away.

Chapter Three

The farther they got from St Anastasia's and its newly installed window, the quieter the incessant thumping became until Cecily finally realised that it had faded away completely. In its place she heard the sound of the waves breaking on the shoreline as she and Raf wandered home along the beach, and it soothed away her headache.

Her lover seemed thoughtful as they strolled, his shoes stuffed in his jacket pockets and Cecily's hand held safely in his. She relished the soft raps of the sand beneath his bare feet and the cries of the seagulls high in the star-studded sky, the cold breeze that ruffled her hair and the twinkling lights of Acaster Garrow, the village that had welcomed her as though she were its own returning daughter.

She had finally come home.

"That window…" Raf paused. They looked at each other and Cecily remembered the first time she had seen Rafael de Chastelaine, standing in a shuttered room on a late summer afternoon. His hair had been tousled then just as it was now, his bright blue eyes shining just as they did tonight. "It's the first time I've seen one blink. I thought only my door knocker did that."

"You saw it *blink?*" Cecily shivered. "There were so many faces on it — did they *all* blink? Could it have been a trick of the light?"

But no matter how much Cecily tried to push it from her mind, the devil in the desert came back to her, that horrible representation of evil. What if *that* had blinked? Cecily shivered again.

"For tonight I'll blame a trick of the light." He kicked at the sand. "But tomorrow I'm not taking my eyes off that devil."

"The devil blinked…" Cecily took in a sharp breath of the cold sea air. Then she asked the man who was half-vampire and could turn into a bat, "How the heck can glass blink?"

"How can a little dhampir get a girl like you?" Raf took a nimble step forwards then turned to face Cecily. He slipped his arm around her narrow waist. "Why does my garden still bloom in winter? They're all mysteries!"

"Because you're magical, that's why!" Cecily pecked him affectionately on the cheek before asking, "Speaking of mysteries — who was Beatrice the Builder?"

They strolled on again, Raf's bare feet splashing in the surf. It must be freezing but, if it was, he didn't seem to notice. "One of my several-times great aunts on the English side, so no fangs. But we think she and me shared a bit of word blindness."

His arm through Cecily's, Raf hopped first on one foot then the other in the seawater, like a child on a summer holiday. "She designed a lot of the house we live in now back in the fifteenth century, but it's been chopped and changed a bit over the years. You should see the buildings she designed and built, Sis. Massive Gothic palaces on the continent, cathedrals, even the odd prison or two. But you won't see the name Beatrice de Chastelaine on any of them, because nobody cared how good you were if you were a lass. She told everyone her name was Benedict, stuck on a pair of hose and started getting more commissions than she could handle!"

Cecily laughed. Who else could a woman like that be related to, other than Raf? "That's an extraordinary story! She sounds wonderful. I don't blame her for dressing as a chap to get things done. I've been tempted myself in the past!"

"Have you heard of the cathedral at Kwaalveld? *The Glass Cathedral*? That's one of hers. It's where the window came from."

"I'd never heard of it before this evening," Cecily admitted. She wasn't embarrassed, though. She knew Raf understood all too well what her life had been until now. "Although I remember reading something in the newspaper during the war about places packing away their stained glass. Did Beatrice design all the windows too? I was trying to understand what the jester had to do with the temptation of Christ in the desert."

"Well, that's another one of those bits of de Chastelaine family weirdness. Kwaalveld was a little scrub village in Flanders once upon a time, a place where plague and crime and war were just occurrences." Raf took off his jacket and draped it over Cecily's shoulders as they strolled. "They reckoned all four horsemen of the Apocalypse had ridden into the village and decided to set up shop there. So because Bea was a de Chastelaine, she did what de Chastelaines have always done, and decided to have a poke about."

"They built a cathedral in a *village*? How very odd! What on earth had Beatrice discovered?"

Raf shrugged and admitted, "Who knows? She didn't leave any writing behind. Piles and piles of drawings and sketches and designs with the odd word here and there, but nothing really written down. She told a story in the window, though."

Cecily stopped. She was gathering her thoughts, trying to knit together what Raf was telling her. But there seemed an impossible gap — how would they ever find out what Beatrice had discovered if she had never written it down? "So what does the jester mean?"

"When she arrived in Kwaalveld, Bea was already sickening with plague. After the doctor saw her, word got out that she wasn't a bloke at all." Raf arched an eyebrow then tutted. "And nobody would go near after that. Plague was one thing but this was a woman *way* above her station. You know, the powers that be are so set that a woman couldn't have designed those buildings that they *still* reckon she was a man! She wasn't though, because we've got paintings of her, letters about her growing up... She was a she, no doubt about that."

He caught himself then and laughed. "I've gone way off the subject, Sissy, sorry. So the only person who'd keep her company was a bloke called *Armand*, supposedly the village idiot. And in the days it took her to die, she never rested. She drew plans for the cathedral at Kwaalveld and when she was too weak to draw, Armand did it for her. She *dictated* the construction drawings for a Gothic cathedral to a so-called idiot! How amazing is that? As a boy who couldn't read and a man who still struggles, I like that part of the story."

"That's remarkable! So —" And now it all started to make sense. Or at least, as much as anything made sense when it involved a de Chastelaine. "Oh, I see... Is Armand something to do with the jester? Is he the fool?"

"She designed that window depicting Armand first as the fool then, in the end of the story, as the ruler." They paused then resumed their stroll, the cliffs rising above but the moonlight illuminating their path as brightly as the sun might. As they rounded a bluff Cecily saw a series of narrow wooden steps that someone had set into the side of the cliff long ago and somehow, before Raf had altered their course towards them, she knew that those steps would take her home.

"When she died, she left the cash to start construction and for the rest of his life Armand oversaw it. The more the cathedral took shape, the more prosperous the village became until it grew into a thriving market town." He stood back a little so she could go ahead up the narrow steps. "The illnesses dwindled to nothing, the crimes and conflicts dried up and Armand, who'd been living in the gutter until he befriended Aunt Bea, was eventually made Duke of Kwaalveld. And the best part is, there's no sting in the tail. He lived to a ripe old age and even made sure Bea came home to Acaster Garrow to be buried in the family vault. It's only recently that things have started getting a bit weird."

As they began to ascend the steps, Cecily noticed the scent from Raf's garden, the heavy perfume of the night-flowering plants contrasting with the sharp briny tang of the sea. Plants that had no right to be in bloom so close to winter in North Yorkshire.

"So the cathedral put paid to whatever horrible business was going on in the village? What an extraordinary story." Cecily paused on the step to glance at Raf, who was framed by the sea beyond, glittering in the moonlight. "And now we have a rattling window... I wonder what Beatrice would make of *that*?"

"You've seen pictures of the Glass Cathedral, as they call it? Windows everywhere. Massive ones like we've been saddled with, tiny ones as big as your hand... They never stopped putting them in until they ran out of wall and it would've brought the place down to add another." Raf frowned, his expression thoughtful. "So they took them out supposedly to protect them during the war but...why not put them back? They're putting in brand-new ones instead. The old are in storage apart from ours. That makes no sense to me."

"Especially if the cathedral was famous for its windows." Cecily sighed and reached for Raf's hand. As she shivered in a sudden gust of sea air, she couldn't help but feel a moment's melancholy. "And when you think of what was lost in all that destruction, why keep beautiful things that had survived hidden away?"

"It doesn't feel right in that church to me anymore. What do you reckon?"

"The thudding, and that horrible atmosphere pressing down and a creature in the glass who blinks — no, something's very wrong."

Raf nodded, then told her, "But everything's always all right at home. And you've got lavender to plant."

The steps led them onto a path that disappeared into a bower of trees, their foliage rich and green despite the season. As they walked together through the sheltering leaves Cecily could see the lawns beyond, lit by lamps that hung on the walls of the house, illuminating beds bursting with colourful flowers welcoming her back to her magical new home. Here it was easy to push the memory of the window to the back of her mind, to focus only on her new life, and to see only the beauty that was hers to enjoy now.

Stained-glass devils can wait for another day.

"So is it sorcery that makes your garden grow like this? Or there something special in the soil?" Cecily asked. She'd spotted a passiflora, something she'd only ever seen in a catalogue before. She was sure its extraordinary layered petals and elaborate stamen weren't supposed to bloom at the same time as dark purple passion fruit swelled on the same stems. Indeed, she wasn't even sure that passion fruit *could* grow in Yorkshire, only yards from the rolling chill of the North Sea.

"There's something special in the air wherever Bea's buildings are found." Raf squeezed her hand. "And maybe the odd incantation now and then keeps the bees happy in their hives."

"I see!" Cecily tapped the side of her nose, a promise that she'd never share his spells. "Do you have their honey? I'd love to try some!"

"For breakfast?" He looked up at the house, his eyes shining like the lights that glowed in an upper window beckoning them. "Does it feel like home?"

Cecily nodded with such vehemence that her hair sprang into her face. She tucked it back behind her ears and answered, "Yes. Oh, I *do*. I can't believe anything bad can ever happen here."

"*Te iubesc*, Captain Sissy," Raf said with such tenderness that she thought her heart would melt. He kissed her very gently then asked, "Ready to visit your quarters, boss?"

Cecily attempted to say *te iubesc* in return, and she grinned because she knew her pronunciation was still more Devon than Carpathian.

"I love you too," she said. "And yes, I do want to look around—with the party and dashing off to see your brother, I barely saw a thing earlier."

"The house can't wait to meet you!" He kissed her nose. "Go and have an explore, see what treasures you can find."

Roses in full bloom crowded the beds, with stocks in all different colours growing between them. Michaelmas daisies spread their white petals to the moon and a bottle brush, another plant Cecily had only seen in a book before, proudly displayed its spiney red flowers. A rich blue California Lilac nodded its boughs of fluffy blooms next to a latticed arch that was busy with jasmine. And she'd never seen jasmine in so many hues all patched together—pure white, intense yellows and soft pinks.

They went through the archway into a walled garden filled with herbs and bean canes, and the beds around were tufted with the leaves of unusually large carrots and onions pushing up from under the soil. The beans and peas were heavy with blossom, even as a forest of weighty pods poked through between the unseasonable flowers. Cecily wondered how the canes could hold themselves up and not topple over. Herbs filled the garden with an extraordinary free-for-all of scents, thyme and rosemary and oregano filling the night air, and Cecily could only imagine the effect it must have on Raf, with his sensitive nose.

They passed through the kitchen door into the house and now, without half the village in the midst of a party in the room, Cecily could see the kitchen.

The room was enormous, with a stone-flagged floor and herbs, which must've come from the garden, drying on a frame that hung from the ceiling. Cecily had no doubt that some of them were for potions rather than cooking as she couldn't identify most of them. A huge range stood in the wide fireplace, old-fashioned but so well-cared-for that it looked almost new. Vast numbers of copper pans shone from their hooks along the walls and china stood on the dresser. The stone flags were worn but the whitewashed walls were bright, and on windowsills and the mantelpiece, and pride of place in the centre of the table, were vases of flowers.

"From the garden?" Cecily asked as she took a gardenia bloom and sniffed it. She already knew the answer even before Raf nodded.

He left her to explore and busied himself rattling about in a drawer, searching for heaven knows what. After a minute or so he gave a cry of victory and pushed the drawer closed.

"Sissy Pincombe!" Raf bowed again and extended his hand. In it was a large, ornate iron key. It looked old and heavy, like the key to a mysterious place. "Every chatelaine needs a key to her own front door."

"Well, I've never had a key that looks quite like this before!" Cecily took the key from Raf and peered at its carvings, wondering if something on the key would wink at her. But for all that it looked so unusual, it appeared to be inert metal. Now the house was empty of visitors she wanted to see more of it, to find her way up to bed, and she came out of the kitchen with Raf at her side, fascinated again by her new home.

"Have a wander if you like," Raf told her. "And maybe you'll wander all the way up to bed. Not that I've been looking forward to it all day or anything."

As they went from the kitchen into the cavernous, cluttered hall, Cecily asked, "About your bed. Do vampires really sleep in coffins — and do dhampirs? Only I don't mind, but I'm not sure about pulling the lid down when we're inside it."

Raf frowned, thoughtful. "I suppose they *could* be called coffins, but we prefer *boxes*. As far as I know dhampirs sleep in beds unless they're trying to impress people. I sleep in a massive bed, can't imagine anything worse that trying to get forty winks cooped up in a coffin."

Cecily sighed with relief. "Phew! I wasn't sure about sleeping in a coffin — a massive bed sounds *much* better!"

"When we visit the other side of the family, I'll show you the boxes if you like? You can even have a try. Nan wouldn't mind."

"As long as they won't think I'm prying."

Cecily went from door to door, guided by Raf. Each room had its own clutter and among it was furniture — much of it old and dark, and some seemingly as ancient as the house itself. Portraits hung in every room and Cecily paused to look at each. Dotted about were elegant gold armchairs and polished side tables, as if each generation had tried to layer something of their era over the house without removing the previous decor. There was even a minstrels' gallery in the high-ceilinged dining room, and Cecily decided that she would eat every meal in there with a gramophone playing above.

Hanging above the dining room's mantelpiece was a modern image, a family group. Mother and father sat side by side in a garden with the sea beyond and around them were clustered five children. Three girls, elegant and tall, contrasted with two miniature boys.

"And I suppose this one's you?" Cecily pointed to the smallest of the children. The grin and the blue eyes gave Raf away, and as Cecily looked closer she noticed the tips of long canine teeth poking from the grins of several sitters. Raf's mother's were the longest, and she wore an enormous shading hat.

Raf nodded and took a step closer to peer up at the canvas. His smile was wistful, his gaze lingering on the pale, delicate features of his late mother.

"Nan did that." He pointed to a cluster of painted trees. "Can you see the hidden bats? Just a bit of family daftness. We posed for it out in our garden."

Cecily squinted and there they were, the bats. Five of them, shielded by the outstretched wings of another.

"That is funny — *and* adorable!" She took Raf's hand and he rested his head against her shoulder, his gaze still on the painting.

"I wish — Mum would've loved you. She taught me about the garden." Raf smiled, his hair tickling her cheek. "And at night we'd spend hours planting and pruning together while Dad played his guitar and the girls batted about and raced each other. Mike used to sit reading comics next to Dad's chair with a flask of tea. There was nothing Mum didn't know about flowers."

"That's a lovely memory to have," Cecily said. She knew what it was to grow up without a mother, with nothing more than memories. It was a pain they shared.

"And when she was gone —" He paused and drew in a deep breath. *Gone. Taken.* "I went into the garden and because she wasn't there, I just didn't know what to do. Then Dad came down and just said, *show me the garden*, and...I felt like I'd woken up. And Mike played the guitar on the patio and the girls started racing and even if we couldn't see her, she was there. We all felt her there. It was like a big hug, and I think she's always been with us ever since."

Cecily linked their fingers and gently swung them to and fro. "I'm sure she has. And I'm sure *someone* was watching over you in that rose garden at Whitmore Hall. They must have been."

"Someone was. Her name was Cecily." Raf lifted his head and kissed her cheek. "I've had a lucky life, but…I wish I knew the name of the man who killed her. I'm not talking about revenge. I just want to ask him why he thought he had the right to take her."

"Then we have to find him and ask. You need to know. Only…" Cecily turned her head and her lips brushed over Raf's hair. "Only I hope he wouldn't—I hope you'd be safe if you met him."

For a moment there was silence, then he admitted, "I promised the family I wouldn't put any of us in danger to find out. That's why I'm not looking—Mum wouldn't want it and nor do they. I remember her by her flowers and the garden, not by the way she died."

"That's for the best." Cecily nodded. "I don't like to think of my mother when s-she was a pale face on the pillow with the sheets all drawn up to her chin. And whenever I smell camphor—I try not to think about it. I remember sitting on her knee while she read to me. That's a much nicer way to think of her."

Raf smiled, then said, "Let's add the three of you to the house? You and Sandy and your mum. We can frame the photos you brought with you."

"Can we sit them here?" Cecily tapped the ancient stone mantelpiece, every inch of which was carved with fantastical beings. Unicorns and mermaids, dragons and sphinxes, a green man with a club and a friendly-looking demon holding up a flagon. "So they're with your family and we're all together."

"I think that'd be the perfect spot." He kissed her cheek again. "They can keep an eye on you, make sure you're being properly looked after by your man."

"I hope they don't watch all the time!" Cecily giggled as she looped her arms around Raf's neck. "I do love you, Raf."

He nuzzled her cheek. "Ready to explore upstairs?"

"Oh, yes!"

They headed off up the stairs, Cecily insisting on pausing at each of the portraits that lined the walls, wanting to know who each person was.

"And is this the de Chastelaine who was given the doorknocker?" Cecily asked as they looked up at the portrait of a man with a pointy beard like Guy Fawkes and a vast ruff. His painting was filled with arcane symbols and he held a gnarled stick that Cecily took to be a wand.

"Rowland and his magic wand." Raf winked. "Bet he said that to all the girls."

They carried on up the stairs, Raf giving a brief history of each of the sitters in the portraits. Each was more fascinating than the next—a mariner who discovered a sea monster, a woman who was holding a shard of the Philosopher's Stone, a man on horseback with his hair flowing in the breeze, his hand aloft as if he were directing the lightning that flashed across the dark clouds above him.

There was so much more to learn about, but they had the rest of their lives together and Cecily was in no rush. Finally, they wandered into the bedroom, Raf allowing Cecily in first, although she insisted on holding her hand over her eyes.

"If I open my eyes and there's a coffin..." Cecily laughed.

She felt Raf's lips against her cheek then he said, "Not quite. Have a look!"

Cecily dropped her hand and found herself in the most inviting bedroom she'd ever seen. Not that she'd many during the course of her life, but it was lovelier even than the several hotels she and Raf had stayed in on their journey north.

The room was wide and looked out across the gardens through the damask curtains that had been left open. The bed was just as Raf had promised, huge and clearly ancient, with intricate carvings everywhere she looked. This room hadn't escaped the clutter — an astrolabe lay on the table, a stack of watercolours leaned against the wall, a knight's helmet with a ferocious metal grin and flowing red plume had been left on its side by the fireplace and a single brogue shoe in what looked like Raf's size sat on the windowsill. But Cecily didn't mind at all.

Cecily slipped her arm around Raf. "It's delightful — I *love* it!"

"I've got something for you," Raf murmured. He kissed her nose then escorted her across to the dressing table. On it was a carved wooden chest, its lid fastened with a flamboyant brass catch. "This is my treasure box. It's full of daft things."

Raf opened the catch with a flick of his thumbnail and lifted the lid, letting Cecily see inside. There was no order — of course not — but a jumble of charms and trinkets, shells and glass, a kaleidoscope of colours shining out in the firelight. He began rifling through with his fingertips, clearly looking for something in particular.

"Ha!" Raf exclaimed, holding out his palm. Something small and white was held there and he said, "Don't worry, this isn't the present. But I thought you might like to see my first baby fang. I got a penny for that."

Cecily leaned down to look at it. The enamel caught the light and gleamed. Although it wasn't particularly big compared to Raf's adult teeth, in a child's mouth it would have been big, a tusk of a tooth. "It's impressive!"

"Nosferatooth." He turned away a little and poked his fingertip into the box, his body sheltering it from Cecily's view. "Right, get comfy. I've got something else to show you."

Cecily sat on the velvet-covered sofa angled towards the fireplace. It was such an opulent piece of furniture that would have seemed grand even in a sitting room, and to have it in a bedroom was wonderfully decadent.

As she closed her eyes again, she wondered what else he could produce from the box.

"I'm ready!" Cecily said, and held out her hand just as she used to when she was a child.

"Open your eyes," he instructed and when she did it was to see Raf down on one knee before her. Cecily knew exactly what was coming now, even as he opened the small red velvet box he held. "Cecily Pincombe, will you marry me? Officially?"

Cecily wasn't looking at the contents of the box but at Raf, at that dear face smiling up at her.

"Officially, yes!" she replied. It was only when she went to hug him that she remembered the box, and there inside it sat a diamond ring. A large stone sat at its centre and it was ringed with smaller stones with a border running around its outside — for all the world, it looked like a daisy worked in gems. Cecily blinked again and again, trying to take it in. But it was so beautiful she couldn't quite believe that it was hers.

"If this isn't your sort of thing—" Raf blinked up at her, his eyes bright with emotion. "You can have any ring you want. Anything for Sis!"

"Oh, please don't think I don't love it, it's just…I've never had anything so lovely before!" Cecily's hand trembled as she took the ring from the box, certain she would drop it. "You are sure I can have this, aren't you?"

He nodded. "I love you." Raf took Cecily's hand and kissed it. "And that ring's been worn by some amazing women in my family. Now it's going to meet the best ever."

"I don't know about that…" Cecily held the ring up to the light and watched as the stones seemed to dance. "How old is it, Raf?"

"Just a couple of hundred years, so it's really one of the newest things in the house." He grinned, the lights glittering on the diamonds. And what a grin it was, showing those keen canines of his.

"But it looks new! Will you put it on my finger?"

Raf took the ring from Cecily with great care. He kissed her hand again then slid the ring onto her finger. It fit so well that it might have been made just for her, the bright gems reflecting the light back at her.

"I'll wear it always," Cecily whispered. Then she glanced at Raf and giggled. "Raf, those fangs of yours…"

"Don't tell me you've gone off them? I'm not going to a dentist," Raf told her mischievously, going even paler than usual. Fearless when faced with the forces of evil, it seemed that the forces of dentistry were rather more threatening. "You're stuck with these here little fangs!"

Cecily peered at his mouth. "Raf, I hate to tell you this but those little fangs of yours aren't quite as small as they were. Is that *meant* to happen?"

"They're not— What?" He laughed and tapped his fingertip to one fang, then the other. Then he grimaced. "I wonder— It must be when I bit you-know-who. You don't mind, do you? They don't spoil my stunning good looks?"

"Not at all—they're dashing!"

"I'll take dashing!" With another kiss to her hand, he hopped up onto his bare feet. "Since we're now living in sin anyway...fancy going to bed and sealing the deal?"

"Oh, yes please!" Cecily ruffled his hair before pulling him down into her arms for a kiss. She was home at last.

Chapter Four

As soon as they arrived at the church for the ceremony, Cecily heard the sinister thumping again, the vibration pulsating through her every limb, leaving her nauseous. But it seemed as though everyone else was oblivious to it. The lane was crowded with locals admiring the large shiny cars and the ecclesiastical grandees who glided out in their silk and brocade robes.

Rad squeezed Cecily's hand. He kissed her cheek then asked, "Are you all right?" He wrinkled his nose. "This place is whiffing of High Church today. They always have the best brandy."

Cecily sniffed as well, but wasn't sure she could smell much beyond mothballs and pomade. "That *thing* is still thumping—do you think it could be Satan in the window? Knocking on the glass to let everyone know it's there! Maybe it didn't want to come to Yorkshire? I can't imagine it'd be fond of a place that calls itself God's own country."

"The devil in the glass?" Raf frowned, then took a little bottle from his pocket. When he unstoppered it to waft it under his nostrils and chase away the smell of incense, Cecily caught a distinct whiff of lavender. "If it didn't want to come to Yorkshire it's not just ugly, it's stupid too. I'll tell you this, I'm not taking my eye off it. I *know* it blinked last night."

"Maybe it'll get bored and...fall asleep or something?" Cecily tried to sound hopeful, although she couldn't convince herself that whatever was generating the infernal thumping was benign. "It might be a friendly sort of creature."

Although *friendly* wasn't the word that came to mind when Cecily spotted an altercation at the door of the church. Michael was in the doorway in his chasuble, offering a painted-on smile to a man in a mitre who was furiously staring him down. She knew that long face with the sharply angled eyebrows and the downturned, sour mouth.

"That's the Archbishop of Exeter," Cecily whispered. "I've met him before. He came to a couple of events at Whitmore School. He looks rather cross, doesn't he?"

The archbishop jabbed his finger towards Michael, something in the way he pointed first into the church then up to the heavens leaving Cecily in no doubt that he was discussing the collapse of the all-important curtain. As he carped and jabbed, the Most Reverend Humphrey Poynting glanced over his shoulder and locked his gaze with Cecily's.

Surely he won't remember me, though? He must meet hundreds of people.

Cecily shone him an awkward smile, then glanced down at her hand clasped in Raf's. He would never remember her. And how could he even recognise her, dressed as she now was in a velvet coat, no longer the wisp of a girl she had been at Whitmore Hall?

"Raf!" A woman in a broad hat burst from the crowds and made straight for him, arms wide, her face powdered. She was easily the most glamorous woman Cecily had yet seen in Acaster Garrow in her patent leather shoes and feather-trimmed silk coat. "I was supposed to be tickling the old organ but they shoved me off the bench in favour of some terrible old bore! Can you believe it?"

"The fools!" Raf gave her a hug of welcome, never letting go of Cecily's hand even as he did. "Mim, I want you to meet Sissy—*Cecily*. My fiancée! Sissy, this is Mim Garrow. Mike's pal."

"Cecily!" Mim boomed. Cecily felt the stares of the various dignitaries around them but Mim either hadn't noticed or didn't care. "I'd heard from the reverend that Raf was bringing a friend home with him. I didn't realise—you are naughty, Raf!—that you're engaged. You vanished in the summer and I had no idea where you'd gone. And now I realise!" Mim unleashed a fruity giggle. "You've been courting, you bad chap!"

"I was just doing a bit of gardening—" Raf began, but he got no further.

"Mrs James, isn't it?" The Archbishop of Exeter was gliding along the path towards them, a towering figure in robes and mitre. He had turned up the corners of his mouth into a benevolent smile and said, "A dreadful shame about the headmaster but perhaps, given his recent troubles, for the best? The Lord has his reasons, does He not?"

Cecily shrank back from him. Why, on her second day in her new home, did her past have to rear up at her like this? It only compounded the malevolent air around the church. The crowd's attention was on her, and wouldn't people be curious why she went by the name Pincombe rather than her late husband's surname?

"Your grace. How pleasant to meet you again," Cecily said, although it was anything but. "Fancy you being in Acaster Garrow... I would rather not speak of my husband, if it's all the same. The entire situation was a painful one."

"Of course." He inclined his head and looked back towards the church. "Well, might I say that the school flourishes under its new guardians and you, dear lady, look most happy. I must beg your pardon, I'm afraid, duties beckon!"

"Curtains are a nightmare, aren't they?" Raf asked innocently. "Hope you get it sorted out before the overture."

Poynting blinked, then said, "Quite so," before retracing his steps and disappearing into the church. As he did the thumping sound grew slower and, for now at least, silent.

Mim linked her arm through Cecily's and she found herself in the middle of the three of them as they headed into the church. Cecily could hear the organ music more clearly now that the thumping had stopped. Perhaps the entrance of the archbishop was what had shifted the player up a gear from a slow, solemn melody to the sort of baroque organ-playing that set Cecily's teeth on edge. It sounded as if at least three people were playing the instrument at once.

The church was already busy and there, returned to pride of place, was the vast velvet curtain. The scent of the freshly delivered flowers that lined the aisles was heady even to Cecily and she saw Raf wince. He peered into one of the bouquets then whispered, "They've sprayed these with scent. They're dying already, look."

The noxious stink of rotting flowers assailed Cecily as soon as she was close enough to see the brown, curling edges of the flowers.

"They should have asked for some from your garden," Cecily said. "Yours wouldn't do that!"

"What an unholy pong!" Mim gagged, wafting her gloved hand back and forth. "I'll have a word with Mrs Ballinger. She always insists on doing the flowers, but my word!"

A young cleric approached and asked with a painted-on smile, "Villagers, yes? Back four rows, if you would. Thank you!" He ushered them towards the pews with sweeps of his hands, where people Cecily recognised from her welcome party were already crowded in. "Come on now, find a place."

"Why can't we sit at the front?" Raf peered round him, looking at where Michael was being harangued by a half dozen similar men, all of whom looked as though they were as thunderous as the archbishop had been. "I'm Reverend de Cha—"

"Thank you!" The man dismissed him with a nod and stepped aside, barring the way of another newly arrived local with an instruction of, "Back four rows, if you would."

Once he was out of earshot, Mim hissed in a whisper, "Dare I point out that the Garrows have had a pew in the front row from the day this church opened? Of course now it's covered in the chubby behinds of archbishops and toadying deacons! It'll need a jolly good scrub before I sit on *that* again."

"Look at poor old Mike," Raf said as they squeezed into a pew as instructed. "This is his church, but they'd put *him* back here if they could."

Mim sighed. "They were going to shove him into the choir stalls but he'll be standing at the back instead. He was able to rebel against *that* at least."

The church doors closed with a bang and Cecily sat straighter, listening for any sound from behind the curtain. She heard nothing save the gentle rustling of clerical robes and the occasional cough, obligatory in any silent church. Mike took up position as the choir rose to their feet and began to sing, their voices soaring in celebration up to the vaulted ceiling. Raf took Cecily's hand but she could feel the tension in him like a physical sensation, a certain tightness in the air.

The congregation joined in with the opening hymn but Cecily merely mouthed the words. She was on the alert. Something wasn't right, but perhaps the fact that the archbishop recognised her had thrown her off kilter. She was aware of some very quiet, benign presences in the church. A long-dead curate was polishing the brass in the baptistry and a knight of the realm sat up from the carving on his box tomb, the dog at his feet swishing its tail, only for him to yawn and turn back into stone as he lay down again. They weren't the source of Cecily's uneasiness. There was something else here, something wrong.

There was a movement at the curtain too as the officious young cleric who had ushered them into the back rows took hold of the end of a length of gold rope. As the congregation sang, he moved with exquisite slowness and she realised, her stomach lurching, that the window was to finally be revealed. With each word the curtain moved a little more, an ever-expanding sliver of sunlight plotting its course across the floor of the church. There was Armand the fool and his followers, there was the delicate face of Christ and soon, too soon, would be the bestial devil, leering out from between hands that seemed to be pressed to the very surface of the glass.

All the congregation, and Cecily with them, lifted their faces to the window. Perhaps it was the trees outside, their branches dipping and churning in the rising wind, scattering the sunlight that fell across the window, that made the glass seem to ripple and stir.

"I preferred the old one," someone muttered from the pew behind them. Mim jogged Cecily's elbow as she failed to stifle a laugh.

If only I could laugh.

But Cecily couldn't.

Raf's head whipped round to look at Mike, then back towards the glass. He kissed Cecily's cheek and, as the singing went on, slipped out of the pew and began to walk along the aisle towards the window. There was a flurry of movement among the representatives of the church but it seemed that nobody dared add to the drama by intercepting him. Yet as Cecily watched her fiancé approach the monstrous window, she heard a series of deafening thuds and thumps, a clamouring that drowned out the soaring hymn, yet nobody else seemed to be aware of it.

Was it Cecily's imagination that the edge of Christ's gown in the window was fluttering? Or that the jester's toes wriggled as his foot met the path? It had to be. But it surely wasn't when she saw the devil blink.

Just as Raf had claimed.

The hymn was faltering as it seemed more and more people began to wonder what on earth Raf was doing.

As the Archbishop of Exeter finally approached him, Michael hurried along the aisle too and the three men began to have what looked like a very spirited, not at all friendly conversation. Raf pointed towards the window, his expression agitated, but the archbishop merely raised his hand and put it over Raf's as though trying to calm him. She could see her lover becoming more exasperated, and a moment before he turned and addressed the congregation, Cecily had already guessed that he was going to do it.

"There's something bad in that window!" he announced. The organ stopped, the choir turning as one to peer at the glass. "We should cover it up and empty the church right now."

"Mr de Chastelaine," the archbishop hissed, "this is outrageous, sir."

"The flowers are dying," Raf told the congregation, gesturing to the curling, wilting blooms. "There're clouds of corpse flies gathering in the corners of the church. The air's going bad. I want everybody to leave just for now, so we can get whatever this is dealt with!"

Only now did Cecily see what she had taken to be a shadow high above seethe and move as what had to be ten thousand flies or more shifted as one.

Screams filled the air as the locals ran, a flurry of Sunday best heading for the door. The choirboys stampeded past the archbishop, a cloud of red in their scarlet gowns, their comics rolled and wielded like batons as they escaped.

Mim and Cecily stayed in the pew as everyone else ran. Cecily noticed Mim's jaw moving as if she were mumbling under her breath. She nudged her and Mim smiled vaguely at her. She seemed to be coming round from a snooze.

"We'll be all right," Mim told her. "We'll stay here at the back until Raf and Mike are ready to leave."

"That is enough!" The archbishop's voice was a thunderclap, and if the terrified clerics had been hoping to leave, now they must have realised that there was no hope of it. Instead they were to remain beneath the fetid cloud of flies as Raf stormed back along the aisle to the pew. He dropped his voice to a whisper and told Cecily and Mim, "I'd rather you were outside. Any chance I can talk you into it?"

Thud. Thud. Thud. Thud.

"It's thumping again," Cecily said, her skull pounding with each blow. "It had stopped but now it's started again."

"What's thumping?" Mim asked, eyeing Cecily with curiosity.

"The window — something in the window is thumping." Cecily clasped Raf's hand, and with her other hand reached for the *cocosul* around her neck. "I'm not leaving, Raf — there must be some way we can stop it, or contain it, or something!"

He lifted her hand and kissed it, then asked Mim, "Whatever you were whispering about, you shared it with Sis, didn't you?"

Mim rested her hand on Cecily's shoulder. "Just a little mutter," she assured Raf. "No time for more, but it's better than nothing."

So it wasn't only Raf who was in the habit of casting spells in Acaster Garrow.

Without another word, the archbishop began the service of dedication, bathed in the light that poured through the newly revealed window. Though Raf sat, he was on the edge of the pew, tense as though he might jump up again and all the time she stared at the images, trying to discern any further movement.

And it was there, of course it was, always on the edge of Cecily's vision. The swish of a cloak, the crook of a finger. The window was alive.

The more the archbishop read of the service, the more the window moved, and the more the thumping and thudding echoed inside Cecily's head.

"Thy servant has sought to advance the goodly order of thy temple," droned the cleric in his well-schooled, measured tones. "Recompense him with thy heavenly blessing, accept his devotion, increase his faith, comfort him with thy favour, protect and deliver him —"

Then Cecily saw it. The devil in the window moved, its fingers flexing, pushing, straining against the glass, and even as Cecily instinctively moved to shield herself from some unknown assailant, Raf bundled her down to the floor, pulling Mim by her shoulder with a cry of, "Get down!"

"Receive him to thy kingdom in the world to come." As the words left the Archbishop of Exeter's bloodless lips, the window shattered with a sound like a glacier breaking in two. Screams and cries went up as Cecily was showered with a spray of broken glass, the edges keen as razors even at this distance.

There was no thudding now. Instead, Cecily heard a dreadful high-pitched scraping, clanking noise, like the workings of an infernal machine. Once the rain of glass had fallen, Cecily shielded her eyes with her hand and peered over the pew. The window had gone, leaving only a fringe of gnarled lead around the frame. High up in the air, the light shining through its glass body, was the depiction of Satan that had dominated the window.

The church was filled with the unholy scrape and clank of its beating wings, its form blocking out the sunlight.

The clerics who had filled the front pews clutched bloodied hands in prayer or held faces that bore the scratches from shards of glass that must have shot out like bullets. They stared at the creature and at their head, uninjured, was the Archbishop of Exeter. He opened his mouth to say something but Raf was already moving into the aisle, speaking in that same melodic language she had heard in the ghost garden that summer, his face turned up towards the devil. The archbishop stepped aside to let him pass, stumbling blindly into the pews, and Cecily watched as her lover drew ever closer to the ghastly creature.

Cecily clung to Mim's sleeve, powdery glass catching her fingers as it lay like dust over their clothes.

"It's so full of hate!" Cecily whispered. "Can't you feel it?"

The shades of the benign curate and the knight had faded away now and all that pervaded the ancient building of stone was fear and enmity.

Mim shivered, her voice tiny as she said, "I've never, ever known the like."

The beast drew back, rearing up above Raf. Then it swooped down towards him but he stood his ground, his voice not wavering. At the last the creature abandoned its descent and instead darted towards the shattered space where the window had once been, disappearing into the sunlight.

Chapter Five

Cecily was glad of the strong, thick walls of her new home. The glass demon had not been seen since it flew out of the church through the gaping maw where the east window had once been, and while she had overheard some of the clerics at the church say that the beast had gone and all would be well, Cecily and Raf were not taking chances.

They had to understand what they had witnessed — and whether the threat was truly over. And the only place they could find out was in Raf's archive.

It was the one place in the house Cecily had yet to see, and after her spirited search the previous evening, she had no idea where it might be found. Despite the efforts of Mrs Hodge, Raf's collection of mementoes from his adventures seemed to be slowly taking over the house, so she wouldn't have been entirely surprised to find it in an outbuilding somewhere on the large estate.

"One good thing I can tell you," Raf said as he took off his jacket and slung it onto a hatstand as they entered the house. "It's definitely not the devil."

Cecily unpinned her hat and, although she removed it carefully, a glittering shower of powdered glass fell from its narrow brim. "Not *the* devil, Old Nick, Satan, Lucifer, etcetera—just *a* devil? A henchman?"

"If only they were that simple, our lives'd be a lot easier." Raf stepped out of his shoes. "Time to hit the books, I think. See if we can find out what sort of a creature hangs about in a stained-glass window. If I had to guess, I'd say demon. Flies, dead flowers, smells like a cesspit… The signs all say demon to me. What's your thoughts?"

"I have to say, I don't know much beyond thinking it must be a horrible beastie!"

Cecily carefully took off her coat and swiped the clothes brush over it, although she knew it needed more attention than that. Her lovely new coat, too. How typical that it would be spoilt by a demon.

Raf watched her, his expression soft. After a few moments he took the coat from her and said, "Mrs Hodge will be able to get this right as rain. Looking after me's never been a picnic!" Then he brushed the tip of his fingers down Cecily's cheek and asked, "Are you all right?"

"A bit…a bit surprised. Rather numb, really…" Cecily caught Raf's fingers and kissed their tips, before saying, "I'm so proud of you, for getting the people out. I feel so uneasy, though—and I don't think it's only because the archbishop recognised me. It's more than that, I'm certain. That *thing*—the demon… It's on the loose, isn't it? What the heck will it do?"

He shrugged one shoulder then admitted, "That depends on who it is. If we can work that out, we can get it in hand. Let's get some food together and take it down to the archive with us. We might need to be down there a while!"

They went to the kitchen and collected together the remains of yesterday's party food, and Cecily made a flask of tea although she suspected Raf might power himself with something stronger. She tried to picture the archive, but all she had for comparison was the school library at Whitmore Hall, a tall narrow room with dark wooden bookshelves that reached the ceiling.

"Ready!" Cecily declared, holding out a basket full of food.

Ever the gentleman, Raf took it from her and, her arm through his, they strolled through the house. Past the portraits they went, the shields and crossed swords and vases and charms that Cecily knew must all have a story of some sort to accompany them. Eventually they came to a small sitting room, cosy and warmed by a fire that roared in the grate. It was decorated in shades of blue and above the fireplace was a large portrait. Even as Raf began to speak, she knew full well who it was.

"*This*," he announced with pride, "is Bea the Builder!"

The mediaeval portrait showed a lady surrounded by the business of architecture. Beside her was an unfurled parchment covered in the confident lines of a building plan, and ink and rulers lay across her desk. She smiled down at them from her friendly, round face. When Cecily peered more closely, she spotted an outfit of men's clothes hanging over a chair in the background, a nod to Beatrice's cross-dressing.

"A remarkable woman!" Cecily said in admiration. *But there is something about her face.* "And isn't she...wait...isn't that the same face as Christ in the church window? That's quite something!"

"A lady of surprises. And *still* keeping secrets." Raf put the basket of foot down on the edge of the hearth and swung the portrait to the left. Beneath it a polished ship's wheel was set in a recess of the wall, concealed by the portrait. It was unlike anything Cecily had ever seen before and when Raf gave it a spirited clockwise turn, the sound that could be heard was unlike anything she had heard either. "This is one of her tricks!"

Raf had to shout to be heard over the sound of grinding cogs somewhere in the very walls of the house and as Cecily watched a vast bookshelf filled with important-looking tomes that covered the wall to the right of the fireplace moved forwards. It swung outwards and behind it she saw a flight of steps descending into darkness. The sound ceased as suddenly as it had started and her fiancé said, "Clockwise to open the archive, anticlockwise to shut the whole house down. Bea built it!"

"Shut it *down*?" Cecily glanced towards the window and the grey day beyond. It looked like an ordinary autumn day, even though there was a demon out there somewhere. "How do you shut down a house?"

"You turn a ship's wheel clockwise." He stooped and picked up the basket. "After you. Don't worry about it being dark, it'll start lighting up as you go downstairs."

Cecily went to the top of the stairs and from somewhere a light came on, just as Raf had said. She held onto the stone bannister that had been carved into the wall and down she went, following the curve of the spiral staircase. Every few steps another light came on and they seemed to have gone some way into the earth before they reached a door at the foot of the stairs.

Raf rested his chin on Cecily's shoulder. He kissed her earlobe then whispered, "Go on, Sissy, open it. It's your archive too. And your weapon store."

Weapons?

Cecily turned the iron hoop and the door swung heavily open. Light after light flickered on inside and she stepped into what appeared to be a vast cavern and as far as she could see was shelf after shelf of aged leather and canvas spines and rolled-up scrolls.

"Somewhere in here we'll find the answer," Raf told her with certainty. "But I can't pretend there's much order to any of it. I do try but the word blindness doesn't necessarily go hand in hand with record keeping. Besides, I'd rather be gardening."

"So there isn't a catalogue or a handlist?"

But she was in for a surprise, because Raf gave a keen nod. "There's one Aunt Augusta drew up in 1816. She almost finished it, but I think she got bored. Do you want it?"

"It's over a century old?" Cecily gazed around at the huge collection and shrugged. "Well, I suppose it's a start..."

Raf handed the basket to Cecily then approached one of the shelves. He rooted through some papers, leaving her to settle as he searched. She took a seat at the long table which had inkwells and pencils along it, like the desks back at Whitmore Hall. A book laid open on the table showed a woodcut of a lamb that appeared to be growing out of a tree. Cecily recoiled and closed the book and poured some tea into the lid of the flask.

As she sipped at it, Raf put a large and rather handsome journal of red leather down in front of her.

"One catalogue, present and correct." He smiled. Then he took a seat at the table and asked, "How does it feel to be on your first proper case? That's what this is, you know. Our first actual job together, working from scratch."

"Nervous, in case we get it wrong," Cecily replied. Then she added with a smile, "Excited, because I really, really hope we can find out what's going on!"

Raf grinned too, his eyes dancing. "I wouldn't normally be smiling after a bunch of folks got showered in broken glass, by the way. But they're all going to be fine and…well, I just still can't quite believe you're here with me. After everything we went through, here we are. And I've still got my shirt on after five minutes at home, it's a miracle!"

"I can't quite believe it either," Cecily admitted. And that wasn't all she couldn't believe either. A demon of glass had escaped from a window right before her eyes. The world was certainly full of some very strange things.

Cecily began to flick through the catalogue, but she wasn't sure where to start. It looked as if all the books had been numbered from one upwards, but in no apparent order unless it was the order they'd been acquired in, or perhaps discovered in piles around the house. The subjects jumped about and Cecily began to wonder if they'd ever find the right book, even if Raf did have it somewhere on a shelf.

"Are all the books down here, or are some of them upstairs?" *In the piles of clutter.* Cecily's heart sank a little at the thought.

Raf scratched his head and admitted, "They're all over the place. There might be a few out in the garage, now I think. One or two in the sheds…" Raf narrowed his eyes, thoughtful. "I always meant to get them in one place, but…I've got plants to look after."

Cecily passed him the flask for a drink. "Raf, darling, *now's* the time. Why don't you go and round them up and I'll start looking down here? You never know, the very book we need might be in the greenhouse!"

"Do you want to plant your lavender first? Your plants have been lucky for us so far."

Cecily had begun to unroll a scroll and held down its edges with large lumps of amber containing long-dead insects. The scroll was covered in a style of writing she hadn't ever seen before, with spotty snakes drawn in the margins. "Raf, my lavender can wait. It's quite happy in its pot."

"We're looking for anything about cathedrals, devily whatsits, all that sort of thing. Anything that jumps out at you." He leaned over and kissed her cheek. "I'll go and start gathering books."

"I'll put away these snakes! These ones look too friendly to have anything to do with devils," Cecily decided, and rolled the scroll back up again.

Cecily began by looking through the books that were piled around the room. One stack consisted almost entirely of books about warlocks — the pile next to it was almost entirely written *by* warlocks. Which was some sort of order at least, except tomes on leviathans, submerged cities and meteors had been interfiled with them.

While she worked, Raf came up and downstairs, his arms filled with books. As he did his shirt became progressively more rumpled and by the time it showed grass stains and soil sprinkles, Cecily began to worry just exactly where he had dug up some of what appeared to be ancient and possibly even valuable volumes. He didn't stop to eat, merely grabbed some food and took it off with him, returning after a few hours with no shirt at all but a crate filled with aging scrolls of paper and sketches tied with grubby and frayed red ribbons. With a brief wave for Cecily, he ascended the staircase again, disappearing to continue his mission.

How will we ever wade through it all?

Cecily tried to sort what he'd found. At least it was a gardening book that had some soil in between the pages, even if it dated from Tudor times. She put it to one side and started to leaf through a primer on angels, hand-drawn and illuminated on every page. It was a beautiful book, and Cecily had to pull herself away from it—she couldn't afford to get distracted while the glass demon was loose.

"That's the last of them!" Raf announced as he came downstairs, carrying a wicker basket in front of him that looked almost as big as he was. He dropped it at the foot of the staircase and sank down to sit on the riser, breathing deeply. "It's a bloody big house when you're searching it for rogue books. I'm knackered! Four hours of climbing up and down a spiral staircase will do that to a dhampir."

Cecily sat down on the step beside him and put her arm around his shoulders. He carried the scent of effort and work. "I haven't found anything yet. But at least we know that. All the books with slips of paper in them like this"—she held one up to show him—"I've flicked through them and they don't have anything in them that we need. But what's in them is on the slip, very briefly, so…so one day we might be able to put all this in order."

If we live to be five hundred years old.

Raf lifted his head and smiled as he met Cecily's gaze. "Do you think we could sell it to the village school as a project? Come and sort the books and we'll ply you with cake and daftness?" He kissed her nose. "Probably won't show them the weapon store though."

Cecily nodded. "We could ask them to help, yes. I don't think we'll ever get it done on our own! And no, we don't want children among the weapons!" She chuckled as she nodded over towards the studded wooden door that kept the weapons secure. "I'm not sure I'm brave enough to go in there either!"

"You've already been down here for hours without any daylight." Raf rested his head on Cecily's shoulder. "Mrs Hodge's left a steak and ale pie for supper *and* got your coat as good as new. We could even have a wander in the garden if you fancy it. Watch the sunset? You've spent long enough in the archive today."

"I have—I'm getting a bit headachey. And dusty!"

"Come on." Raf rose to his feet and held out his hand. "We could take your lavender for a walk too. Not that I'm fretting about her sitting in her pot when there's a whole garden waiting to meet her."

Cecily only realised how tired she was as she mounted the stairs. How Raf had managed to go up and down them so often, his arms full of heavy volumes, she couldn't imagine. In the kitchen Cecily collected the lavender cutting from where it was waiting on the windowsill. She'd sat it there so it could see the garden even if it wasn't yet in it.

"Where would you like to go, little plant?" Cecily asked it. The new, tender shoots branching off from the old twig seemed to wave at her in reply. "Do you speak plant, Raf? What did it say?"

Raf cocked his head and nodded as though listening intently to the cutting. After a few moments he said, "She'd like to go under the dining room window with Mum's tulips, because you can see the sea from there. And don't fret about us planting her in the autumn. The de Chastelaine garden doesn't worry about little things like seasons!"

"Sounds like an excellent spot!" Cecily linked her hand with Raf's as they headed outside. The cool evening was full of birdsong and together they strolled across the lawn. Here in the sea-scented air it seemed unthinkable that the glass demon was out there somewhere, but she knew that together they'd find it. And as they strolled, the locket containing her brother's picture around her neck and the pot of lavender in her hand, Cecily felt that sense of contentment all over again. Even with that infernal creature of glass loose in the world, she wasn't facing it alone.

"Just about here?" Raf nodded towards a colourful border beneath the window, filled with tulips in every imaginable hue. It was like a rainbow bursting from the earth. It reminded her of Raf. "What do you think?"

"Perfect." Cecily hitched up her new dress and knelt on the lawn beside the flowerbed. She scraped a handful of dirt aside with her hand. "It'll look beautiful here, and the bees will love it!"

Raf knelt beside her and added his hand to hers, helping her dig. He pecked a kiss to her shoulder as they worked. "Look at you, digging without a trowel. No wonder we fell for each other."

"I'll make a terrible state of my nail polish, but I don't care!"

"I'll paint them for you," was his answering promise.

Once the hole was deep enough, Cecily helped the cutting out of the pot and she and Raf patted it down into the flowerbed.

"A little bit of Exmoor in Yorkshire!" Cecily rested her head on Raf's shoulder. "I hope it grows big and strong."

"She will," Raf told her, his voice gentle. "And she'll soon be keeping the tulips in line. Pie and plotting time?"

"Yes!"

Just as they'd got to their feet, Cecily heard someone calling their names. She held Raf's hand.

He whispered, "Mim and Mike approaching. Shall we be nice or shall we hide?"

Cecily chuckled. "Let's be nice!"

And just as she spoke, Mim and Michael appeared around the angle of the house. Michael was a picture of anguish and Mim was pale as paper.

"Oh, there you are!" Michael said, hurrying his pace. "We rang the doorbell but no one answered!"

"Busy planting," Raf told them with a welcoming smile. The newly arrived couple were muffled in coats and hats, at odds with Raf's bare feet and naked torso. As he stepped forwards, Cecily saw again the layered jumble of tattoos that covered his back, each one a totem or charm. "We're just about to eat supper. Will you join us?"

Michael shook his head. He was panting as if he'd been running. "Thank you, but no. It's the village, Raf. It's Acaster Garrow. Something terrible's happening."

"Has the glass demon attacked someone?" Cecily asked.

"*It* hasn't," Mim tutted. "But plenty of other people have. There was a brawl in the street at the market this afternoon. A dozen people or more, fists flying and the *language*! I've never heard the like in Acaster Garrow!"

Michael wrung his hands. "It's dreadful, Raf. I was asked to break it up and the things they said to me! Unholy things. I've never been spoken to like that before. And especially not by my churchwarden and the Sunday school teacher. It was as if they were possessed, I tell you."

"Bloody hell." Raf sighed, raking his hands through his hair. "It's not a very nice question, Mike, but…any sign of flies?"

Michael gulped. "Here and there. Gathering. You can hear it, a buzzing noise. It comes and goes. But when that brawl was going on, there were clusters of them on the awnings of the market stalls and they were crawling over the walls."

"And when they brought the catch in from the trawlers, the fish were all covered with horrible great flies." Mim grimaced. "And rotten in the nets. The same with the milk churns. Clustered with flies and curdled almost as soon as the cows were milked."

"Right." Raf sounded thoughtful. And determined, Cecily thought. "Me and Sissy are going to scour the books and see if we can find the demon's name. Can you two keep an eye on the village and Mim, I know it's asking a lot, but…keep the protection up if you can?"

"Of course." She smiled. "You've explained to Cecily, I assume?"

"You perform spells?" Cecily asked. "It's all right, I've seen Raf do it too."

"Well, you see, Mim isn't quite what she seems." Michael raised an eyebrow, and Cecily struggled to understand what he meant. It was left for Mim to reach out and lay her gloved hand on Cecily's arm, her smile warm.

"They're trying very tactfully to tell you that I'm a witch," Mim confided with a roll of her eyes. "And I'm very glad that you're here, Cecily. The more of us against that thing, the merrier!"

Cecily could think of no one less like a witch than Mim. The elegant woman with perfect makeup — a *witch?*

"I'm awfully sorry if I seem surprised, only…I don't believe I've ever met a witch before. I'm not one myself, I should add. But Raf says I'm a sensitive."

He nodded. "Last night Sissy could hear that thing in the window knocking to get out. She's got a hell of a gift." Raf squeezed Cecily's hand. "I think it's still here, you know. I don't know where, but it's here."

"I can't hear it anymore." Cecily lowered her head. It felt like a failing, because if she could hear it then they might be able to find it and stop it ruining life in Acaster Garrow.

"You mustn't blame yourself," Michael told her. "Those who forced that window on us, they're to blame for this. Certainly not you."

"Come into the house," Raf told them all as he began to amble along the lawn with Cecily's hand safe in his. "If you're not going to eat, you'll at least have a drink. I reckon it's a demon. What do you think, Mike? Any clues from Him upstairs?"

"I've asked the Lord to watch over us and to enter the hearts of the people of this village and work his peace. But if a demon is already moving in them…"

Michael shook his head. "I've never seen such a thing, but a demon seems most likely, it's true. Before it got out, it looked for all the world as though it had been squashed between the glass by a butterfly collector. Yet it's *made* of glass. What a thing!"

"This calls for *țuică*!" Raf closed the kitchen door when everyone was safely inside, then opened a cupboard. He looked suddenly as though he had remembered something and asked Cecily in a whisper, "Sis, can you sense anything? It's not around? Not listening?"

"No, I can't sense anything at all." Cecily took some glasses down from the dresser and set them out on the table. "This house feels so friendly and calm — nothing like how it felt in the church. But it must be in the village *somewhere*."

"If it's a demon, we need to know its name." Raf uncorked the bottle. "Once you have the name, Sis, you can call a demon to you. You can't control a demon with it whatever the storybooks tell you — heads have been lost when people got that bit wrong — but you can summon them. And because demons are incurable show-offs, they'll always answer a call. It doesn't make them any less dangerous, but at least we'd have some way of keeping it where we want it."

"Quite right!" Michael said. He pulled a chair out at the table for Mim. "Worked a treat when we were sent to sort out that poor lad in York. You must remember, Raf? It was kept all very quiet — the Church doesn't like exorcisms to be talked about, but the family were convinced there was devilry, and so many strange things had been going on in the house... Raf here found out the demon's name and joined me in the chanting and we got that little toerag out, didn't we!"

"Sent it packing," Raf agreed. "Just so we know, Mike, what's the Church position on all this? Has the archbishop thrown his hands up and said, *nothing to do with us, mate*, yet?"

"Oh, of course!" Mike sighed as he sat down. "Exeter went off to the hospital — unscathed, because that's just his luck — and made a big to-do and said the workmen hadn't put the window in properly and it fell out. I ask you, what a lot of old nonsense. Then I received a telegram, just as I was about to head off to sort out this brawl. He demands I not say a word to anyone, and that all we saw was a trick of the light!"

Raf drew in a disapproving hiss of breath then handed a glass to Cecily and one to Mim. Michael picked up his own. Mim took a sip, frowning thoughtfully.

She looked as though she might have something to say, Cecily thought, and after another sip she murmured, "Funny thing... Did you notice, Mike, the children? The adults were brawling but the children were playing on the beach as they always do."

"It hasn't affected them, then?" Cecily swallowed a mouthful of the liquor. "So there's hope."

"There's always hope." Raf reached out and took her hand. He was right, nobody knew that more than Cecily because she had endured. Through sadness and grief and the brutal marriage in which she had been trapped for so long, she had endured. And survived.

Chapter Six

Cecily worked in the archive long into the night with Raf, but she was still struggling to find anything. When they did eventually find a book on demonology, it was so old that it was missing several pages and those it still had were tattered and stained.

It seemed an impossible job, and the next morning, when Cecily groaned at the thought of going into the archive again, Raf told her to go out and get some fresh air. How like him, to shoulder the burden that he was all too willing to relieve her of. He would exhaust himself if she let him.

"I've got that note to post to Harriet, to tell her we arrived in one piece," Cecily said. Harriet, Cecily's old friend, was still at Whitmore Hall, the wife of the new headmaster. "I'll have to go down to the post office in the village, but I promise not to get into any brawls!"

"While you're doing that, I'll get out of bed," Raf promised, watching her from where he was propped up against the pillows. "And I'll drag myself back down to the archive and try to find a picture of our ugly new pal. That's the good thing about a house like this. You can find pictures everywhere you look."

As Raf said that, he cast a very meaningful look at the carved headboard of the four-poster bed where they had spent the night wrapped in each other's arms.

"Grinling Gibbons put a goblin on this bed after it kept stealing his tools at Windsor. The goblin, not the bed." He gestured to the intricate carvings of fruit and flowers that wrapped around the posts. "Have a look at the headboard and you'll see Francis de Chastelaine freeing the little bugger in a Welsh forest, where it hooked up with a whole bunch of its kind and discovered the joys of fresh air and the company of lady goblins!"

"And that's your ancestor there, with all the hair?" Cecily pointed at the headboard where a man stood among trees with a *creature* — she couldn't think of any other way to describe it — nearby.

"Yeah, can you see the similarity?" Raf turned his head a little, angling his chin upwards. He put one hand on his hip and gestured vaguely with the other, approximating the pose of his ancestor. "With Francis, not the goblin."

"Your hair's not as wild!" Cecily ruffled it then said, "It is now, though!"

He caught her hand and asked, "Sure you don't want me to come down to the village with you?"

"We can't waste time, can we? And I'll hurry. I'll be fine." Cecily leant down and kissed the end of his nose. He stroked his hand through her hair and smiled.

"I'll be working hard, Captain, I promise."

"If you're still in bed by the time I return..." Cecily chuckled as she headed for the door.

When she glanced back Raf blew her a kiss, then made a show of drawing up the covers as though he was about to go to sleep again. He wouldn't, of course, because she knew he was as dedicated as she was to ridding Acaster Garrow of its unwanted pest.

As Cecily wandered down into the village, she began to wish she had asked Raf to come with her. The atmosphere was as oppressive as if a storm was about to break. In the lane she saw a dead magpie, and farther along a fallen branch that she hadn't noticed before, the torn splinters of the tree's trunk gaping like an open wound. When she passed the gate into a field the cows were standing close by, swishing their tails and watching her as she went by as if they thought she were about to spring.

A woman cycled past and Cecily recognised her as one of the attendees at the welcome party. She had given Cecily a homemade jam tart and made sure she was plied with tea, but today the woman merely scowled at her, muttering something under her breath as she pedalled away along the road. Cecily took a deep breath and walked on, reminding herself that this wasn't Acaster Garrow, but the malign influence which it currently laboured under.

Once she reached the parade of shops where the closest thing to Acaster Garrow's village square was found, it was clear there was something amiss. Not one person was happy. Everywhere she looked there were people with clenched fists glaring at one another, their voices raised.

Cecily unbuttoned the top of her overcoat and clutched the *cocosul* around her neck. She dodged past a pulsating mass of corpse flies crowded into the angle of the lintel as went into the post office.

The little shop was hushed but the air seethed just as it did outside, crackling as though heavy with approaching thunder. When Cecily approached the counter, the postmaster took the envelope without a smile, muttering under his breath all the time. As he inspected it, he asked, "Nothing else you need, *Miss*?"

And there it was, so much bile in that one word. As if it was the business of *anyone* whether Cecily was a spinster or a widow. She clenched her teeth, biting back every invective she could have spewed, and instead grasped the *cocosul* even tighter.

So tight that the worn leather thong snapped.

"No, no, thank you, I don't need anything else today, thank you." As she shoved the necklace into her pocket, she added, her tone sharp, "And I would kindly ask that you keep your considerable nose out of other people's business. Good day!"

"Oh, madam doesn't need anything else, nor does her little foreigner now he's got a scarlet woman living under his roof," huffed a woman who had joined the small queue behind her. "How about a ring on your finger? Or isn't that how incomers do it?"

"How about a fist in your gob?" Cecily retaliated as she swept out of the post office.

What a bloody place, and what nosey bastards!

Cecily stormed back home. She made the return journey twice as fast as the journey there, and uphill too. She would have a word with Raf about his rude, insinuating locals. Maybe they should leave, go and find somewhere better to live, somewhere without ill-mannered imbeciles — Acaster Garrow was filled with them.

A whole village stuffed to its rotten gills with village idiots.

They would be so much happier somewhere else, somewhere far away from Raf's beloved Yorkshire. Even that made her roll her eyes as she thought of it. He'd spent his formative years in the splendour of a Transylvanian castle, but he'd chosen to live in this stinking hole of a village stuck up in the middle of nowhere? He was too sentimental about his precious family tradition by far. Raf de Chastelaine was just one more village idiot.

A castle, for heaven's sake!

As Cecily neared the gates of her new home she saw a figure emerge. It was a woman, dressed in a coat of dark red and a hat to match. Long feathers stood out from the wide brim, showy and overdone for a village morning. Showy and overdone were the kindest words Cecily would apply to a woman of this sort.

"Morning!" Mim called, an infuriatingly fake chirp to her tone. "Raf's hard at work. I promise I didn't distract him! I just wanted to update him on— Are you all right, Cecily?"

"Why wouldn't I be?" Cecily snapped. "Are *you* all right, prancing about in scarlet?"

Mim frowned, then asked, "Would you like me to come in with you? I don't think you're quite yourself."

And how would you know?

The scarlet woman.

Cecily stormed towards her front door. "There's nothing wrong with me—not a damned thing! But how everyone *must* interfere! *Are you all right, shouldn't you be wearing a ring,* blah-de-bloody-blah! I don't want to hear another word of it. Not one word! And if this is what village life is like, I'm bloody well buggering off!"

"Have you been down to the village?" Mim reached out and flicked her fingertips across Cecily's shoulder, swiping away a large black fly that she hadn't even noticed was there. "Let's go and see Raf together. I think perhaps you're under the influence of our unwanted glass visitor."

"How dare you! No, I am not! And you stay away from him, you keep your talons off my fiancée, you harlot!" Cecily drew the enormous key from her pocket and tried to get it into the lock but it was so huge and heavy that it wouldn't catch. "Oh, damn this door and damn this house and — damn you all!"

Mim took a few steps towards the gate, clearly torn between staying where she was and running away from the scene of her grubby little liaison. She *should* run away, Cecily decided furiously. She wasn't needed or wanted here, sniffing around Raf in Cecily's absence. What had the two of them been up to anyway?

"What the hell are you staring at, woman?" Cecily finally got the key into the lock and opened the door. She didn't want to go in, but she didn't want to stay out. She didn't want to be anywhere because wherever she went, she wasn't wanted.

Raf was crossing the hallway, looking like an unmade bed as usual in trousers and a shirt that looked like they'd never seen an iron. And no shoes, for goodness' sake. Didn't Mrs Hodge look after the clothes of the man who paid her wages? Did nobody take any pride in themselves in this godforsaken place?

Oh, no, he's going about like that because he's had to dress in a hurry.

"We're leaving!" Cecily announced. "Well, *I* am. I suppose you'd be quite happy here on your own, though, wouldn't you? Roaming about like an overgrown child with your harem of harlots to fawn over you!"

Raf blinked, then grinned. *Grinned.* As if it were funny to drag a woman to the other end of the country just to go behind her back with a creature like Mim Garrow. Skulking about behind closed doors, making fun of her. Laughing at her.

"You had me going there, Sissy." He chuckled. "You're home just in time. Mim came round to drop off some jam tarts for you. Kettle's on, shall we—"

"I don't *want* a cup of tea! I want you to bloody well explain yourself, you miserable little man!" Cecily threw her hat onto the pile of rubbish that had taken over the hallway. One more piece to add to the clutter wouldn't make the blindest bit of difference after all, and she added her new coat to it. It landed on a fishing rod and looked like the beginnings of a scarecrow.

Raf approached, a little more cautious now. He held out his hand. "Sissy? What's up?"

"Up? Up? Nothing's up at all! Apart from all those inbred fools in the village poking their noses in and you and Mim enjoying your *delights* behind my back!" Cecily dashed tears from her eyes. "Why have you done this to me? Why did you bring me here just so everyone would mock me?"

"Why—" Raf took Cecily's hand. "I love you, Sissy, and the village does too. I think you might be under that creature's influence, and you need to fight it. You *can* fight it."

Cecily snatched her hand away. "I'm not! And I've got the *cocosul*—you said it would protect me!" Cecily gulped back her tears. She felt wretched, hopeless. And bloody furious. "Why Mim? Aren't I enough for you? She's so glamorous and I'm a dreadful frump. I should never have believed you! You don't love me. You say you do, but you *don't!*"

"I *do*. Charm or not, you know that I do. You're my whole life. Come on, you *know* that I do. This isn't you." The grin had vanished from his face now, replaced by a look of false, infuriating concern. "And if the *cocosul* isn't strong enough, we'll find another charm that is. Please though, Sissy, fight it. Remember Exmoor? Remember dancing together and going on that river cruise in York and — Look at the ring I gave you. You're my everything."

"I'm *not!* You're laughing at me!" Cecily wrenched the ring from her finger and threw it at Raf. "It's a rubbishy bit of tin and it doesn't mean anything at all. None of it means *anything!* And you can have this piece of tat back *too!*"

Cecily grasped at her neck for the *cocosul*, but it wasn't there.

Good.

He caught the ring and closed his fist tight around it. "This isn't you, Sissy." Raf took a step closer. "Where's your necklace?"

"I don't know," Cecily replied coldly. "I don't care, either!"

"You must've dropped it in the village." His tone was urgent. "I'll run down to the post office, see if I can find it on the road. Promise me you'll stay here?"

Run down to the post office.

Run to your fancy woman's house, more like.

"Say hello to Mim from me, won't you?" Cecily grabbed her coat. "I'm going for a walk in the garden. Not that you'd care. I might just keep going and tumble off the edge into the sea! You'd be glad of that, wouldn't you? Then you can have Mim as often as you choose!"

"Please don't go far, Sissy. Promise me?" Raf opened the door. "Please."

Cecily shook her head. "You don't care, Rafael, so why do you pretend?"

"I painted that charm with my mum when I was a lad. I don't want it to be lost. Come with me, help me look." He stepped into his shoes. "I'm going to find it and bring it back to you, because I love you. And you can fight this."

Cecily's tears broke their banks. She felt so alone, so bleak, all the happiness she'd found now vanished. She shivered as her sobs racked through her. "Why do you keep saying that when it's not true? You don't love me. No one does. No one *ever* has."

Raf closed the door. "Forget the charm. The charm doesn't matter." But she didn't want the door closed. Or open. She just wanted him to go away and leave her alone. If that meant a fruitless search for the necklace in her pocket, it was one way to get rid of him. And to prove that he was really going to see *her*.

Cecily sank down on the last step of the staircase, her head resting against the newel post as she cried. "It's here, in my pocket."

Cecily held it out to him on the flat of her palm. "Raf, you're wearing shoes. Are you going somewhere?"

And as she looked at him, Cecily's heart reached out to the man she loved. She wondered what on earth Raf seemed so het up about, why his usual carefree expression was knitted with concern. *What can have happened since I came downstairs?* Then his face seemed to crumple with emotion and he murmured, "I really thought it was lost... And you with it."

"Why? I'm here!" Cecily smiled as she patted her pocket. "I've got to go into the village and post the letter to Harriet. Now where have I put it?"

"Sissy." Raf crossed the hallway and knelt on the floor in front of her. He reached out and took her hand, holding it gently, almost gingerly. "You went to the village and somehow, I don't know how, the *cocosul* fell off your neck. While you weren't wearing it, you were… I don't know what you'd call it. You were under the influence of the demon. You've just read me the riot act, accused me of not loving you… there was no getting through to you. You know I love you, don't you? More than anything?"

I – What?

"I know you do, and I adore you!" Cecily closed her hand around his. "What do you mean? I haven't been to the village yet. But the *cocosul*… Oh, the leather's broken. It must've fallen off!"

"You've been to the village and you've come back." He kissed her palm. "The demon makes people say things they don't mean. It fills them with malice and suspicion. I'm going to nip upstairs and grab another bit of leather for your pendant. Will you hold on to it for two minutes until I get back? Don't let go."

"Of course. I've got it, I won't lose it, I promise, darling. I know how important it is to you." Cecily kissed the pendant and held it. He rose to his feet then kissed the tip of Cecily's nose and stepped up onto the staircase.

"Two minutes," Raf promised. "You keep hold of that pendant."

With that he bounded off upstairs, leaving her alone.

Cecily got up from the step and noticed her hat on the top of Raf's clutter. She slipped the pendant back into her pocket and reached for the hat.

If only Raf tidied up after himself, the house would look a lot better. How could he live like this, with mounds of rubbish everywhere?

Cecily hung her hat on its peg. Her gaze fell on an elegant woman's umbrella in the stand by the door.

A red one.

Mim's?

Cecily picked it up and hefted the cane handle. It had a fringe all the way around it too.

Oh yes, just the sort of thing for a scarlet woman!

Cecily banged her way out of the front door and stormed off up the driveway.

I'll crack the bloody thing over that bitch's head!

Clutching the umbrella, Cecily marched to the end of the driveway then hoisted herself over a stile and strode across a field. The ancient chimneys of Mim's house appeared over a box hedge, which no doubt Raf had kept trimmed. He had pointed the house out to Cecily on their way to the church, and of course he must've laughed behind his hand to tell her because he had evidently been a frequent visitor.

Cecily took Mim's driveway at a run and before long she had crossed the stone bridge over the moat and was across the courtyard. The house's hotchpotch stone, brick and timber frame frontage seemed to goad Cecily, as if the only function of its shifting styles was to deliberately confuse her.

Cecily heaved the bell pull at the front door, a growl in her throat as she yelled, "Open up, you damn whore, you can't hide from me! I've got something of yours — you can bloody well have the horrible thing back!"

"Cecily?" Mim opened the door just a little. *You'd do well to keep your distance.* "Where's Raf? Did you go home?"

"He left me. He left me all alone!" Cecily wailed. She shoved her toe into the gap between the door and the jamb and tried to wedge in the umbrella too. "Is he waiting for you? Were you going back? Is that it? You couldn't wait, could you? I haven't even married him yet and you're taking him away from me!"

"Cecily, stop it!" Mim backed away from the door, murmuring something under her breath. Some sort of incantation, probably, something else to steal Raf away. How could Cecily hope to compete with this tart and her black magic? With her crimson coat and her feathered hats and her rouge?

Slut.

Cecily shoved open the door and forced her way into the dark, wood-panelled hallway, brandishing the umbrella at Mim.

"Was it raining, was it, when you arrived?" Cecily jabbed the umbrella at Mim as if it were a sword. "Then when you were sneaking off again you forgot it! Well, it's proof, isn't it! Proof of you and him! Oh, you can have him. I've had my fill of this place and all of the blighters in it!"

"That's Mrs Hodge's brolly!" Mim backed away along the hallway. "Cecily, this isn't you!"

"You're lying! It's *yours!* It *is!*" Cecily swished the umbrella from side to side, nearly knocking over a tall vase full of dried grasses. She was gaining on Mim with every step.

"Sissy!" Raf's voice was loud enough to stop even Cecily in her furious tracks. She turned to glare at him and he advanced into the house as though he were approaching a wild animal, a picture frame tucked beneath his arm. He held it up and in it she saw a picture of her mother, willowy and pretty, smiling as she held the hands of Cecily and Sandy, her two toddling children. "Look, Sis. It's your family. *We're* family, me and you. We're getting married. And I've got your engagement ring safe too. Will you put it back on?"

The umbrella fell from Cecily's hand and thumped against the floor. Her mother...her lost mother. "Mummy?"

She tore her eyes from the photograph and glanced up at Raf. "How did you get that?"

"We brought your photos with us when we left Devon. Do you remember? And when we stayed in London, I surprised you by having this one framed." He smiled, his expression kind. "That little shop we found in Belgravia, remember? Where the bloke behind the counter thought I was Russian and wouldn't be told otherwise?"

Cecily tipped her head to one side. Something sparkled at the edge of her vision, something white against the dark red clouds in front of her eyes.

"I...I think I remember... We drove ever such a long way. For days and days and days we drove. And we came here." She looked at the photograph once more. She remembered warmth and love. She heard the memory of laughter. "Mummy. And Sandy. But they've gone... Everyone goes. Everyone always does and you will too."

"They're always with you, they're never, ever gone. They love you, just like I do," Raf told her in a soft voice. "And I'm not going anywhere either. Do one thing for me, Sis. Just have a look in your pocket and see if you can find a little painted stone. I won't ask anything else, just hold it up if it's there."

Cecily folded her arms petulantly. "Why should I?"

"Because you're stronger than that demon is. You're the strongest person I've ever met, and I live in *Yorkshire*."

Something white and crystalline flashed bright in Cecily's vision and she wasn't so sure now that Raf was lying to her. She sunk her hands into her pockets and found a handkerchief, a coin purse, a hair grip.

And a stone.

She pulled it all out and laid it on her palm—and blinked.

"Where am I? Raf, what's happened?"

"Don't let go of that stone." Raf put the picture frame he held carefully on a side table and hurried to join Cecily. He took her face in his hands and kissed her, murmuring, "I love you, Sissy. I'll always love you."

"I love you, too. Raf, I'm so scared..." Cecily wrapped her arms around him.

As he strung a new length of leather through the hole in the pendant that rested on her palm, Raf told her what had happened. He explained the rage that had seized her, the trip to the village, the fury he had faced as soon as the pendant left her hand. And she remembered none of it.

"There we go." He tied the pendant safely around her neck. "My magic cock, eh, Sis?"

Cecily giggled as she put her finger to her lips to shush him. "Mim might hear!"

"I meant the painting on your pendant," was his innocent reply. Then he turned to Mim. "You know Sis wasn't—"

But Mim shook her head and smiled. "Oh, I know. Get home, you two, and be very careful. I'm worried it's only a matter of time before someone does a real injury with all this aggression, and this isn't that sort of place."

"Not before my girl puts her engagement ring back on," Raf said. "It's missing her!"

Cecily took the ring from him and put it back on. Bashful, she held her hand out to Mim to show her the ring. Then she was about to put her hand back in her pocket when she spotted a red umbrella on the floor. She picked up and said, "Oh, Mim, is this yours?"

"Mrs Hodge's brolly!" Raf laughed. "She'll be looking for that next time it rains."

Cecily tucked it under her arm. "Better bring it home, then. Sorry, Mim… Maybe we can have a cup of tea and cake one day soon? Once all this demon business is over with?"

"I'd love to." Mim beamed. She reached out and squeezed Cecily's hand, the gesture one of unmistakable affection. "We'll soon send the blighter packing, never you worry. Then tea and cake for us girls!"

"Yes, we will! Take care!" Cecily waved to Mim as she and Raf headed outside. "I'm so embarrassed, Raf. I'm so sorry…"

He hushed her with a kiss and tucked the picture safely beneath his arm. "You shouldn't be. Let's get home, get the door locked and get onto the books again. We need to find its name."

Chapter Seven

They took a pot of tea down to the archive with them and set to work again. Raf helped Cecily carry the enormous tomes to the table, and he held down the pages as she read through them. Occasionally he would take a sniff from the little bottle of floral scent he carried, using it to block out what to him must be overwhelming odours from the oldest of the volumes, those coated in a century or more of dust.

Cecily needed a magnifying glass for one book and, as she ran it slowly over the page, she realised what the book contained. "These look like spells – I should be very careful and not read any out! This one's to get rid of ingrown toenails. I didn't know there were spells for such things."

Raf nodded and told her, "Dad's favourite is one to banish mould from cheese. We're practical, us de Chastelaines. I just eat the cheese before it gets mouldy. Or cut it off and eat what's still there!"

Cecily laughed as she closed the book. "I suppose there might be demon-banishing spells in there. We'll keep it to one side. But we need the blighter's name first, don't we?"

She ran the back of her hand over her forehead. "Let's get another book down…"

Straightaway Raf leapt to his bare feet and made his way to the ladder. He climbed it and called down, "What do you fancy? Bound in suspicious-looking leather or so old it probably sailed with Noah?"

"Don't suppose any demons stowed away in Noah's boat and kept their feet dry when the flood came?" Cecily peered up at the shelves. "It's worth a look, isn't it?"

Raf drew the ancient book out, leaning his shoulder against the shelf as he opened the cover and peered at the pages. He was tireless, Cecily thought as she watched him. Her lover put everything he had into everything he did and through it all, he kept smiling. And she loved him for it.

But he looked as though even he might be flagging.

Cecily climbed up the other side of the A-shaped ladder. "Are you tired, darling? You work so hard."

"I'm —" Raf closed his eyes for just a moment. "I love this village. To see it falling apart because of some rotten thing— At Whitmore Hall there was something to work with but this? The Church has washed its hands of the whole bloody mess. They've left us to it." He smiled, his eyes twinkling. "Lucky there's a dhampir and a sensitive here to save the day!"

"Not to mention your huge archive!" Cecily leaned forwards across the platform at the top of the ladder to kiss him. He sighed against her lips, sinking into the kiss for a long moment.

"Did you notice," Raf murmured, "that I avoided the obvious *huge* joke?"

Cecily held her pendant. "Were you going to say something about a *huge cock*, Raf? Only I'm far too innocent to know what that would mean!"

"It's only a little pendant," he observed of the painted cockerel. "No *huge cock* there. Only a magical one."

"Thank heavens." Cecily rested her head on her elbow. "Was I horrible earlier, Raf? I'm so sorry. I didn't mean it. It was so strange, but I can't remember any of it—it's as if it happened to someone else."

"You weren't yourself. Nobody is. But now you're back." He put the book down on the edge of the shelf and kissed her again. "Promise me you won't dwell on it? Because if you do, I'll have to take your mind off it with something fun."

Cecily raised an eyebrow. "And just how would you do that?" But she knew, and she grinned because she remembered a hotel room in Stratford-upon-Avon, when a line a schoolboys filing past outside had reminded her of Whitmore Hall. And Raf had kissed all the sadness away.

"Well, I'll start by getting off this ladder." Raf kissed Cecily's nose then hopped down from the ladder. "Shall we see what happens next?"

Cecily stepped down and met Raf at the foot of the ladder. There was a promise glittering in his eyes and he put both her hands on his shoulders and kissed him. He wrapped his arms around her waist and held her as the kiss deepened, his body pressed to hers. She thought again of the *slightly* bigger fangs her dhampir now possessed and a shiver went through her, a shiver that she knew he couldn't fail to notice.

In reply Raf dropped his mouth to her neck. He drew in a deep breath and whispered, "You're wearing that perfume we bought in Oxford, aren't you? The one that reminded me of the garden."

She nodded. "It's my favourite scent. And I know how much you love it."

"When you're not wearing any scent, you still have a fragrance like flowers," Raf murmured, nuzzling her shoulder. "I'd know it anywhere. Like a summer morning and lavender in a coastal garden."

"Do I?" Cecily ruffled his hair then kissed his ear. "You smell like the earth after it rains. Always."

"Do you like it?" He blinked up at her.

"You'd never find the like of it in a bottle. And that's why I love it."

"Once we've sorted out our pest problem, I want to get back into the garden," Raf told her, but she knew there was more to it than that. His tone was too full of mischief to be innocent. "Now, it might be winter, but this skin of mine is still *very* sensitive to sunlight. It'd be a big help to me if I knew a gorgeous woman who might help me put my sun lotion on. Someone who wouldn't mind massaging it in all over."

Cecily began to unbutton his untucked shirt. "That's a tall order, Raf, but I don't mind helping!"

"Well…if you *insist*. You do have a good technique." He nuzzled her throat, kissing his way up to her jaw. "Talented hands. Sensitive in every single way."

Cecily trembled with need at his kisses, her fingers fumbling on his buttons. "Oh, Raf… I want you, you dear, dear man."

"We could take a bit of time off from saving the world and just…I want you, Sissy." His hands slid over her back, caressing and gentle. "It's been a hell of a morning already. We've earned a moment to ourselves."

Cecily brushed her hand over the front of his trousers. "I rather think you're not suggesting we rest for a cup of tea?"

"I'm suggesting," he began to unbutton her dress, "that we behave in a way that no respectable librarian would approve of in a priceless archive. What do you say?"

"Raf!" Cecily giggled as she swept his shirt off and down his arms to pool on the floor. "Well — as long as we don't damage anything… And who's here to see us anyway?"

He gave her a very approving look as he eased her dress down her shoulders and lower, the soft fabric whispering against her skin. How wonderful it was to have nice clothes at last after so long making do, but how much better to take them off at moments like this.

Cecily unfastened his trousers and as Raf rarely wore braces they dropped from his waist with little effort. His compact, toned body always excited her and she held him close against her as they kissed ever more passionately. She felt the weight of the charms he wore against her breast as they embraced and his practiced hands moved over her underwear, unfastening a lace here and a button there. He was utterly without any trace of embarrassment in his nudity and since they'd been together, so was she. She no longer felt gawky and ugly, awkward and unloved but… Maybe it wasn't *British* to say it, but she felt strong and beautiful.

Cecily felt like someone worth loving.

"*Te iubesc,*" Raf breathed, his voice low with desire as he revealed her body. All she wore now was the pendant and her locket, both of them warm against her skin. "My Sissy."

"I want you, Raf..." Cecily whispered. The confusion she had felt earlier still washed against the edges of her consciousness, and she wanted closeness with Raf again, connection. Something that would soothe away the bruise. "Here?"

"Anywhere you like," he whispered, kissing her again.

Cecily took his hand and led him to the chaise longue. She moved aside the pamphlet box that she'd left on it earlier and drew Raf down to it. "There's something rather louche about these sofas, don't you think?"

"There should be, because they're ours," Raf teased. "A sensitive like you should pick up something from this one though. Something *very* louche. Are you getting any tingles?"

The chaise longue had a decidedly saucy air, as if Cecily could hear the echo of a brazen giggle. "I get the feeling we're not the only people to have ever sat on it like this."

"You might be onto something with that," he told her, easing her down onto the soft cushions as he kissed his way over her throat. "You're a bloody talented woman, Sissy. And smart. And that makes you even more sexy."

Cecily stroked his face, circling her thumb against his skin. "Sexy...!" She giggled, the word sending a forbidden thrill through her. She tangled her legs with his and finally crossed hers around his waist. "You're caring and lovely and handsome and *everything* to me."

"And you're the only girl I've ever met who keeps a magic cock around her neck!" With that pronouncement,

Raf ducked his head lower and kissed the pendant, then the locket too. Then he dipped lower still, teasing the tip of his tongue against Cecily's nipples.

Cecily laughed, but it soon dissolved into a sigh as he caressed his tongue against her. She was desirable to him, and it still surprised her how aroused the thought of it could make her. She ran her hands over his tattooed back, stroking his firm, muscled body, breathing in his scent of earth and gardens.

Whoever would imagine Cecily Pincombe, timid, withdrawn, afraid, would be reclining on a chaise longue with her very own dhampir? Yet she was and as their bodies finally joined, *reclining* was the very least of what they were doing.

They kissed deeply, their bodies moving together in perfect time as if they'd been lovers for years, not months. Raf knew instinctively how to make Cecily gasp and she moaned into their kiss, not wanting the pleasure or their kisses to end. As they made love, the lingering sense of something out of kilter finally fell away. The unease, the sensation of having been cruel but not knowing quite why or how, left her with every moment that slipped by. Instead she felt nothing but safety and desire, caught in the love they had for one another, the love that had never wavered no matter what had been thrown at it.

Cecily drew Raf closer and closer to her, her body fluttering around his as her climax drew near. She moaned his name, gasping with pleasure. He caught her earlobe gently between his teeth, nibbling and teasing again before he whispered breathlessly, "I love you."

She shivered with pleasure, every part of her trembling as her climax rushed through her. She cried, holding Raf tighter, the sensation of his body moving against hers making it seem as if her pleasure had no end.

There was no coming down from it, just a soaring joy that only intensified when Cecily felt Raf surrender to his orgasm. His hips thrust hard and fast then with a cry of her name every muscle in him seemed to tense as one as pleasure claimed him, sweeping her along with it all over again.

Finally, Cecily fell still. She gazed at Raf, his head cushioned on her chest. "I love you so much, Raf... I love every bit of you."

Raf traced his fingertips down her side, sighing with contentment. "You're the best thing that's ever happened to me." He lifted his head a little and she felt his tangle of charms pool on her skin. "I love you."

Chapter Eight

There was no time to slouch. Dressed again — or at least, Cecily was, and Raf had his trousers on once more but not his shirt and certainly not his shoes — they were back hunting through the archive for any hint as to who the demon from the window could be.

While Raf went up the ladder to fetch down some more books, Cecily wandered over to the weapons store cupboard. Considering that there were books in every nook and cranny of the house — Cecily had found a grimoire under the kitchen sink when she'd gone back upstairs to make more tea — she decided it was worth seeing which tomes might have made their way into the weapons store.

The door was set in the wall, and when she opened it, she discovered not a cupboard as such but a whole room. The walls and shelves were heavy with items, blunderbusses and sabres, flint-studded nets, gauntlets and chainmail. There were more gentle pieces too — sticks that Cecily assumed were wands, folded cloth, and a wad of what looked like sheep's wool that sparkled gold.

No, not Jason's golden fleece? Surely not.

"Found anything good?" Raf called. "Have a look at the longbow on the back of the door. Robin Hood twanged that once upon a time!"

"Goodness me! And what's in *here?*" Cecily took a wooden case down from the shelf, about the same size as a shoebox. "Is anything going to spring out if I open it?"

Raf ventured into the doorway and paused. Then as he moved closer, he advised in a suspiciously cheery voice, "It shouldn't, but…open it slowly, maybe? Just in case?"

Cecily turned the box so that it faced away from her. She nudged open the catch and took a deep breath before carefully lifting the lid. It swung open with surprising ease for a case that was so old, and nothing burst out of it. So she looked inside.

"Rulers, compasses, set-squares…" Cecily picked through the contents then glanced at Raf. "Bit too old for you to have used at school!"

"Just a bit!" Raf dipped his head towards the box and inhaled deeply, taking in the scents that Cecily's merely human nose wouldn't be able to discern. "Maybe…" He frowned, then inhaled again. "There might be a hint of incense but I wouldn't swear to it. Too old for much to have lingered, which is a shame. Are you getting anything from it?"

Cecily took one of the compasses and closed her eyes. "Someone sitting by a window. For the light. Drawing and drawing… I'm looking closer… It's a cupola on the paper, I…"

Cecily's hand trembled and suddenly she was turning the compass, then adjusting its width and turning it again. She had no idea what she was doing, her hand no longer under her own control.

"Raf, I'm not doing this... The compass is."

"A cupola," he said thoughtfully, taking it all in his stride as ever. "And how does this feel to you? Are you happy with it or is it feeling off? Because we can put them away if you'd rather."

"It feels — content." Cecily watched, fascinated, as the compass took her fingers for a dance in the air. "Does that make sense? It's a tool, and it wants to do a job. It wants to draw."

Raf nodded. "Shall we give it some paper and see what it wants to tell us? If it's been kept down here, it's probably mostly benign. It looks it, at least."

"Yes, it's worth a try." Cecily couldn't put the compass back into the box, so she headed out of the weapons store, the compass apparently guiding her. "It seems to know where it's going. Do you think it...no, it's silly of me to say so, but do you think it might have belonged to Beatrice the Builder?"

Yet Raf didn't seem to think it was silly at all. He paused and tapped his fingertip against his chin, apparently considering the question.

"Something drew you to that unremarkable box. I wonder if it called to you," he mused, laying out a sheaf of paper on the table. "I've heard of it with sensitives before, but...do you think it might've? Saw a gorgeous girl and thought, *here we go!*"

"I don't know, I really don't!"

The compass was on the paper before Cecily had sat down, and was dancing off with such energy that she struggled to force a pencil into it before it was off again.

Round and round it went, sketching out a cupola. Then it stopped and fell sideways onto the paper as if it were tired. Cecily unscrewed the pencil and it took on the compass's energy, darting across the paper.

"Whatever is going on, Raf?"

He sank into the seat beside her, watching as the pencil lines grew bolder, sketched feverishly in Cecily's uncontrolling hand. Yet she felt nothing malign, no force, only the sure knowledge that this pencil needed to draw whatever it was working on. And it looked like—

"It's a cathedral," Raf realised, his voice a wondrous murmur.

"Is it? Any cathedral in particular? Look at the arches on the windows!" Cecily laughed until a thought struck her. "I never thought I'd ever— It's not the one that the window came from, is it?"

He nodded, slipping his arm protectively around her shoulder. "I'm not sure if you can talk to a pencil or— Bloody hell, let's try. Weirder things have happened to you and me." Raf kissed Cecily's cheek. "Can you ask it if it's Bea's equipment? If you don't mind chatting to a pencil."

Cecily nodded. "Did this set once belong to Bea de Chastelaine?" she intoned.

The pencil stopped. Then moved suddenly to the very corner of the page and in an old-fashioned hand, wrote, *Aye*.

Raf peered at the word for a second but Cecily waited to see if he needed her to read what it said. His brow furrowed then he smiled and said in his own Romanian accent, "Aye! That's a Yorkshire lass, is that!"

"Am I channelling Bea?" Cecily asked. "It's odd, I don't feel she's here, really. But her tools are, and that's something."

"I think...yes. You need to be all right about it, though." His arm tightened around her shoulder. "Are you? Remember that you're in control, you're the one who calls the tune."

"I could put all these tools away whenever I choose," Cecily said, all the time the pencil dragging her hand across the paper, leaving another part of the cathedral's plan in its wake. "But I don't mind. I want to see what she has to show us."

Raf nodded. "Maybe she'll show us how to deal with this bloody pest problem!"

The pencil continued to move, undaunted. After going through four pieces of paper for different elevations of the building, the fifth piece turned into a detailed plan for what looked like a side aisle. Cecily watched in amazement as under her hand there appeared columns with spiralling designs, different on each as they surrounded the window. And still the drawing went on, one pencil after another growing blunt and replaced by Raf.

As the hours passed and the endless supply of sharpened pencils continued, Cecily realised that Raf's newly sharpened canines had their practical uses too. What started as a silly bit of show to make her laugh eventually became just part of their routine as amanuensis and aide. She drew, he whittled the pencils back to sharpness beside her. Sometimes he used a pencil sharpener but more often than not a few strokes from his teeth did the job.

Even when Cecily yawned and began to tire, the pencil still moved. More and more detail from the cathedral emerged—the pews, the enormous incense burner that hung down from the ceiling, the vast pulpit...

"Isn't it supper time?" Cecily asked, but apparently pencils channelling long-dead architects never rested.

Raf nodded. "Mrs H didn't show up today—too busy being as bad tempered as the rest of the village, I expect. But we've got plenty in. I'll nip up and put together a ploughman's if you fancy."

"Would you? I don't think I ought to stop—I might miss something if I do."

But what, Cecily wasn't sure.

"I'll bring supper down to you." Raf kissed Cecily's cheek as he stood. "But I want you to rest tonight. The pencil might not need it, but you will."

With another soft kiss, he left her alone.

The pencil twitched towards another piece of paper and Cecily dragged the paper across the table to her hand. She wondered what on earth was coming out of the pencil then, until she realised it was the inner workings of—*something*. A gear, and perforations in stone, and perhaps a plumb line which caught against a ratchet.

"Come on, Bea, back to the cathedral. Is this part of your designs for this house?"

There was no answer, other than the pencil now drawing with more furious speed, filling in detail after detail of the mechanism.

She didn't know how long passed before Raf returned but when he did, he was carrying two plates laden with food. There was cheese and pickles, ham and colourful fresh salad and, from the bag that hung from his wrist, Cecily could see the top of a seeded loaf. A beer bottle peeped from each of his pockets and even as the pencil continued to move, she realised that she was ravenous.

"Supper!" Raf called. "Time for a break, Bea the Builder and Sissy the Sensitive."

Cecily sat back in the chair, resting, but the pencil was still going in her hand. "Erm..."

Raf laid the feast out on the table as he said, "Take a rest, Sis, the last thing I want is for you to exhaust yourself with this business. The pencil can wait while you eat."

"Can you help me take it out of my hand, Raf?"

Cecily clasped at her fingers, trying to unlock them, but she couldn't. And neither, it seemed, could he. Nothing seemed to loosen her grip on the insistent pencil. Instead, it continued to sweep and glide over the page like the ballet shoes of the story Cecily had read in childhood. She was entirely in thrall to the pencil and Raf's efforts to help were apologetic and careful, her lover mindful of doing any injury to her in the process.

When the tip snapped, she reached for another even as they both tried and failed to arrest her wayward hand. Raf tried melodic incantations and rather more forceful ones too, bellowing arcane words with all the ferocity of a blood and thunder preacher, but still the pencil wrote.

"What happens if—" Raf snatched the paper from beneath the tip but the pencil kept on drawing, on the surface of the table this time until the paper was restored. Then it retraced the lines that had been missed, continuing on its way. And all the time her wrist grew more tired, her eyes more bleary.

"Bea!" Raf called the name into the cavernous room. "Bea, give Cecily her hand back before it drops off. Sis, can you make any contact with her, do you think? Should I fetch the portrait down here?"

"I'll have to try... It's cramping up..." Cecily let her gaze rest on the wooden case and whispered, "Bea, let me rest. Just for a little while. Please. Didn't *you* rest when you were drawing these things? Please, Bea...*please*."

As they waited for a reply, Raf closed his hands over Cecily's shoulders and began to mutter a soft incantation. In it she heard her own name and that of Beatrice too and she knew that he was adding his voice to hers, asking the long-dead woman to give her some time to rest.

The pencil's furious pace slowed and finally, in the middle of a line, it stopped then fell out of Cecily's hand.

Cecily sighed with relief and tried to rub the cramps out of her hand. "I thought it'd never stop! And it wasn't even drawing the cathedral anymore—I don't know *what* that is. A portcullis or is it something for dumping boiling oil on your enemies?"

But Raf set the page aside. "First we eat, then we'll have a proper look. You need to get your strength back. I've never seen anything like that!"

Cecily flapped her hand about, trying to relieve her cramped fingers. "Really? So that's not exactly normal, then? I mean...in the realms of...the sort of thing you deal with."

"Automatic writing? Yeah, that's nothing new, but...usually you *can* put the pencil down." Raf caught her hand and rubbed it vigorously between his own palms. "She can't just take ownership of your hand when she fancies it—you never know where that might end!"

"I might punch a stonemason!" Cecily laughed. "And I wouldn't be very popular if I did that."

They moved from the table to the chaise longue and brought the food, Cecily blushing as she remembered what they'd enjoyed there earlier. Now the delights were perhaps a little less earthy, but no less welcome. They snuggled together and tucked into the food Raf had gathered, sipping at the bottles of beer and sampling what he proudly declared was *the best of Acaster Garrow's crop*. Cecily could believe that too, and it made her determination to rid the village of its unwanted new arrival more acute than ever. They might be safe here in Raf's charmed home but out there in the little village that had made her so welcome, things were far from serene.

Soon enough their break was over and Cecily returned to the table. The pencil twitched as if it were being drawn like metal filings to a magnet, but Cecily didn't pick it up. "Raf, *what* is this mechanism meant to be for? Have you seen it before?"

Raf's pressed his fingertips to the page and drew it across the tabletop towards him. Then he leaned closer, peering at it, turning the paper until he had scrutinised every possible angle. With each second that passed his frown grew deeper and when he lifted his hand up to ruffle his hair, the expression on his face was nothing short of perplexed. He blinked at Cecily, rolling his eyes up towards the heavens as he considered his next move.

"Do you know what I'm going to do?" Raf made a fist and rapped on the desk. "I'm going to build it. I've always been better with my hands than my brain, so let's make it. We've got the plans, we've got enough bits of wood and what have you. It looks like it *should* be massive, but we can scale it down."

"Excellent!" Cecily sat back down again and drew in a breath. The pencil rolled over the table towards her and stopped next to her hand, nudging it like an animal after a treat. "I better get back to this drawing…"

Raf nodded. "I'll stay here in case you need me. I'll get to building when it's daylight." Then he grinned and shrugged. "I mean, I don't *need* daylight but… nobody wants me hammering after dark, do they? They're all grumpy enough already."

"Stand by to sharpen more pencils!"

Cecily laid a new sheet of paper in front of her and the pencil hopped into her hand. And she was drawing again.

This time it looked like the detail of a window, but not the one she had seen in the church, although its style was similar and appeared to be another from the same cathedral. The jester appeared again, a crowd apparently jeering at him, and above Cecily drew Adam and Eve in the Garden of Eden. The snake was wrapped around the trunk of an apple tree, but what seemed to excite the pencil was a worm poking its head out from the fruit in Eve's hand.

So much so that the pencil demanded another sheet of paper just to draw the worm and the apple in more detail.

"It's going to be a long night." Cecily sighed.

"Lucky I've got sharp teeth," was Raf's reply as he kissed her cheek. "We'll need a holiday after this."

"We've only just had one!"

The hours ticked by and Cecily could no longer hold up her head. She was tired in every bone of her body, but still the pencil moved. When she rested her eyes, she would open them a few moments later to discover that the pencil had carried on without her.

"Raf, I'm going to have a nap." And she rested her head on his shoulder and fell asleep.

Even in her dreams the pencil kept moving, and she heard the fearsome sound of those glass wings, the horrified cries as the window exploded. But she felt Raf's embrace too, and was aware of his protection even as she slept.

Chapter Nine

When Cecily awoke the next morning, she and Raf were on the chaise longue, asleep under a blanket. She had no memory of getting there. After kissing Raf's cheek, she flexed her fingers. The pencil was long gone, it seemed, but her fingers were grey with pencil lead.

Cecily sat up and looked over at the table. She was alarmed at the sight of the pile of paper on the table, and when she got up to have a closer look, careful not to disturb Raf, she wondered how any of it could be of any use. Window, after window, after window and finally the huge piece that had been foisted on Acaster Garrow's church.

Cecily peered at it and wondered. She had the oddest feeling that there was something in the drawing that was telling her something, but all she could see were the crowds with the jester and the central depiction of Christ and Satan. There was nothing new to see.

She went back to the chaise and crouched beside Raf.

"Breakfast?" she whispered.

He blinked awake and peered at her through bleary eyes. Cecily saw them swim into focus, then grow bright as ever.

"Breakfast," Raf agreed. He sat up and stretched his arms above his head, catching sight of the pile of paper that waited for them on the table as he did. His mouth fell open and he whispered, "Bloody hell."

"I *know*... If anyone ever wants to rebuild that cathedral, we have the plans for it!" Cecily combed her fingers through Raf's hair. "Before we get stuck in again, let's get some fresh air. And breakfast. I'm famished."

He rose to his feet, still stretching his arms. "Bacon sandwich on the beach? I'll cook it. You've done enough. You need to rest."

"That would be divine!" She glanced over at the table again. "I hope like hell we haven't wasted our time, Raf. It's drawings of windows. There's no names on any of it. Maybe we should've persevered with the books?"

But Raf took her hand and drew her into his arms. Then they were dancing towards the staircase as he sang, "Bacon for now, windows for later! And a cup of builder's tea!"

They scuffed up the stone steps and danced on their way to the kitchen, Cecily chuckling. Her sense of guilt at leaving the archive and thus the mystery unknown for the duration of breakfast began to dissolve. They'd never get anywhere near to unravelling the mystery of the glass demon if they were exhausted.

Bea watched from her portrait as they twirled and whirled across the little sitting room and along the hallway. Even in the kitchen Raf held Cecily in his arms as long as he could, eventually admitting defeat only when he clearly realised that he couldn't boil a kettle, fry bacon and dance too.

He settled Cecily in a chair and returned to the range, calling out, "Should I chuck a nice fried egg on your sandwich an' all?"

"Go on, I've got Bea to feed as well!" Cecily kicked up her legs and laid them across the chair next to her.

"The sea looks stormy." Beyond the window the sky was iron grey, and though Cecily couldn't see the ocean from her seat, her heart felt a touch of heaviness when Raf said, "The birds aren't singing. Everything's wrong out there."

"Are we really the only people who can do anything about it?" Cecily asked, her throat dry. "Mim and Mike, they can help, can't they?"

The smell of frying bacon filled the air and Raf closed his eyes, drinking it in. He smiled, then opened his eyes again, meeting her gaze with his own. "Mim's doing what she can to keep people safe. Mike's doing the same thing but without magic. He's talking to people, trying to keep them from forgetting who they are and what this village means to them. But we need to get on top of this."

"How can something like that just disappear? It's hardly inconspicuous!" Cecily shook her head. "Although I suppose it's a big village. It could be *anywhere*, and if we started beating about looking for it all those angry villagers would be after us!"

"That's what worries me." Raf poured out two cups of tea and shovelled the usual spoons full of sugar into his own. Then he began carving off thick slices of bread from the loaf. "How long before they find their way up here?"

"You said you can close the house. Could you? Would there be time?" Cecily dropped her feet from the chair and brushed the crumbs from the table, readying herself for breakfast even if she wasn't ready at all for anything else.

Raf piled an egg and slices of bacon onto the sandwiches as he said, "There'd be time. Nobody's going to hurt you, Sissy."

"They were so nasty yesterday, Raf. So horrible and cruel. There's evidently *opinions* about the fact that we're in this house together and we're not married, yet they'd kept it to themselves until the glass demon loosened their tongues."

Cecily watched his face, wondering if she should add the other barbed remark about *foreigners*. Even if he'd inevitably heard similar jibes before, they would still wound, she was certain of it.

But Raf shook his head as he wrapped the sandwiches in baking parchment. Then he took a small bottle that she recognised as his homemade sun lotion from the windowsill and put in into his pocket.

"That's not them speaking, remember that. It's that creature." He picked up the parcelled breakfast. "And if anything happens and you need to close up the house, wheel anticlockwise. That's all you need to do and the house does the rest."

Let's hope things never get that far.

"Breakfast." Raf held up the sandwiches. "You bring the tea!"

Cecily followed Raf into the garden, carrying the cups and careful to avoid the tea from sloshing over. She dismissed the thoughts that worried at her — *What if Raf is outside when the house closes up? What if I'm trapped on my own and something happens to him and I can't help him?* – and thought instead of their breakfast outside. She wasn't used to such a thing, as breakfast was a meal that for years she had eaten in silence in a tiny kitchen under the eaves. Never, ever outside.

What struck her as they strolled across the lawn together was the uncanny silence. Raf was right, there were no birds singing, and not even the clamour of gulls sounded along the cliffs. All she could hear was the insistent hiss of the waves and their own feet on the grass, Raf's bare, Cecily's shod. They wandered through the trees and down the steps onto the beach, where Raf held out one of the sandwiches to her.

"I'll swap you." He grinned. "A sandwich in return for a cuppa and a kiss."

Cecily's heels sank a little into the sand so she didn't have as far to lean as usual when she kissed him, and nearly dropped her sandwich in their exchange.

"It's such a lovely spot," she said. "And it'll be lovelier still once we've sorted out the demon."

Something about that seemed to tickle Raf and he laughed as he settled down to sit in the sand, his legs stretched out before them. He peered up at Cecily and asked, "Will you be all right on the sand? Do you want my shirt to sit on?"

"Would you mind? I haven't chosen the best dress to wear on the beach, have I!"

It wasn't the best dress to wear in an archive either, a wool crepe frock with large embroidered flowers around the skirt and a ruffle at the hem and the cuffs. Of course, she knew that Raf wouldn't need asking twice and moments later he had peeled off his shirt and laid it out on the sand, an impromptu picnic blanket for her. Cecily saw him glance up at the sun, failing to make much of an impact thanks to the heavy clouds above.

No need for lotion today, it seemed.

Cecily carefully sat down and stretched out her legs. She settled her teacup on the sand and began to eat the delicious sandwich.

"This *is* good—and you said you couldn't cook!"

"I can fry." He smiled. He was doodling in the sand with his big toe, Cecily realised, watching as Raf drew a heart. Then he nudged her and said, "I'm not just good at frying. I'm a romantic too."

"You are," Cecily whispered. "You're very romantic indeed. Let me…"

Cecily took a mouthful of tea then got to her feet. Still eating her sandwich, she grabbed a sea-roughened stick with her other hand and wrote in the sand *C & R*. Then she drew a huge heart around it.

She laughed, but before she could stop it, the stick, still in her hand, was drawing of its own accord.

"Oh, not *again*…."

"Bloody hell, Bea, give her a break," Raf called to the heavens.

Cecily began to recognise the figures—the people who were in one of the jester's crowd scenes in the window that the demon had escaped from. But drawn in the sand with a weed-strewn stick they were abstract, depicting only the outsides of some of the figures—an upside-down *V* for a hat, a Greek *E* for the folds in a robe, an *S* for an elaborate scarf and…

"Raf, come and look. Is this a word—a word from one of your spells maybe? I think it's an *H* now—there's that person in the crowd with their arms up in the air, it must be them. And what's that? An *M*—the shape made by someone's jerkin and jacket, I remember. And another hat! *Veshmv?* What on earth would that mean?"

The stick flew from her hand and imbedded itself on one end in the pebbles, as if declaring a full stop.

"Veshmv?" Raf rose to his feet, chewing the last of his sandwich as he took his place beside Cecily. He drank some tea and drew the small bottle of lotion from his pocket. "Will you do my back while I have a think?"

Cecily brushed the remains of her breakfast sandwich from her hands and took the bottle. The beguiling scent of herbs and gardens rose as she opened the lid, and she began to smooth the lotion into his back. Raf cocked his head to first one side then the other, looking at the images she had drawn with the stick.

"V or...could it be N? She was like me, remember, not good with words and letters." He chewed his thumbnail. "*Neshmn* sounds like gibberish too, doesn't it? Could it be another language?"

"Maybe...unless...well, it looks like an upside-down *V*. But if you put a line through the middle, it becomes a capital *A*. Which would make it..." Cecily mouthed the word before saying, as quietly as she could, "Aeshma."

From far above there came a strange sound and one of the dark clouds lowering above them seemed to pulsate, as though the sky itself were coming alive. From within the cloud rose the demon made of glass, its wings unfurling and blotting out what little of the sun there was with their dark, painted surface.

It opened its mouth and let out a screech the like of which Cecily had never heard before, a long, snake-like tongue darted out to lick the glass surface of its maw. The creature hadn't changed form, hadn't solidified or become flesh and blood. It was still a thing of stained glass, yet somehow animated, alive with malice, and it turned its bright yellow eyes on Raf and Cecily and howled.

Then, with a noise like a lightning strike severing a tree through its heart, the cloud thundered down towards them. Raf turned and seized Cecily, bundling her close to his body and bringing her head down to his shoulder. In the moment before Cecily instinctively closed her eyes she knew what the cloud was and her stomach turned in on itself.

What must have been thousands of flies swarmed around them, the buzzing deafening in her ears. Over even that though Cecily heard something else, a clanking, grating sound as the demon's glass wings carried it towards them. Raf was bellowing something, the words lost in the beating of innumerable wings before the cloud of flies ascended once more and disappeared out over the sea. In the centre of the cloud was Aeshma, glass wings snapping back and forth as it disappeared into the mass of insects.

Cecily stared after them in stunned silence. She had summoned a demon by its name, but had it gone? Had it really gone?

"Don't worry, I won't ever be repeating its name again! But that's *it*...the demon's name. And it was written in the window all along, only it'd been disguised!"

"Sup up," Raf said. "Then it's back to the books for you and I'll see exactly what you drew last night. We'll find it soon enough, should be a matter of time now we've got the bugger's name! If that's all right with you, Captain? If you'd rather do the carpentry, I'll muddle through the grimoires!"

"No, I don't think we want me anywhere near the carpentry!" Cecily finished her tea in one swallow. They had a name now, and those feelings of hopelessness that had assailed her before seemed very far from view.

"I wish Bea had built a fly swatter into the house." Raf grimaced, then shuddered deeply. "I don't mind much but bloody hell, they're dirty things. They smell putrid, like the grave. Be glad you don't have my nose."

"How horrible!" Cecily remarked. "I didn't notice them smelling of anything at all. Where have they come from? Has the demon conjured them up, or are they all swarming to him from the four corners of the Earth?"

But even Raf didn't seem to have an answer to that. He shook his head, then drew Cecily to him, holding her close. She heard him sigh and knew that he was gathering himself, clearing the stench that had assailed him from his senses.

Cecily combed back his hair only for it to flop forwards straight away. "Come on, let's go up to the garden—all those lovely perfumes will help you."

"Flies." Raf gathered up his shirt, still keeping her close. "First it's murderous rose bushes, then it's flies… I think the garden's probably a good idea."

Hand in hand they went up the steps to the garden. Its many scents seemed as welcoming as an embrace to Cecily and she could only imagine what it must smell like to Raf. He could, she supposed, identify every bloom that contributed to the perfume, a feat no mere human could ever be capable of.

Raf led her across the lawn towards the lavender they had planted with the tulips and there he drew in a deep breath, then another. He closed his eyes and kissed Cecily's cheek, letting his lips linger against her skin.

"Is that better?" Cecily asked. Her cutting had taken root, it seemed, already having doubled in height if not more, with unseasonable dark blue wands of tiny flowers lending their scent to the breeze. Raf nodded, his breathing more regular as he rested his head on her shoulder.

"Sorry about that," he murmured. "That stink was — I never want to smell that again."

"Let's get to work — the faster we put a stop to this, the sooner that smell will be gone for good!"

Armed with fresh cups of tea, Raf and Cecily descended into the archive once more. Raf gathered up the plans for the mysterious mechanism that Cecily had drawn, tucking them under his arm as he leafed through the others, choosing a few more to add to his stash.

"I'm away up to my workshop," he said, brandishing the stack of pages that he had collected. "If you need me, call. I'll hear you, don't worry. Sure you'll be all right?"

Despite the horrors of the demon, Cecily was enjoying her sense of purpose. *We'll get rid of it somehow, we will!*

"I'm *very* all right! We'll have this nonsense licked in no time!"

Cecily got to work. Now they had a name, she returned to the shelves with renewed fervour. She had something concrete to look for now and after about an hour she had laid her hands on just the thing. A book with a leather cover that was crumbling away, its parchment pages looked freshly minted although it must have been centuries old. It was a demonology, and she didn't dare read any of the names aloud.

She found Aeshma on the second page, an ancient demon of wrath from the Zoroastrian tradition. Aeshma was in opposition to truth and obedience, stirring up violence and brutality.

But there were no tips in the demonology about what to do if Aeshma decided to take the form of glass. Cecily sighed and looked back at the drawings of the windows.

And slowly but surely, one by one, she found more letters in the stained-glass designs and matched them up with the demonology. The demon Az watched Judas as he hanged from a tree, his purse of coins at his feet. Belial chased the Hebrews with the pharaoh's men, the tide forever about to close over his head. Krampus was in another window, Amdusias in another. And more appeared in each and every window design that she looked at.

Cecily furled the drawings under her arm and lifted the heavy demonology.

"Raf! I've found something!" she called as she made her way upstairs.

As she reached the sitting room where Bea watched placidly from the canvas, it occurred to Cecily that she didn't actually know where Raf's workshop was. Yet she could hear distant hammering and, sensitive or not, she had an idea that following the sound might just lead her to her lover.

Cecily set off through the house and out into the garden. She walked around the perimeter towards a cluster of outbuildings and saw Raf's little car sitting in the middle of the courtyard, the gardening implements he had carried all the way from Devon now unpacked.

The hammering was louder than ever and Cecily peered over the top half of an open stable door and found herself looking into Rafael de Chastelaine's workshop.

It looked like a place where Father Christmas and his elves might toil as Christmas approached, filled with little projects and experiments, with items being repaired or perhaps even being created. Sketches were pinned to the walls here and there, along with intricate diagrams and designs, all of them drawn by Raf, she suspected. Tools hung from wall-mounted racks and elaborate pieces of machinery stood on benches whilst Raf, humming merrily to himself, worked at a bench with his back to her, the tattoos glistening beneath the slick of lotion she had applied.

"Hard at it, Captain," he called, sawing a piece of wood that rested atop the bench. Beside it she could see a scale model of the drawing Bea's pencil had created beginning to take shape. It was as tall as Raf's torso and constructed from what seemed to be a dozen different types of wood. "Come in and tell me what you've found."

Cecily crossed the room quickly and told him, "There's a demon in every window. Each window's design spells a name in the lead, and each window contains a figure which must be a demon. The worm in the apple, it's —" Cecily held back the name. "I can't say it, of course, or I'll risk summoning it, but they're not very nice at all."

"*Every* window? That's a lot of windows. Which means a lot of demons." Raf put the saw down on the bench and slipped his arm around Cecily's waist. "I've been looking at the plans you drew and I was wondering... There are elements in it that Bea built into our house here, but when we close the house down, it's to keep the outside from getting in."

He spread out the pages he had brought up to the workshop, fanning them over the bench. Cecily could hardly make head nor tail of what she was looking at at first but then she realised that it was cross sections of the cathedral walls, intricate architectural plans that had flowed from the pencil's tip. There inside the great stone walls were hidden ropes and pulleys, cogs and gears that powered vast spiked portcullises that hung ready to drop and contain the congregation.

Why would anybody want to, though?

There were huge metal gates that might turn the cathedral into a fortress, trapdoors that would plunge people down onto the stone floors of the crypt fifty feet below and even vast guillotine blades that looked as though they might slice through a hundred necks at a time, like a knife would cut through butter. And on the machinery, she saw dozens of intricate symbols that she had initially taken to be rivets or screws. Now though, as Raf held up a magnifying glass and allowed Cecily to examine her work more clearly, she recognised the marks as hieroglyphs, symbols of a language that she certainly didn't understand.

Why on earth would anyone build such monstrous things into a place of worship, especially Beatrice de Chastelaine? It made no sense whatsoever.

"Bea booby-trapped Kwaalveld," Raf explained. "But not to protect it from what was outside. These traps are all triggered from *inside*. They're meant to keep what's in from getting out. You see these little symbols you drew? They're everywhere, dotted all over the cross sections, on every bit of machinery. You've drawn them under the font, scratched them into the ceiling, behind the memorials...too small for anyone to see if they didn't know they were there."

She looked down at the sketches as he indicated the strange marks that Cecily had drawn with her own hand, under the guidance of Beatrice de Chastelaine's spirit.

"I've got some of these same symbols tattooed on me and they're scratched into the plaster of this house. They're protection marks, little charms to keep us safe," Raf explained. He fanned out another sheaf of papers, ancient this time, and Cecily realised that she was looking at plans of the house in which she had come to live. Beatrice de Chastelaine's original architectural drawings for her own family's home.

"I don't reckon Kwaalveld was just an unlucky village, with its plagues and disasters and all that. My mum was a vampire, I've got relatives in Transylvania who'll tell you they watched the pyramids being built — we know the veil can get stretched from time to time." He paused, looking down at the drawings again. "I think someone tore a hole right through it at Kwaalveld and all sorts of nasty little buggers came pouring out. What Bea built wasn't only a cathedral. It was a prison."

Cecily stepped back in surprise. Yet as she ran it through her head again, it all made devastating sense. "A demon prison? Oh, I see! And they were all squashed into the glass like flies in amber! Until Aes — until that *thing* escaped. Without the symbols cut into the walls or and with no portcullises to bind it, no wonder it got out!"

Raf picked up a drill, its bit as fine as a needle. "According to your plans, this cross-beam was covered in tiny holes, through from one side to the other." He put the bit on the newly sawed piece of wood. "But they were dealing with pieces of stone almost as tall as me. Why would you need to make holes in that? Imagine the work it'd take."

Cecily couldn't even begin to wonder why anyone would design such a thing, even in what seemed to be a prison for these hellish monsters.

"Read me what you've found about our escapee and I'll crack on with drilling. I've got a fair whack of work left to do." Raf glanced up, his smile filled with mischief. "Just don't say its name."

"Don't worry about that, I've made that mistake already!" Cecily laid the demonology on the workbench and turned to the page near the front that she'd bookmarked with a slip of paper. "The demon's legendarily bad. It says here that the name gives the Georgians their word for the devil. And it's possible it's in the Apocrypha, too, as—well, I won't say that name either. Just in case." Cecily settled on a stool beside the bench and read on. "It's the demon of wrath, the antithesis of obedience. And someone with a very similar name was once worshipped as a false god. That's quite a fall from grace, isn't it? False god one minute, trapped in a window for hundreds of years the next! It can be driven away by the recitation of a particular prayer, but whatever it is, some creature got inside the book and expired right across the rest of the entry and the ink's gone. A huge moth or something."

"That sounds about right." Raf kept drilling as he spoke, creating a growing pattern of holes in the piece of wood. "Be glad it wasn't a fairy. They've got a habit of springing back to life when you least expect it. Whatever that was though, it's definitely not going to be springing anywhere. So we know its name, but we don't know its prayer."

Cecily closed the book, superstitious that the moth might revive after all. She watched Raf as he worked, fascinated by his dexterity. She wouldn't have known where to start. "What on earth are those holes for? It looks like a piece of wood that the worms have got at."

"Can you imagine doing this through those great pieces of stone?" He nodded towards the wooden frame. "I reckon it looks like the surround for the demon's window, so it'd be a lot more solid than this, but the design's what we're trying to understand. None of the others have got this weird, drilled stone built into them, so I feel like we need to know why. What made *that* demon special enough to get the big window and the whatever-it-is stone?"

Cecily shook her head. "Aren't we lucky it's turned up in Acaster Garrow?

"Yeah, let's send the Archbishop of Exeter a thank you card and a big bunch of blooms." He laughed. "I'll probably be a few more hours here. Do you fancy helping?"

"If you think I can. I'm not very good with my hands."

He nodded towards a pair of heavy gardening gloves at the end of the bench. "There're some glass off-cuts on the shelf above the paint brushes. See if you can find something that's more or less the right size for this frame? You'll need the gloves — don't want you cutting yourself after we saved your hand from Bea!"

Cecily put on the gloves and went to look at the pieces of glass. They lay in a stack, all different sizes, some clear, some green, some pink. "It was a strange old thing, you know. Bea had my hand but I didn't feel as if she was present, not like when I channelled before."

"In an ideal world, which Yorkshire usually *is*, you'd have time to get to know what you're capable of," Raf said as a large spider scuttled out from behind the glass and darted away to safety. "But we've been chucked into this one a bit. I think we should use it as an excuse to have a very long, very sunny honeymoon."

Cecily found two pieces of glass that looked about the right size and carried them over to Raf. "Where shall we go? Scarborough?"

"That's a day trip but if you fancy Scarborough, we'll go to Scarborough." He pecked a kiss to her cheek then peered down at the cluster of charms he wore. After a few moments he lifted one from the tangle and Cecily recognised it as the piece of bone that he had showed her when they'd shared his humble bed in Devon. He had told her then it was from Egypt and she had dreamed of the place, exotic and so impossible that it might be on another planet. "I was thinking more along the lines of...Egypt?"

Cecily chuckled awkwardly. "Oh, I'd love to, but aren't you terribly busy? It's such a long way to go, after all. And how would you manage with all that sun?"

"I've got the recipe for my sun lotion just right now. All I need is someone to lather it on." Raf moved the drill bit again, ready to make the next in the growing number of holes. "Last time I was there I had to rely on a bloke called Masudi to do it. Amazing bloke — you'll love him — but not my first choice for the job of lotion application. We made sure to talk about manly things while he did it, just to be proper Yorkshire."

"Don't you worry, I'll handle it!" Cecily placed the glass down on the workbench and wiped the dust and cobwebs away with a cloth. "And hopefully we'll have a quiet time. As long as no one's opening any pyramids while we're out there— Who knows what might escape!"

Raf's laughter filled the air but she saw his brow furrow. Then he lifted his chin and sniffed the air before whispering, "Chocolate cake. Who do we know who—"

"Yoo hoo!" Mim's voice called from outside. "Hello? Cecily? Rafael?"

"Are you there?" Michael was with her too, then.

"Chocolate cake and incense." Raf winked. Then he called, "Workshop!"

Cecily took off the gardening gloves and tried to tidy her hair. She hoped it didn't look too obvious that she'd slept in her clothes.

"Hard at work?" Michael said as he stepped into the workshop, a very gentlemanly hand on Mim's elbow as he led her inside. "I cannot tell you how lovely it is to be met by smiling faces."

"We come bearing gifts!" Mim held up a cake tin, brightly patterned with vivid green Christmas trees. "How're you feeling, Cecily? You look a lot more like your old self."

Cecily welcomed them in, making space for them to sit on the stools that were piled with strange machinery and tools. "I *am!* I'm so, so sorry, Mim. Was I beastly?"

"Oh, no more than anybody would be living with Rafael," she joked. "Michael's been in the village. It's not a happy place is it, darling?"

Michael shook his head. "I've lived here for most of my life and I can honestly say that I've never seen the like. Awful."

Cecily noticed red scratches on his face, heading down under his collar. He evidently saw that Cecily had spotted the blemishes and he touched his fingertip to his sore skin, wincing. "Courtesy of one of the ladies who does the flowers at church. She tried to tear my dog collar off me while hissing something about false gods."

"Bloody hell!" Raf put the drill down, his expression shocked. "Have you cleaned that up? I've got some witch hazel in the kitchen if you need it."

Witch hazel.

Cecily caught Raf's eye and she knew that he was thinking the same thing as her. It was the first gift he had ever given her, when he had been an exotic stranger and she her husband's slave and prisoner. *"Witch hazel from the garden"*, scented with lavender, to dab on the bruises her spouse had left on her body.

But those days were gone. Now she was loved.

"Haven't had a chance yet," Michael replied. "I had to run to Mim's because they were throwing manure at me! And the dashed blinking flies were having a field day!"

"Manure?" Cecily shook her head, shocked. "This is all too horrible for words. But Raf and I are onto something." She showed them the sketch of the window, tracing her finger across Aeshma's name in the figures in the crowd. "We know who the demon is—but don't say the name aloud!"

"It summons flies." Raf grimaced and picked up his discarded shirt. "Thousands of flies."

Mim clutched the cake tin to her bosom. "Flies? Oh, heavens, Michael says that the village is overrun with them. They're perching on people like horrible canaries!"

"It really is vile," Michael agreed. "And the place reeks. I can *still* smell how bad it is. And just think how unsanitary! Those clods of manure I had to dodge nearly flew after me, they were so riddled with the damn insects. We thought we'd come here, though. The gardens always smell so nice!"

"You did right!" Though Cecily could see concern behind her lover's smile, his good humour strained with worry for the village and the people he loved. "Shall we get a cuppa and some cake and sit out on the terrace? I'll grab that witch hazel for you, Mike — you need to clean that before it goes bad."

Cecily picked up the demonology. She didn't want it to leave her sight. "Cake and tea — I think we could all do with some!"

Ten minutes later they were settled on the terrace with tea and cake, the air so chilly now that even Raf had put a jacket on over his shirt. As Michael dabbed at the scratches on his face and neck with Raf's witch hazel, Cecily watched her dhampir potter up and down the beds of flowers, gazing at them. Occasionally he took a bite of cake, but she could see that he was deep in thought.

From here they could see the village in the near distance. A fearsome dark cloud hovered above Acaster Garrow, the occasional pulse within telling her that the flies had not gone far after they'd swooped over the beach and she shuddered, wondering again where Aeshma could be hiding.

"I had a devil of a time in the village — quite literally!" Michael, his hands trembling, tried to hold his rattling cup and saucer carefully on his knee as he spoke. "I went down there on my bicycle and hopped off it to break up another fight and within moments a crowd were kicking my poor bicycle—including Wilkins. He's our local constable, for heaven's sake! The wheels are all twisted, the frame bent—and they threw it, hurled the thing up over my head and it's now dangling from the sign outside the pub! There was a woman lying on the pavement who'd been walloped over the head by another woman's handbag, and when I knelt beside her to help her up, she spat on me. Then I got the scratch, then they started to pelt me! And all around me, the whole time I was there, the dreadful stink of those flies and the buzzing...like low, murmuring voices. Everything's turning sour. The dairyman poured out his milk into the drain and the cats came to taste it and soon ran off. All the meat in the butcher's is crawling with flies and the vegetables are a rotten mess. The bread and cakes in the baker's window are pulsating with maggots. Aside from how they're behaving, the people of Acaster Garrow may very well starve if we can't shift the demon. Whatever are we going to do?"

Raf reached into the plants and plucked out a vivid red tomato. He weighed it in his hands as he said, "There's half a dozen bikes in the shed. Help yourself and when we get yours down, I'll make it good as new." He took a bite of the fresh tomato and paused, then swallowed. "Dad would say this needs a sprinkling of salt."

With that he trotted across the lawn and into the kitchen. Mim opened her mouth to speak when, from inside the house, Raf suddenly shouted, "Salt!"

"Salt?" Cecily got up from her deckchair and wandered over to the kitchen door. "It's on the table, I think."

Raf met her on the threshold, the salt pot in his hand. "It's a massive bloody saltcellar!" He caught Cecily's arm, excitement glittering in his eyes. "That's what the holes are for!"

Cecily hopped up and down with childlike glee. "The demon was held in with salt? Oh, yes, Raf! That's *it!*"

"Mim, Mike." Raf turned and put the salt pot down on the worktop. "Can you go down to the archive with Sissy and search everywhere for any mention of this demon whose name we won't say just in case. We want to know everything about it, from it shoe size to its favourite biscuits. I need to finish my little building project, just to be sure. Do you mind?"

"Of course not," Michael said. He finished his tea with a Raf-like slurp and rose from his chair. "Ladies…?"

"We'll bring the cake." Mim smiled. "This is your house, Cecily. Lead the way!"

Chapter Ten

Leaving Raf busy in the workshop, Cecily took Michael and Mim down to the archive.

"It's no tidier than the last time I saw the place." Michael sighed. "But we're lucky to have such a collection—you never know what you might turn up down here."

Mim paused at the bottom of the spiral staircase and let out a long exhalation. Then she asked, "Where on earth do we start? And, Cecily, what *is* this name we can't say?"

Cecily laid the demonology on the table and turned to the page. She covered the demon's name with her hand and said, "Don't say it aloud."

Then she drew her hand away and revealed it, a name written with a flourish of ink.

Aeshma

Mim and Michael leaned over the page and read.

"And it's in the Book of Tobit too? Gets about, doesn't it!" Michael said. "I've always been rather fascinated by the Apocryphal texts, although they're not recognised in my church. Lots of interesting creatures in there, and to think one of them's at large in Acaster Garrow…!"

Mim mouthed the name silently once, then again. Then she nodded, as though satisfied that she wouldn't forget it. As she lifted her head she seemed to notice that Cecily was watching and told her, "Now I know what to call it, I can strengthen the protection spells. They're little match for something of that magnitude but they're all we have at the moment. I worry that someone's going to be killed, Cecily. The village would never forgive itself."

"The fights have been violent," Michael told them. "Horrible. Only fists, but it won't take much for someone to get hold of a knife, or a firearm—" He bowed his head and pressed his fingertips to his forehead. "No, I mustn't think of that. I mustn't."

"We'll find something. I know we will." Cecily pointed to the book of spells as she pushed the ladder a little farther along the shelves. "Mim, would you have a look through that book? It's full of spells, only I would imagine you'd need to know what you're doing to read it and not conjure goodness knows what. Would you mind having a look through it? And Michael, what do you think the prayer might be that repels him?"

As Michael considered the question, Mim dutifully took down the book of spells and retired to the table where Cecily had spent so much of the past few days. She opened the cover and began to read, her head bowed.

Michael tapped his chin in thought. "It must be Zoroastrian. There are some books on that particular faith in the collection somewhere, but I couldn't hazard a guess… Let me look at the Book of Tobit, though, and I'll see if that offers any clues."

He went over to the shelves and ran his finger along the spines. Meanwhile Cecily climbed the ladder and took a volume from the top shelf. The book was a good couple of feet high and when she opened it, balancing it on the platform at the top of the steps, it turned out to be a book about sea creatures. Back it went, and she reached for another.

After a while Cecily found another demonology, and this one didn't seem to be inflicted with dead moths posing as bookmarks. She carefully brought it down, trying to avoid damaging the tooled leather cover with its dancing monsters highlighted in gold leaf.

And when she laid it on the table, she saw a name scratched into the flyleaf.

Betrixe de Chateline.

"Oh…"

Mim blinked up at her, her expression questioning. "Is it a good *oh*?"

"Possibly." Cecily turned to a full-page depiction of Satan on his throne, tiny demons circling him like flies. "I think this might once have belonged to Beatrice the Builder. It's page after page of demons, but it's all written in Latin!"

Mim looked towards Michael and laughed. "Luckily we have a vicar. Michael, would you mind translating?"

"Oh, of course! I'm no closer to finding the prayer, by the way. Do let me put my Latin to good use." Michael put aside the notebook he had been writing in and came to have a look. "Goodness me, this is quite a tome. And it's been in the family a fair few years." He turned to the entry on Aeshma. "Now, here's our chum who's running riot in the village. But there's a note here in the margin, in English, I think. What does that say? *Salt*, by the looks of it. Or at least, *salt* plus a couple of extra letters. *Sowlte!*"

"Left by Beatrice, perhaps?" Cecily wondered.

"So Rafael was right," Mim said. "It makes sense, after all. Salt *is* useful when it comes to matters like these. We'd need an awful lot of it though if we were to salt the whole village!"

"Could we? Would it work?" Cecily clasped her hands, hopeful that they might have the beginnings of a plan. "If the demon's been held in that window all this time with salt..."

"But we'd need so much of it." Shaking her head, Mim frowned. "How could we ever hope to contain it forever if we can't even find it? And we daren't call it by its name because of the damnable flies!"

"It must be in the village *somewhere*," Michael said. "If we can contain it here, then we can destroy it — or at least send it packing down below."

"There's lots of demons in the other windows." Cecily started counting through the heap of papers. "And all those windows are in a warehouse somewhere. But I suppose they'll all get a mention in this book too."

And they did — one after another, Michael translating the entries for each one without saying their names aloud and Cecily and Mim making notes as he went.

It was an enormous number but Aeshma in the huge window seemed to be chief of them all.

"So we have to trap it," Cecily realised, the full horror of the situation now dawning on her. "Because what if it summons all the others?"

"*My name is Legion: for we are many,*" Michael intoned. "They like to work in a gang, these demons. I would be very surprised if Ae — *our chum's* next move isn't to summon its friends and turn Acaster Garrow into a new Kwaalveld. We've *got* to contain it. Oh, it's chosen the wrong village, that's for sure!"

"That's fighting talk for a vicar." Raf laughed as he descended the stairs into the archive. "I think Bea wanted us to see how she managed to contain it. She was very ingenious!"

Cecily trotted over to him. "You've worked it out? What does it do?"

He put his arms around Cecily's waist and kissed the tip of her nose, then gestured with his head towards the staircase. "Come up to the kitchen and see?"

They headed upstairs, Cecily bringing the notes from Michael's translation. As they entered the kitchen, Cecily saw that Raf had finished mocking-up a wooden version of the mammoth contraption she had drawn. It didn't have the grandeur of the east window but that wasn't the point. The point was to demonstrate how it worked and as she looked at the perforated block, not resting on the other uprights at all, but suspended by a number of taut lengths of rope, she was none the wiser.

"So this is where Bea had our pal held." He nodded to the structure. "It was sandwiched between two panes of glass and hers were tighter together but I've had to leave a gap so a little bat can fit in and demonstrate. There's a massive chamber above the window and in the bottom are hundreds of holes. Under it there's a sort of...I don't know what you'd call it, but it's this block, covered in more holes. Now, the holes don't match up, so the salt in the massive chamber can't fall out, unless..."

Raf slid one finger between the panes of glass and tapped it. As he did the drilled block trembled and shifted, releasing a sprinkle of salt from the chamber above that fell like sand in an egg timer between the panes.

"Give me a moment." He left the room and Cecily heard the telltale tinkle and rattling of falling charms. A second later Raf returned to the kitchen in his familiar form of a tiny pipistrelle. He neatly slid between the panes of glass and batted the tips of his wings against them, earning himself a shower of salt. Cecily heard again the thumping that had assailed her at the church, and realised that Raf was right. The demon had been held in place for centuries because its every movement had caused the blocks to shift and the salt to fall, weakening it. Now there was no salt and those ceaseless thumps against the glass had finally secured Aeshma's freedom.

"Incredible!" Cecily gasped. "We found Beatrice's book, by the way, her own demonology. And she'd written *salt* – more or less – in the margin. This *must* be it!"

She came nearer and offered her palm out for Raf to perch on. He emerged from between the panes and settled on her hand, shaking his salt-covered head.

"Well!" Mim laughed and peered more closely at the structure Raf had constructed. "The question is, where on earth do we find *that* much salt? I'm not sure I dare even go into the village, let alone pop to the shop just before closing time!"

Cecily stroked Raf's fur, helping him to brush away the salt. "I don't suppose we could use the sea?" she suggested.

"I'm not sure how we could, but it gives us a safe border on one side of the village, at least," Michael said. "But all the shops have salt. The fish and chip shop definitely will, as well as the general store. The butcher and the fishmonger salt things…and it's not as if they have any food to salt at the moment anyway. Question is, how do we get it?"

Raf can pick locks.

And after their weeks travelling together and a few spirited lessons, Cecily could certainly give it a go too. She might not be up to his standard, but she could do it when she had to.

"Do the shops shut at five?" Cecily asked. "If we wait until it's dark…"

"The sun's already setting, it'll be pitch-black in half an hour." Mim tapped her fingernail against the glass, watching the salt shimmer down. As she did Raf rose from Cecily's hand and, after a little pirouette of thanks before her face, fluttered out into the hallway.

Michael shifted from foot to foot, clearing his throat. In a rather strained voice said, "I hope we're not countenancing theft. *Thou shalt not* and all that."

"But if it's the only way we can defeat a demon, I'm sure your boss won't mind too much," Cecily replied. But it was clear from Michael's expression of horror that he didn't agree.

"Thou shalt pick a lock and take some salt," Raf said as he pottered back into the kitchen, dressed once more. "So long as thou leaves some cash on the counter. Sound fair?"

"Erm..." Michael ran his fingers through his hair. He was evidently struggling with an internal conflict and finally he answered, "Well, all right then. It'll be paid for, at least."

Raf ducked his head and dusted the remaining salt from his hair as he pulled open a drawer. Cecily recognised the little parcel of lockpicking tools immediately, remembering when she had first seen them in Whitmore Hall, before they were as familiar as they were now.

"I'll do it," he told them. "I don't want any of you putting yourself in danger and we don't know how the village will be by now. If anyone's getting a black eye or worse, it's better that it's me."

"I'm coming with you," Cecily announced. "It's not safe if you're on your own."

Raf shook his head and told her, "I'd be happier knowing you were safe here."

He'd told her to stay out of trouble once before, of course. She'd ignored him then too and if she hadn't, he'd be dead. There was no way Cecily was going to listen today either.

"And I'd be happier being with you," Cecily said as she stroked his cheek. "I'll throw on one of my old frocks and my sensible shoes and I'll be ready."

"No rush," Raf said. "Let's wait until a little bit later, give time for people to get home and settled. Mim, can you search out a really, really strong salt circle incantation while we're in the village? I'm going to circle Acaster Garrow all the way round, land and sea. Mike, if I'm doing the salt, I'll need you up above looking down to make sure it's a solid circle. I know you don't like to, but I need a bat."

Michael swallowed. "You — you want me to bat? Oh. Well…" He glanced at Mim and something unsaid passed between them. "Seeing as it's an emergency…of course."

"I don't want to know," Raf told his brother, clearly reading something rather saucy into that look. "Right, let's get a list together of where there's salt to be had, then we'll be able to get in and out as quick as we can."

"Perhaps when we have the list, we could draw a rough plan of the village and we can work out a route from shop to shop?" Cecily suggested.

Raf nodded and together the four of them drank tea and, with Cecily thankfully in sole charge of the pencil now, they drew up a list of the places in Acaster Garrow where salt might be found. The time ticked on as Michael sketched out a plan of the village and, eventually, they had a route which would, Cecily hoped, see them safely home without too much trouble.

Raf and Cecily said goodbye to Mim and Michael at the front door.

"Don't worry, we won't tidy the archive!" Michael joked.

Raf slapped his shoulder and warned, "And don't eat all that cake either!"

Chapter Eleven

It was odd being back in Raf's car again, not relaxed and happy on their long tour of England, but furtively creeping through the dark night down to the village.

She could sense a tension in him even as he tried to be as chipper as ever, telling her, "When we've been on holiday, let's teach you how to drive. It's easy, even I can do it!"

Cecily patted his leg. "Yes, maybe. Isn't that where we're parking just over there? Behind the blacksmith's?"

She peered out of the window at the space behind the blacksmith's shop, wondering if it was discreet enough. And wondering if, when she looked outside, she'd be face to face with Aeshma.

Not this evening, it seemed. Not yet, anyway.

Raf parked the car beside the blacksmith's van and climbed out. He paused and listened intently to the sounds of the village, then beckoned Cecily to follow.

Cecily kept low, listening out for any sound. She heard radios blaring from the cottages near the blacksmith's and the distinct sound of raised, furious voices. She couldn't hear any laughter at all.

Cecily's pulse thudded in her ears as they emerged from an alleyway into the main road through the village. Keeping in the shadows, they crept as light on their feet as cats to the first place on their list. Raf made short work of the lock on the general provisions shop and together, they stole inside.

"We're looking for the massive sacks," he whispered. "I don't need to tell you. You've bought salt!"

Cecily glanced about the shelves, wrinkling her nose against the smell of decaying food. Even in the weak glow of one of Acaster Garrow's few streetlights, she spotted some salt. "There! Behind the counter, there's a sack or two just on the floor. Do you think there'd be more in the storeroom?"

Raf nodded. "Keep out of sight. I'll go and see what we can grab." He kissed her cheek. "Love you!"

Cecily blew him a kiss, then she crouched down behind the counter. Someone was shouting upstairs, stamping across the room above. Outside, she heard yelling.

If only there had been another way, but if they'd travelled farther afield, they would have lost valuable time.

Minutes seemed to pass before Raf emerged from the storeroom, hefting three enormous sacks of salt in front of him. He might be small, impish as Cecily had thought on their first meeting, but she knew that he possessed reserves of strength that would be a challenge to a man twice his size. Perhaps it was that Transylvanian ancestry of his.

"Five's a good start," Raf whispered. "Reckon you can manage one if I take these? I'll come back for the last couple."

"Yes, I can manage!" Cecily took one of the sacks from him. "Oof! That's heavy!"

Raf left a handful of cash on the counter and together they lugged the sacks back to the car. This time Cecily stayed with the vehicle as she waited for Raf to return with the other two. Though it was a matter of a couple of minutes, she felt as if she barely dared to breathe, the raised voices seemingly louder when she was alone. Flies buzzed overhead and she grimaced, retreating into the safety of the car.

Yet perhaps they were blessed after all because they went from shop to shop taking salt and leaving money, unobserved by any except the flies that seemed to be clustering in every doorway. In the butcher's and the fishmonger's he made copious use of his scent bottle against the putrefaction but with her help they cleared the stores of every grain of salt they could find. Soon all that remained was the fish shop and, as the axles of the Austin testified, they had plenty of salt with which to encircle Acaster Garrow.

"Oi!" The shout ripped through the night air as a figure crossed the street heading straight for them. "Is that Raf de Chastelaine, is it? And his fancy woman? Is it? You bloody foreigners, skulking about in the night like you think we don't know you're there—who do you think you are?"

"Bill!" Raf beamed, turning to face him. "Any chance you could open up the chippy? We're starving!"

"Starving? All the fish rotted and there's none coming out of the sea. I'm closed, you beggar — get out of it!" Bill swatted Raf away. Or at least, he seemed to, but he was being pursued by flies that seemed to increase in number the more he tried to bat them away.

Raf stepped in front of Cecily, shielding her from Bill and the cloud of flies. He asked casually, "How much would you want for your stock of salt? You name the price, mate."

"*Salt?* What the hell do you want *that* for? There's no bloody chips to sprinkle it on! Have my bloody salt and sod off!"

Bill banged open the door of the fish shop, and as Cecily recoiled from the stench of rotten fish, she wondered how on earth Raf hadn't passed out. He looked a little wobbly though and took a step back from the door, holding his hand to his chest.

Bill whipped round and grabbed Raf by the collar of his shirt and lifted him off his feet. Cecily wanted to cringe back but she clutched Raf's arm.

"What's the matter with you, you weird little squirt? And your freakshow beanpole missus?"

"Chippy Bill," a young female voice said from the shadows, "you're breaking curfew. Get back indoors or we'll put you back indoors. Now what's it to be?"

"Little Ivy Bamforth?" Bill dropped Raf and took a step back into his shop. "You, you little pest!" But he was still shrinking back indoors, step by step.

A little girl stepped out of the shadows and in her wake trailed what looked like two dozen children or more, accompanied by what seemed to be almost as many dogs and cats. Some carried bird cages or fishbowls and one or two held little hamster cages as though they were the most precious things on earth.

Ivy Bamforth, however, carried only a long, thick branch, and she held it out towards Bill.

"Inside, Chippy Bill. And if Raf wants salt, you'll give him salt." She weighed the stick in her small hand. "Go on then!"

"You don't scare me, little 'uns!" Bill said, even though the children clearly terrified him. He vanished into the shop and after clattering about inside for a few moments, returned with a sack of salt. And even the saltshaker from his counter. "Have it, Raf, you blighter! Go on, take it all! Go on! Before the kiddies come after *you!*"

Raf pressed some money into Bill's hand and told him, "Cheers, mate. Now get that door locked."

Bill almost threw the salt at them, then slammed the door in their faces. He drew down the blind on the door with a snap and was gone.

Cecily clutched the tall saltshaker and turned to look at the children and their entourage of pets.

"Isn't it past your bedtime?" she asked with kind concern, in the tone she would have used on finding one of Whitmore Hall's pupils wandering the corridors after dark. Ivy shrugged but beneath the bravado Cecily could see a frightened little girl.

She shifted from one foot to the other and told Cecily, "Everybody's shouting and carrying on. They don't notice if we're there or not and the houses are all filled with flies!"

"Ivy, you're only eleven. You can't just roam the streets," Raf said kindly. "Are you keeping the adults in line?"

Ivy nodded. "They're going loony at each other, but not at us. It's like we're invisible."

A little boy behind her said, "It's horrible indoors. It's more fun outside!"

Cecily whispered to Raf, "They're not affected. The demon can't get at the children."

He wafted the scent bottle under his nose as Ivy asked Cecily, "What's up with the two of you, anyway? How come you're not loony an' all?"

"We…" Cecily glanced at Raf. How much did they know about what went on in Raf's house? How much did they know about Aeshma? "We have charms against the demon."

"I'm looking after the children. The babies are getting on all right, they're still getting fed and burped but…nobody notices us." Ivy seemed to accept the explanation without question. "And we're all getting scared to go home."

From behind her came a chorus of agreements, some firm, some fearful. Cecily's heart went out to them all, like a flock of lost lambs. But lost lambs who had happened on a very unusual couple of shepherds.

"Give us a minute." Raf smiled, turning away. He waited until Cecily had turned too and asked, "What're we going to do?"

"Bring them home," Cecily whispered. "There's so many rooms in our house, we'd barely notice them. And we've got plenty of food. We can't leave them here—we can't leave them to get hurt."

"That thing, it feeds on fear and hate. It's a matter of time before someone takes it out on one of the children." Raf nodded, his mind apparently made up. "But we have to let their parents know. We can't just take them."

He glanced back at the children and asked, "Where did you all sleep last night?"

"In the church. We stayed there today as well," Ivy said. "But the little ones got scared when the flies came in. Then we heard Bill shouting and came out to help. We'll sleep on the beach tonight, down by the caves."

"No, no you won't." Cecily crouched down in front of Ivy and the little boy next to her reached out and patted Cecily's hair. She smiled at him, then told the children, "Would you like to come to our house? There's plenty of room for all of you."

Ivy studied Cecily's face, then smiled at what she saw there. She turned to her following and asked them, "Who wants to go up to Raf's house tonight?" She looked back and asked Cecily, "Can we bring the animals? The birds and rats and that're all in cages and the fish are in bowls. We can manage to carry them. It's only the cats and dogs who need a bed."

"Of course you can bring them," Cecily said.

With a firm nod, Ivy asked again, "Who's for it? Say aye." Up went a chorus of agreement. "And who's not? Say not!"

Silence.

"That's agreed, then!" Cecily turned to Raf. "Do we leave a note on the door of the pub, so their parents know where they are?"

The little girl spun on her heel and asked, "Just...don't tell them tonight? Tomorrow when the sun's out we'll come back and see them." She dropped her voice to a whisper. "We've told the little ones it's just a game. Like a pretend treasure hunt or something."

"Very wise." Raf smiled. "And you know that this isn't your parents at all, don't you? You know it's that thing that came out of the window making them do this."

To Cecily's relief, Ivy nodded. "We love them just the same, we just wish they'd stop shouting."

"Me and Raf, and Mim and Reverend Mike, we're going to stop them from shouting—very, very soon. I promise," Cecily said. "We'll fit the smallest of you in the car, and I'll walk with the rest of you."

Raf nodded and promised, "And tomorrow, when the sun's out, we'll come back to the village and get all this sorted."

The procession wound down the alleyway to the back of the blacksmith's where Raf's car was waiting for them. Cecily fitted the three smallest children on the passenger seat, with one crouching in the footwell, and sat two more on top of the bags of salt.

"Hold on to the strap," she told them. "But Raf won't be driving very fast."

She picked up another of the children, a little girl whose bunches were coming undone, and balanced her on her hip. She passed the girl the shaker. "And here's the saltshaker. We might need it."

A saltshaker versus a demon. But it was the only weapon to hand.

"And a big stick," Ivy reminded her as they set off. "I didn't sleep last night. I kept count of all of us just in case somebody got lost." She smiled up at Cecily. "But nobody has. We're all here and so are our pets *and* our toys. I've always been one for counting."

Raf drove only as fast as Cecily and the children could comfortably walk and she wondered again at the little girl who had marshalled her peers and their pets so ably. A little girl like this might go far one day, Cecily thought, glancing at Ivy as they walked.

Ivy looked up at her, then tucked her long hair back behind her ear and said, "My mum and dad own the pub. Dad brought the beer to your welcome party! He said it's about time Raf had a sweetheart."

"What a kind man," Cecily remarked. "I know he isn't at the moment, but nearly all the grown-ups…they're not very well. But they'll be better again soon, won't they?"

Ivy nodded. "That's what I told the others. They don't love them any less, they're just not very well tonight. Like when I had the chickenpox." She smiled. "But I got well right enough, and so will they,"

"Good, that's the right thing to say." Cecily shifted the girl she was carrying to her other hip. "I don't suppose, aside from your parents behaving oddly, you've seen anything else that seemed strange?"

Ivy looked thoughtful then said, "There's the flies and last night…" She glanced over her shoulder and dropped her voice to a whisper. "Last night there was a big *thing* sitting on the cliffs at midnight. I thought it was a bird but…I could see the moon through its wings. And it made a strange noise, a bit like when Mum puts the bottles in the cellar but…horrible. All clanking and noisy."

Ice filled Cecily's spine at Ivy's words, and she shivered. The girl had seen Aeshma. "On the cliffs? It looked a bit like a bird? If you see it again, run and hide, Ivy — do you understand? It's not a nice creature."

The little girl on Cecily's hip began to grizzle and Cecily gently swayed to try to calm her. "There, there, don't be frightened."

But they were so exposed out in the lane and every yard they walked seemed to take forever.

Raf leaned out of the car and called to Cecily. His voice was light though she recognised from his words that all wasn't well.

"Sissy, why don't you sprinkle some salt as you walk, like Hansel and Gretel?" he asked. "I'm just going to sing one of the old country songs, a travelling song."

And she knew then that something was coming.

"Come on, let's sprinkle the salt." Cecily shivered again, ice in her veins, but she wouldn't let on to the children that she was frightened. The little girl in her arms giggled as she shook the salt onto the road. "Still got your stick, Ivy? Good lass."

Raf began to sing his song, a gentle incantation that somehow calmed Cecily's fluttering heart in her breast. Overhead she heard the fearsome sound of the buzzing flies yet Raf kept singing and the children, though they glanced up at the insects that were almost within touching distance of Cecily's scalp, seemed almost serene. Even the animals they had brought with them kept pace. No dog barked, no cat howled, and as if by a miracle, no child panicked.

It's the song, she realised. *The song's keeping them calm.*

But then there came another sound, the glassy clanking of wings, the screech of the doomed, and from the head of the clouds she saw Aeshma descend like a tempest, the stars shining through its glass body. It opened its wings and arms wide and threw back its head, letting out a howl of damnation.

The false god's scream blotted out the lilting melody of Raf's song and he raised his voice to combat it, but Aeshma's scream was unending, louder with every second that passed until Cecily thought her head might burst with it.

In her arms the little girl flinched, burying her face against Cecily's shoulder, and she heard fearful murmurs from the children, growls from the dogs that grew more anxious as Raf jumped out of the car and advanced towards the demon. He held one of his charms before him and the gentle song was replaced by a shouted incantation, good bellowed in the face of evil.

"Shhhh, children, it's all right," Cecily whispered, trying to stop the tremble in her voice. She wasn't sure they'd hear her over the demon's roar. "Uncle Raf will look after us…"

But could he?

From above, Cecily heard the sound of leathery beating wings. It wasn't Aeshma, and when she dared herself to look up, she almost screamed in horror.

The other demons were coming—because what else could that be with such a huge wingspan flying above them?

"It's the vicar!" Ivy cheered. She turned to the other children and as they followed their leader's example and began to roar their approval, she shouted, "Raf and Reverend Mike'll sort the bugger out!"

"That's Mike?"

Cecily squinted up at him. He was several times the size of Raf's pipistrelle, but she couldn't fathom how he could fight off Aeshma. Until a dust began to rain down on them, but what dust could be raining from the sky unless—? When Cecily poked out the tip of her tongue, she tasted salt.

"Mike! Mike! Mike!" Ivy led the children in a chant, thumping the stick on the ground as she did like a warrior giving a war cry. Aeshma threw its head back again, this time not in triumph, but in agony. The flies clustered around the demon, shielding it from the torturous rain of salt, and as one the cloud and its infernal leader ascended towards the heavens. They moved fast, faster even than the bat that Michael had become, and as they hit the clouds they merged with the night, leaving the fetid air silent once more.

"That's how we do it in Transylvania *and* Yorkshire too," Raf shouted, jubilant. But Cecily felt his exhaustion in her own bones even as he raised his hands above his head and applauded. "Go on, vicar, chase him back to hell!"

Michael looped and swooped overheard, coming low enough for Cecily to see an empty salt packet in his claws. Then he seemed to wave with one wing and was off, heading over the brow of the hill towards Raf's house.

"Sorry I said *bugger*," Ivy told Cecily. "But they *did* get the bugger."

"Onwards to the house, troops," Raf announced to the children as he climbed back into the car. "We'll pretend it's a castle tonight!"

"We're nearly there!" Cecily tried to urge the children on. She couldn't imagine how tired and hungry the poor mites were, yet none of them complained. They all stoically carried on, helping one another along with their cargo of pets, dolls, teddies and toy boats.

Once they turned in at the top of Raf's drive, Cecily saw lights on in the house ahead and Mim and Michael — who was fastening his shirt — came hurrying towards them. Raf parked the car and climbed out. He helped the children down and announced, "I hope you're all hungry, because we've got piles of food inside. Come on in, honoured guests, and take the weight off your feet."

Ivy stood back and watched the children file into the house like a sergeant major counting off her troops. Each received a pat on the back or shoulder, a little sign that they'd done well. In went children, cats, dogs and everything in between, until only the adults and Ivy remained outside. With a smile, she held out her stick to Raf and told him, "I don't think I'll need this tonight, will I?"

"Not a chance," Raf replied, taking it from her. "At ease, general. Cake's waiting."

He watched as Ivy trotted after the others, then said, "Bloody hell, Mike, I— Thanks. Thank you."

"We've found a spell," Michael told him. "Mim was practicing it and I batted over to the village to see how you were getting on. But I saw *him*, and I had grabbed some salt in case he tried to—well, he did, didn't he? All's well, though. Everyone's here, nice and safe."

"Those poor little lambs," Mim whispered, shaking her head. She patted Cecily's hand. "I'm so glad to see you back safely."

"The kids slept in the church last night. They were going to try and sleep on the beach this evening because all their parents are bothered about is fighting each other." Raf looked up at the sky. "And that bastard's getting stronger on it. Tomorrow we have to move against him but for tonight, I'm closing up the house. I'm not risking any of you or those children. We *all* need to rest tonight."

Chapter Twelve

As soon as they were all safely inside, Cecily began to settle the children while Raf prepared to shut down the house. She rounded up quilts and cushions and pushed armchairs and sofas into the great hall so that they could all sleep together. Tonight, being surrounded by their pets and their friends would be a tonic for the children who had been chased out of their homes. As Michael helped Cecily, Mim laid out food and lemonade and bowls of water for the animals and a strange calm descended over the house.

Perhaps Raf was singing again.

Cecily brought round a bowl of hot water and a flannel, trying to clean the children as best she could. She passed them brushes and combs and sat with them while she secured buttons that had been nearly pulled off and patched up coats that had been torn on sharp branches. She found comfort in these little jobs, a way to fight off the demon's chaotic influence by holding on to normality.

When Raf finally joined the group, he was a bundle of lighthearted silliness, but she could sense the tension in him. To the children, of course, he was simply Raf, all smiles and songs and expressions of amazement at Mike's heroic intervention. Raf perched on the edge of the window seat, helping Cecily with the needlework as jam tarts and sausage rolls did the rounds, washed down by fresh lemonade. His hands were nimble on the needle and thread and as he worked Raf sang the song that had calmed them again, teaching the children the words as he went along. It was a language that none of them spoke but they joined in with gusto through mouthfuls of pastry, singing through yawns and smiles. Their treasured toys were set beside their impromptu beds or cuddled in grateful arms as Raf turned what was very nearly a nightmare into a relaxed party. Their animals were safe too, the cages and fishbowls stowed away out of the reach of the cats and dogs who curled up with their companions, as calm as the children.

Cecily smiled at him as he sang and worked. He was so kind to the children, patient and fun, and she wondered whether they would ever have children of their own. Maybe they would — one day. And for now, it was enough to daydream.

"This house was built by a lady called Beatrice," Raf told his rapt audience. "And though she made it look like a house, it's really a castle. I want you all to count to ten, then I want you to shout *abracadabra*, and when you do, the portcullis will drop, the shutters will close and we'll all be safe as houses until tomorrow. It might be a bit noisy, but don't be scared because we're all knights and this is *our* castle — there's nothing scary here. In fact, if *I* were a rotten old fly or an ugly old thing made of glass, I'd be scared of us — we're an army of Yorkshire folk! Captain Sissy, would you lead our count?"

He rose from the window seat and kissed Cecily's hair. Then he left the room and she heard him singing his gentle song as he went, heading for the ship's wheel that would turn the house into a fortress.

"Ready, everyone?" Cecily began the count. "One… two…three…"

Deep in the house she noticed a vibration that grew stronger and stronger and rattled the windowpanes. Some of the children had noticed too and glanced at her anxiously, but Cecily still counted and the children joined in.

"Four…five…six…"

The children counted along with her now and Ivy clapped her hands in time with the rhythm until, on ten, the house rang with a cry of, "Abracadabra!"

As the word echoed through the halls, the vibrations ended in a series of thuds and clunks that sounded like gears sliding into place. With a metallic *thump* Cecily heard shutters close over the windows, hidden by the bright curtains, and from the outside, the metallic slice and clang of what sounded like portcullises thundering down to the ground. For a moment there was silence, then Ivy laughed and announced, "We did it, knights! We defended our castle!"

"That's it, soldiers, the castle is secured!" Raf bounded back into the room as a cheer went up, his expression bright with mischief. He looked at the assembled faces, all turned to him in anticipation. "Time my heroes were in bed. Everybody under the blankets and I'll tell you a story from Camelot about a bunch of knights just like you. We only have good dreams here."

Cecily helped tuck them in. Some of them were so little that it hurt her to think of how frightened they must have been, wandering in the village with no aim other than to escape the irrational wrath of the grown-ups. They had been through enough horror for a lifetime these past few days. Ivy had kept them safe and together, but she deserved to be a little girl again.

At least the children in the house would be safe tonight with their pets and toys beside them.

As Raf told his story the children settled into their makeshift beds until, one by one, they were all slumbering. Only then did he fall silent and lean back into the window seat, letting out a long sigh of exhaustion. As he did Cecily realised that she could hear another voice singing that calming song somewhere in the house. It was Mike, she knew, easing the children safely to sleep as Raf told them tales of Camelot and the knights of Acaster Garrow.

Cecily pulled Raf to lie sideways on her lap and rumpled his hair. "You were so brave earlier," she whispered. "You took on a demon."

"These children…" Raf sighed, stroking his hand gently over Cecily's knee. "I don't want them to remember this night and be frightened. I want them to remember it and be proud of what they did. They're a little bloody army, this lot, and you're the general. I'd face a hundred demons to keep you and these kids safe."

"Oh, Raf…" Cecily was silent for a moment as she stroked his dear face. Then she said, "Knowing the children had run from their angry parents reminded me of when I was small and Father would go into his rages. And me and Sandy wanted to run away, but we didn't dare leave Mummy. You and I could never have left these kids wandering about like they were, not when we could help them."

Raf tipped his head back. He blinked up at Cecily through tired eyes and told her, "You're the kindest person I've ever met. I love you."

Cecily shook her head as she twined her fingers with his. It was only when she yawned that she realised how exhausted she was. "No, *you* are. And we both need to sleep."

"Camping indoors." Raf smiled as he sat up and snuggled into her arms. He kissed her, the gesture filled with nothing but love. "Life's one big adventure in Yorkshire."

Chapter Thirteen

Serving breakfast for thirty people would have daunted many a person, but not Cecily — having spent almost all her life living at a school, she knew exactly what to do. She found the biggest pan Raf owned and made an enormous bubbling vat of porridge. The children decided from an array of jams and marmalade from the pantry what to stir into their bowls and breakfast became an adventure.

But the house was still closed up. At least they had passed a quiet night, but Cecily dreaded seeing beyond the shutters at what the demon might have done in the hours of darkness. It was Raf who braved the unknown that awaited them outdoors in the end and had anyone been watching the house very closely, they might have spied a tiny bat, barely noticeable, emerge from a space no bigger than a letterbox which was revealed when a bolt was drawn back within the house.

After all, as Raf pointed out to Cecily before he left her with Mim and Mike to serve breakfast, "Even a fortress needs the odd bit of modification."

Ivy helped serve her young friends and the atmosphere was just as Raf had wanted, one of camaraderie and somehow, perhaps as a testament to him, fun. Even the younger children seemed at ease, chattering excitedly about their nights of adventure and all the tales they would tell their parents upon their return.

But Cecily couldn't settle while Raf was gone. She did her best, tidying the children and supervising the washing up that several of them volunteered to do. And yet the thought of him out there, beyond the safety of their home and in the presence of that beast of glass, worried her.

Ten minutes after the little pipistrelle had left the house Cecily had a sudden sense that Raf was near. It was so clear, so palpable, that she might have heard his voice or felt his touch, but she had done neither. She couldn't even see the little slot through which he had made his exit, but somehow she knew that he was back, and the relief that washed over her was like a wave breaking over the beach. As she finished settling the children all Cecily could do was wait, picturing Raf as he dressed and put on the tangle of charms then made his way through the house on his bare feet in search of her.

Mike and Mim were engrossed in helping the houseguests with their porridge, setting out water and food for the pets, but Cecily's gaze kept darting towards the door, willing Raf to appear there.

And, eventually, he did. One minute the doorway was empty and the next it contained Raf de

Chastelaine, large — or small — as life. He was leaning with one shoulder on the doorframe, his hands in his pockets, and he greeted Cecily with a wink and a mouthed request of, "Got a minute?"

As casual as he looked, Cecily wasn't convinced that all was well. She hurried across the room to him. "What is it?"

He stepped out into the hallway and caught her hand. Then he took a deep breath and shook his head.

"There's flies everywhere out there. The house is clear but once you get into the village… If the kids had tried to sleep on the beach last night, I don't want to think about what might have happened to them." Raf paused and rubbed the tip of his nose, as though the stench he had caught before had somehow stuck on him. "There must be a million or more. It's like a smog. I don't know what we're going to do but I'm not taking children down there."

"They'll have to stay. And what about the salt? We have to do it today." Cecily glanced back into the room. "Can we leave the children in the house unattended? It'll be such a huge job, though. And what if the circle is broken? And Mike said he's been trying to find the prayer that will fight off *you-know-who* and he hasn't found a thing. It could take days of searching through every last book down in the archive. What are we going to do?"

"I thought…" Raf frowned, clearly considering his options. He seemed paler than ever, perhaps thanks to the memory of the flies. The very thought of it was sickening, it made Cecily's skin crawl on her bones. "What if I do the salt-sowing on my own or me and Mike? It's a start, but it's a massive job with — We need help, Sissy, and we can't ask the kids to do that."

With rising desperation, Cecily asked, "Is there anyone you know outside Acaster Garrow who could help? Aren't there other people — dhampirs — *anyone* who we could ask?"

"That's what I'm thinking too," he replied. "But that means someone has to leave the village to get the messages out. One or two have telephones but the folk I'd want on our side don't all live in houses like this, if you get my drift?"

Cecily's mind was filled at once with ruinous castles and dilapidated abbeys, a pale figure peering from a casket in a cobwebbed vault.

Or perhaps Raf meant they lived in modest cottages that didn't have a telephone.

"We have to at least try, don't we?" Cecily said. "If there's only us to do it, then…then we have to do it."

"We'll get Mim and Mike on it after I've had my breakfast." He kissed Cecily, holding her hand tighter than ever. "So long as only one of us leaves, we should still be able to hold the fort here. I can nip out tonight, pick some more locks, grab some more food… We're not quite under siege just yet."

Cecily tried to sound optimistic, even if she was struggling to feel it. "There's a sack of oats in the pantry — there's enough for two more breakfasts for us all. There's flour — I can make some bread. And there's a roll in the bread-bin — I kept it back for you. I thought you might be hungry after you flew."

"Starving," Raf admitted. "Let's both sit down and get some food inside us. And if the kids ask, this is all still part of the game. You're doing an amazing job, you know. I don't know how we'd be getting through this without you keeping us all together."

Cecily shrugged as they headed into the kitchen. "It reminds me of the times we got snowed in at Whitmore Hall! The boys loved it but trying to make the food stretch over several days was a challenge."

"And that's before we think about feeding all the pets," he realised as a little boy scurried past in pursuit of a marmalade cat, his laughter tinkling like a shop bell. Raf watched him go, then continued into the kitchen after Cecily. At the sink Mim was washing up what seemed like every piece of crockery in the house, a curiously glamorous figure even now, though a lock of hair had fallen into her face and she kept blowing at it, trying to clear it from her eyes. Eventually she murmured a few unheard words and the hair magically swept back into place, before promptly falling forwards again.

"What a few days it's been," Mim said cheerily to the new arrivals, but her drawn face made her look as tired as Cecily felt. "And to think Chief Scout Baden-Powell would have us do this every weekend if he could!"

"I hope he doesn't. I'm not very good at tying knots!" Cecily laughed. "I'll give you a hand in a second, Mim—Raf, I'll just get your breakfast."

Raf was polishing off his second sugary cup of tea when he stopped dead, the cup halfway to his mouth. Around the house Cecily could hear the children playing, their laughter warm and filled with hope, but here in the kitchen she felt her blood freeze. He sniffed at the air, the tip of his nose twitching, then whispered, "Oh bloody hell, what's this now?"

"Is it the flies?" Cecily asked. She could barely force the words from her constricted throat.

He shook his head then said, "I can smell... It's like a dirty nappy?"

"Oh, has one of the little ones had an acci—" Mim was silenced by the sound of a frantic knock from outside, but it didn't sound like a knock on the door, rather a knock on metal.

Is that what the shutters are made of?

"I'll go and see what's up," Raf told them, his voice hushed as though whoever was outside might be able to hear. Then he pushed back his chair and stood. He paused, preparing himself for whatever was lying in wait, then set off to meet their visitors.

Meet, not welcome.

Cecily decided to follow. She picked up the saltshaker from the table in the hallway—she didn't expect Aeshma to be polite and herald its arrival with a knock, but it paid to be prepared.

At the front door Raf paused for a moment as though gathering himself, but when he opened it, all Cecily saw was a solid piece of dark wood, ribbed in metal and studded with iron. It looked more like something from a fortress than a house on the idyllic Yorkshire coast and she wondered again at how *closed* the house must be from the outside. Very, it seemed. They really *had* been safe last night, from earthly threats, at least.

Raf whispered, "Stay behind me, Sis," then pressed his hand to one of the studs. A tiny window in the wooden shield opened, letting in a shaft of light. Raf leaned forwards and peered out as he asked, "Who's there?"

All Cecily heard at first was a fretful baby's cries, followed by a man's furious voice. "What have you done with our kids? Where the hell are they?"

And behind him now a chorus of voices demanding to know the same thing.

A woman shouted, "You're like the Pied bloody Piper. Give them back! What've you done with our children?"

"Bloody foreigners!" a male voice bellowed. "Taking our children! Bring them out then get back to wherever you come from!"

"The children are all safe in here," Raf told the unseen mob. Perhaps it was tiredness, because his cheery demeanour seemed to have fled when faced with this new assault. "You ought to be bloody ashamed of yourselves, the lot of you. I don't care whose influence you're under, your kids spent the night sleeping in the church because they were too terrified to go home!"

"Rubbish!" The woman's voice wasn't quite so certain as it had been though. "I don't believe you!"

"Believe it!" Raf rested his palm on the door. "They look to you to love them, to keep them safe. Instead you were that busy fighting amongst yourselves that you scared the poor little mites away! They came here last night and with that bastard flying around, you should be glad they did!"

From outside Cecily heard a murmur of conversation, but it wasn't angry. Instead she recognised the sounds of realisation and caught the sound of names, of parents faced with losing their most precious things in the world.

"Those kids need you to care for them." Raf rested his other hand on the door and closed his eyes. Cecily watched him, wondering if this was the start of some new protection incantation. He certainly seemed primed for something. "So you either push off and clear your heads or remember what's *really* important. Your children are safe, but they're staying here with us until you lot start acting like parents again!"

"We're sorry — we're so sorry." The man at the door was weeping, barely able to restrain his sobs. His fury had broken and around him Cecily heard the others began to sob their apologies too. Raf's words had reached through the fury, it seemed, and pulled out the love that existed in Acaster Garrow. "We just want them back!"

"You're just one bloke, Alf," Raf said, his tone more kind now. "What about the rest of them? Where's Chippy Bill, who nearly put me on my arse last night? His little ones are safe here with their goldfish and cat. Will he come forward and speak?"

"I'm here..." Bill sounded contrite. "I don't know what was the matter with me. Our baby was crying his head off this morning, and only then we realised the other little 'uns weren't around. He's rocking his pram backwards and forwards yelling for want of Mabel and Bert."

"What do you remember of the last few days?" Raf asked as he reached back and took Cecily's hand. She already knew that the answer would be very little, just as she had remembered nothing of her own fury, so dark had the cloud that had descended been. As dark as the fog of flies. "Is anyone out there still going nuts? What about those who don't have children to worry over?"

"I don't remember much at all," Bill admitted. "Everything was red. There was Little Bill to look after, but everything else? I don't know."

Cecily held her breath, as though this was a moment to be remembered. Was it really concern for their children that had woken then from their rage? At Bill's words Raf nodded, then asked, "Can you ask them all to be quiet for a moment? I want to hear if the birds are singing again."

"Pipe down, you lot!" Bill called. The adults fell silent but there was still grizzling from the babies outside. As one, they all listened, and from somewhere overhead came the gentle sound of birdsong. It was like the dawn breaking after a moonless night, bringing with it the promise of a new, bright day. As the birds united in their chorus Raf let out a sigh of relief and turned to face Cecily, wordlessly waiting for her to give her verdict.

"The demon's gone?" Cecily began to smile. "Maybe you and Mike managed to chase him off last night, with your chanting and Mike's salt. So it's all over?"

Raf shook his head and lowered his voice to a whisper. "I don't know about that." He twitched his nose and closed his eyes for a second or two. "There's still a whiff of rot in the air. The flies aren't so far away."

"Please, Raf," a woman called from the garden. "We want our Ivy home."

He took another deep breath then whispered, "I think…it thrives on hate, but these parents love their kids. And their love is stronger than *its* hate. Like me and you, it couldn't claim you, could it?"

It almost did, but we've come through.

Raf squeezed Cecily's hand and asked, "Shall we open the house? What do you reckon, Sis?"

"You might be right. Bill's so changed since last night." Cecily unfolded her arms. "Let's open the house."

She saw a spark of affection in Raf's blue eyes in the moment before he turned back to the door and said, "Can everyone stand back from the walls? I'm going to open the shutters and fetch the kids. Give me five minutes but if any one of you start up with it again...those kids are going nowhere!"

"Stand back!" Bill shouted. "Stop slouching, there— stand away! He's opening the shutters!"

Raf closed the little hatch, then the front door too. He slid the massive iron bolt into place and asked Cecily, "Would you mind letting the kids know that their folks are here? I'll go and spin the wheel, let some light into the place!"

"With pleasure!" Cecily kissed him then hurried back to the children.

They all stopped and looked up at her as she went into the room. They'd folded the blankets and stacked the cushions and mattresses and had been playing with their pets, but a sense of anticipation was alive in the air. The children wanted to go home as much as their parents wanted to have them back. Their love was stronger than all the hatred and terror that the glass demon could muster.

"Your mums and dads are here to take you home. And they're all excited to see you again. Uncle Raf's about to open the house—shall we watch?" Cecily opened one set of curtains, presenting them with the view of the metal shutter that had drawn down over the window outside.

The children clustered around her as though waiting for a story and, from deep within the house, she heard the tremoring gears and rumbling mechanisms. Faced with the new dawn, the children no longer seemed so fretful at the sound as they had last night. As the shutters parted and began to slide back into wherever it was they were concealed, bright sunlight poured into the house, bathing them all in its glow. For the first time in days the sky above was a vivid autumn blue and there on the lawn birds hopped and pecked at the grass, the simple sight winning a cheer from the children. They understood what it meant, too. It meant that for now the horror had passed.

Ivy reached up and tapped Cecily's arm. She asked, "Can I go first? I want to be sure for my mates."

Cecily put her arm around Ivy's shoulders. "You can, Ivy. You're a very brave girl."

Cecily headed to the door of the room with Ivy, and the rest of the children followed behind. She peered into the hallway and saw Raf going back to the front door.

He put his hand on the bolt then with a command of, "Just stay in the garden," for those outside, drew it back. With a smile over his shoulder towards the children, he opened the door. Ivy waited near him, her hands knitted behind her back.

Cecily came forwards, leading the children to their parents. They were cautious, whispering amongst themselves. The parents gathered around the door, peering into the house.

"They've all had breakfast—and they've all behaved!" Cecily told their parents. "They've all been very good."

As the words left Cecily's lips, Ivy streaked out into the morning and flung herself into her parents' embrace. Seeing that, any last remnants of doubt Cecily might have had melted away and the children swarmed around her and out into the daylight.

Raf muttered something under his breath then stepped back to join Cecily and whispered, "Just something to keep the dogs and cats safely indoors so we don't lose any."

The laughter and happy tears of the parents made it clear that they were no longer under Aeshma's malign influence. It wasn't salt or a banishing prayer that had done it, it had been love.

Cecily took Raf's hand and smiled at him. "As much as I'd like to have children, that's probably too many!"

Raf cocked his head to one side. He studied her, a gentle smile on his face, then asked, "Would you really like to? Lovely willowy dhampirs who take after their gorgeous mum?"

Cecily kissed his cheek. "Of course I would! And why not strong impish dhampirs like their handsome father?"

"Maybe we should have a couple in that case." Raf slipped his arm around her waist then dabbed his fingertips against his eyes as he watched the happy reunions taking place in the garden. "You know, just to be sure?"

"At least," Cecily said. Some of the families had started to head out of the garden, making for home. She hated the thought of the demon waiting for them in the village after they'd been so safe the night before. "Raf, shouldn't we go with them?"

"Just before anyone runs off," Raf called, halting them in their tracks as he and Cecily headed out onto the lawn, "some of you've got toys and animals to take care of, so come in and Mike and Mim will help you gather them up. Then let's all of us walk down to the village together. I'll lead, if that suits everybody?"

The children cheered and ran back to the house, towing their parents behind them.

They made quite a procession as the children, their pets and their parents went down to the village, with Raf and Cecily at the head. Michael and Mim followed behind, and they all sang — or at least attempted — Raf's song, which had calmed the children the night before.

The animals trotted neatly alongside their families and Raf held Cecily's hand tighter than ever as the clouds of flies came into view over what should have been a pretty village. Soon the other residents would know they were approaching, and only time would tell if they too would join the procession or labour under Aeshma's influence.

As they neared the first house on the road into the village, the front door banged open and a furious woman emerged and barged her way to stand in the middle of the road.

"What's with all the noise?" she yelled, her hands planted firmly on her hips.

Cecily halted. But even as the procession pulled up behind her, she saw something stir in the woman's expression. From her deep scowl there began to emerge a smile.

"Just look at them kiddywinks with their cats and dogs!" she said, a completely different person to the woman who had bellowed at them moments before.

"Come and walk with us?" Raf gestured to the group. "And fetch your neighbours out too. Our Ivy'll teach you the song. The flies *hate* it."

And as Raf spoke, the cluster of flies that were around the windows of the house lifted as one and rose into the sky, heading towards the village.

"Thank heavens they've gone!" the woman said. She hurried with glee to the next house and knocked at the door. "Doris? You in there? Come outside!"

And soon Doris joined the procession, and Doris called for Winnie and Douglas and Winnie and Douglas fetched half a dozen more until the entire village of Acaster Garrow was marching together. At the head of the march, striding beside Raf with a rolling pin clutched in her hand so tightly it might have been a sabre, was Mrs Hodge, the housekeeper whom Cecily suspected would brook no nonsense, whether from demons or dhampirs. Some of the villagers hobbled on sticks, supported by the hands of their fellow residents, some were pushed in prams, but everywhere the people of Acaster Garrow strode the tide of flies fled in the wake of their song until the cloud pulsated and hovered above the sea, forced back from the land it had terrorised.

When the villagers reached the village green, Raf stopped walking and held up his hand. He hopped up onto the varnished wooden bench and addressed the residents.

"What's happened in Acaster Garrow these past few days has taught us all a few things." He put his hands on his hips, his voice a rousing shout. "And now we're going to teach that rotten old bugger from the window a few things in return, all right?"

Everyone threw their hands into the air and roared in agreement, the usually quiet Cecily included. Here among the assembled villagers, she really believed that they could see Aeshma off, that its legion of flies was no match for Acaster Garrow when they marched with Raf at the head of the little Yorkshire army.

"We're going to start today. Those of you with little ones, get them home, give them a cuddle and count your blessings they're the brave, fine knights they are. If you've got shops to open and farms to tend or boats to fish from, it's time to get back to work and I don't want a *single* cross word, not one, because that's what that thing feeds on and if we feed it, it's going to get stronger. We work together here and we do it with a smile. And can someone let Mike get his bike down!"

Raf rubbed the back of his neck, clearly just a little troubled by the ever-brightening sun. "The rest of you, we need every able-bodied person we can get. Because we're fighting back! And I need to get out of the sun, so if you've got a day to spare to win your village back, let's go to the pub and get planning!"

Chapter Fourteen

Quite a crowd volunteered to go to the pub, and trade at the bar was brisk for Ivy's parents, Walter and Pearl. Cecily had never been allowed in pubs when she was Mrs Headmaster, but here in Acaster Garrow the pub wasn't the den of vice that her husband had painted such places to be, it was the centre of the community.

People had *usuals* and favourite seats, even tankards with their names on them waiting behind the polished bar. Cecily could get used to visiting the pub, she decided as she carried two foaming tankards of beer across the taproom to Raf. He looked relaxed again after the tense stand-off of the night just gone, settled and happy but with a determined gleam in his bright blue eyes. He was making plans, she knew.

"On the house," Cecily told him. "They wouldn't hear of me paying. And you know, I thought the beer would've gone off, but it's really good."

"Beer's exempt from evil, that's good to know." Raf laughed. "A gorgeous woman with two tankards of ale, safe and sound in the de Chastelaine Arms. What more could a bloke ask?"

He glanced towards the bar that spanned the length of one wall. Behind it Ivy was kneeling, peering into a mirror that covered the wall, a little paper bag of liquorice beside her. On the mirror, pieces of stained glass spelled out the name of the pub, and after she popped another piece of liquorice into her mouth, Ivy leaned forwards and breathed on the mirrored surface. Then, in the newly formed cloud on the glass, she began to draw a castle with the tip of her finger. The fearless general and protector of the village children was a little girl again, even if that innocent stained glass made Cecily shudder at the very sight of it because it had her thinking of the demon again.

Stop it.

It was nothing but a perfectly innocent-looking piece of glass, but it would be some time before Cecily could look at a window like that again and not remember the moment when the demon burst out from it. One day perhaps that anticipated threat would be gone, but that day hadn't arrived just yet, and with a last glance back at the glass Cecily took a deep, grateful mouthful of her beer, steadying her nerves.

"With this many people, Raf, we'll be getting that salt circle down in no time," Cecily said. "And for as long as the circle lasts and the demon's contained, we've got time to find the chant that'll banish it!"

Raf took that as his cue. He banged his tankard on the table until the chatter in the pub grew silent and he had the attention of its patrons. Only then, as the villagers hung on his every word, did Raf outline his ambitious plans to create a circle of salt around the village, a circle of salt that would hold the hellish creature inside it and let them deal with Aeshma once and for all. It would take nerve and bravery, Raf admitted, something that Acaster Garrow had in spades, and though there would be fear, it was fear that they couldn't give in to. Raf's words were as rousing as the demon's threat was immense but Cecily knew that, with everybody's help, they could do in an hour or two the same job that might've taken Raf, Michael, Mim and her a whole day.

And that was even supposing that the furious villagers would have let them do it in the first place.

Now there were no furious villagers to contend with though, and together the people of Acaster Garrow and Raf drew up plans for the salt circle that would contain Aeshma and keep the demon's influence from spreading farther into the country. The scheme would involve cars and boats, vans and tractors and Raf would travel every step of it, ceaselessly chanting the incantation that would bind Aeshma within the circle. Even Michael would play his part, flying above the village to ensure that the circle wasn't broken. If it was, Aeshma would escape as surely as night followed day.

"Together we can see it back to hell," Raf told them as the plans were finished. "But it has to be as a village. It's going to do all it can to divide and conquer, but we'll stick well and truly together!"

A young farmer banged down his tankard on the bar. "When do we start, Raf? I'm ready to get my tractor revved up! Sooner we get shot of that clanking bastard, the better!"

"Let's start now, take it by surprise!" Raf clapped his hands together, urging them on. "Everyone go home and grab all the salt you can find. Knock on your neighbours' doors and get theirs an' all. While you're doing that, I'll draw up the route and we'll meet back here in an hour. Let's show it who it's messing with!"

As the crowd roared its approval, there was a glorious moment in which it seemed as though they had already won. Then from the behind the bar Ivy gave a scream, silencing the cheer in an instant. Above it, louder than any voice, there came a piercing, ear-splitting shriek that Cecily knew at once.

Aeshma.

There was a rumble like distant thunder then hell swept into the little pub, bringing chaos with it. The bottles that clustered along the pub's shelves smashed to the floor as Aeshma burst through the stained glass behind the bar and took shape in front of them, splinters of glass flying together, impelled by some unearthly force. It'd been hiding there all that time, watching, listening, biding its time until it could erupt from the glass. No wonder Cecily had felt so uneasy — she'd sensed it there without knowing it.

Aeshma flew up to the ceiling, shrieking again, its hideous wings scraping and clanking with every beat. The sound in the low-ceilinged pub was unlike anything Cecily could have imagined in her most terrifying nightmares, like a thousand nails raking over glass.

False god, bringer of wrath...

Raf virtually dived across the taproom towards the bar and seized up the salt pot that stood beside a jar of rotting picked eggs. He drew it back and, like a priest wielding an aspergillum, began to dash salt against Aeshma as he recited the same words he'd bellowed at the demon in the lane the previous evening. The creature seemed to fill the air with a sense of evil, the glass tongue whipping like a flail, but Raf barely flinched even when it drew a slash of blood across his shirt. He held his ground, pushing the monster back across the room, his voice steady, as loud as it was commanding.

Daylight shone through Aeshma's body as the demon grew closer to the window, forced farther and farther into retreat by the swirling grains of salt. Then with the sound of splintering glass the demon was outside, the shattered window left in pieces in its wake. Aeshma hovered above the road, only yards from a man up a ladder trying to rescue Michael's bike. Then the glass demon screeched again and flew at the village pump, bursting its metal with a howl, before it ascended on the force of the pump's fierce jet of water shooting into the air.

And just like that, Aeshma was gone.

"It bit me!" Ivy shrieked, emerging from behind the bar. Her hand was held tight against her body and she was shivering as though plunged into cold water. "Mum, it bit me! It bit me!"

Cecily could tell from Ivy's tomato-red face that it hurt, while her shivers were growing more violent by the second. "Pearl, have you got any aspirin? Ivy needs to lie down."

And hopefully that would be all. If the child started rampaging through the village with a host of flies, Cecily wasn't sure what they'd do.

Ivy, however, looked a little bit woozy. Her legs buckled and her mouth fell slack, silencing her tears. Her eyes rolled back in her head then, with a groan, she fell unconscious into her mother's arms. The insensible little girl gave a sound like a hiccup, her lips parting very slightly. Just enough to allow a fat, black corpse fly to crawl out of her mouth.

* * * *

Cecily and Raf followed Pearl upstairs to Ivy's bedroom, Mim hurrying behind. The little girl made no sound apart from her harsh, shallow breaths, and every one of them sounded like agony.

Ivy's bedroom was small and cosy and its window looked out onto the street where, unseen by the insensible Ivy, a team of villagers were still trying to turn off the impromptu fountain that had shielded Aeshma's escape. Her friends' laughter as they ran back and forth through the water was lost to Ivy's ears, loud and delighted as it was, but Cecily didn't want to shut the window. She wanted Ivy's room filled with the sound of her happy friends, because that sense of a community that was almost a family was what had saved Acaster Garrow once already — perhaps it could save Ivy now.

Pearl laid Ivy in her bed, the mother's sobs pitiful as she settled beside her daughter, stroking back her hair with trembling fingers. Apparently unaware of his own injury from that terrible glass flail, Raf knelt beside the bed and lifted Ivy's hand, inspecting the bite closely. He bent closer and sniffed the small but angry wound, the teeth marks more like the slashes left by the blade of a knife than the bite of any creature from this world or another.

After a minute or so had passed in silent contemplation, Raf reached into his pocket and withdrew a little bottle of witch hazel like the one that he had once given to Cecily, before they had saved each other.

"I made this. It's for helping wounds. Dress Ivy's hand with it every hour," he told Pearl softly, watching her to ensure that the message cut through her shock. "Mim, would you sit with Pearl and help nurse little Ivy? You know Mim, Pearl, she's got the skills this here fighter needs just now. You couldn't have a better practitioner looking out for her."

"Thank you, Mr de Chastelaine," Pearl said, taking the bottle. As she began to apply the ointment to Ivy's hand, she said, "It caught you, though—you're not sickening too?"

He shook his head. "I'm all right, just a bit of a cut. It bit this little one, but she's a hell of a fighter. She'll soon—"

Raf fell silent. He lifted Ivy's hand again and Cecily followed his gaze to the wound, her heart leaping at the sight before her. Ivy's hand had already started to change, and the change didn't look like it was for the better. Narrow black lines traced the shape of Ivy's veins like the surface of a leaf, spidering out through her hand with the bite wound at their epicentre. They reminded Cecily of the leading in the windows at Whitmore Hall, the leading in the church too. And between those spiderwebbed veins, black as night, the texture of her pale skin was... *What* was it?

What's happening to her skin?

Oh no, it can't be glass.

But as Cecily watched the brittle sheen spreading over Ivy's hand resembled nothing other than glass.

"We need a belt," Raf said quickly. "Something to use as a tourniquet. And a bowl, quick!"

Without waiting for a reply Raf bent his head and put his mouth to the wound. He drew his breath in with one deep inhalation, his lips clamped over the bite on Ivy's pale hand, the hand that had wielded that protecting stick just last night. For a moment Cecily wondered what he was doing, then she realised that he was trying to suck the poison out.

And he needs a tourniquet.

Cecily took the sash from her dress and passed it to Mim. "Use this," she said.

As Mim tied the sash tight around Ivy's elbow, Pearl rose shakily to her feet. On the windowsill there was a pretty dish of pale blue china, filled to the brim with seashells that Cecily imagined Ivy must have collected from the beach. Pearl emptied the dish with great care before bringing the dish back to Raf, her lower lip wobbling with barely contained distress. The poor woman looked stricken, her gaze never leaving her daughter's unmoving face.

Raf drew his mouth away from Ivy's hand and spat a mouthful of viscous black fluid into the dish, from which a smell like rotting meat began to rise. It didn't look like blood at all, and Cecily knew that must be Aeshma's poison. With a sigh Raf rocked back on his knees and peered down at the wound again, studying it. All the time he was fanning his hand beneath his nose, and Cecily knew better than anyone that if the smell of the fluid was bad for her, it must be nearly unbearable for him.

"That's slowed—" He flicked his head up and exclaimed, "Window!"

Cecily pulled the sash window closed just in time to prevent a thick swarm of flies from entering the bedroom. She stepped back from the glass as the insects slammed into it, entirely blocking out the daylight like a blanket.

"I've seen this before," he told them. "If we can get rid of it, even if we can chase it off a fair way, it's like the psychic hooks break and it'll lose its influence over her. Ideally we get rid of it permanently. And we have to do it fast."

He's seen it before?

Once again, Cecily wondered what bizarre sights Raf had witnessed in his unorthodox life. Was a girl turning into glass really not so unusual to him?

"Then we get rid of it," Cecily said. "However we can."

"Right." Raf took a deep breath despite the odour, then murmured something in a language that Cecily didn't understand. It sounded like one of his incantations. "Pearl, you and Mim just need to keep Ivy cool and that tourniquet tight. Don't worry about her arm. I've…said a few words. They'll help. I'll send Walter up and…this might sound a bit unorthodox but give her lots of hugs. Hold her hand, talk to her, read her stories. *Don't* lose hope. Love and hope are two of the strongest weapons we have against that bastard."

They stepped out into the hallway, alone once more. Only then did he admit, "We can't take *her* away from it. If we try that, she might never wake up. We need that thing to leave Ivy. She can't outrun it."

What a horrendous possibility, Cecily thought with a shudder. *And what a vile creature it is.*

Cecily took Raf's arm as they headed downstairs. "Do you need anything, Raf? A drink or a sit-down?"

"I need a hug," he admitted. "And if I'm salting Acaster Garrow, I'll need my sun lotion. I could feel my shoulders getting sore out on the green. It's a good sign, though, to have the sun again."

They stopped on the middle of the stairs and Cecily hugged him. She didn't want to let go of him, but the longer they stayed there, the longer Aeshma would be at large. With a sigh, she took Raf's hand and they carried on downstairs.

Chapter Fifteen

The wind at the cliff edge was bracing, but nevertheless the Acaster Garrow volunteers were ready to draw the salt circle. Michael, transformed into a large bat once more, perched on Raf's shoulder, and Cecily stood beside him, ready with a megaphone. Once again they were like soldiers going into battle, waiting for the word from their commander to go over the top and face the unthinkable enemy.

From here they could see the de Chastelaine Arms where Ivy languished between life and death, her skin hardening into glass with every passing minute. The walls of the pub were hidden beneath a solid shroud of corpse flies so thick that it seemed as though the very building were alive. It glistened jet-black, pulsating with the innumerable insects that made up the swarm, but the people of Acaster Garrow were ready to fight back at last.

Raf had divided the route into relays, with nobody required to do more than a few miles whether on foot, bike, boat or tractor. The only person who would be present for the entire circle was Raf himself, chanting his ceaseless incantation, and Cecily, there simply because she wouldn't dream of sending him out alone. Michael would watch from above, ensuring that the circle wasn't broken and watching for any sign of Aeshma's return. If it did return... Well, they would deal with that if it happened.

If, not when.

"Mike's written down the incantation phonetically," Raf told Cecily, handing her a piece of folded paper. "If anything happens and I can't continue, you need to finish the circle and speak the words. Promise?"

Cecily swallowed as she took the piece of paper. She didn't dare begin to imagine what could stop Raf from finishing the circle, and she glanced up at the lowering cloud overhead, where even now Aeshma might be waiting.

"Of course I will," Cecily said. "But let's hope nothing *does* happen. If you start feeling ill, you must tell me, Raf."

"I'm not going to turn into glass," Raf told her gently, taking her hand in his. "But if it comes after us... It might come after us. We just need to be ready. I wish you'd stayed at home, Sissy."

"Nonsense," Cecily said with a grin. "And after all these people volunteered to help...it wouldn't be fair if I'd stayed safe at home."

Raf kissed Cecily's cheek, then pressed his mouth to hers as though that gentle peck hadn't been enough. Only when they parted did he pick up the megaphone and announce, "Acaster Garrow, let salt circling commence. And if you're listening, you-know-who, you've got two choices. Leave the village, leave Ivy be and take your stinking flies with you, or stay and find out what happens to demons who get above their station and try to take on Yorkshire. Now let's spread some salt!"

So it began. Michael took off with a great flap of his wings and soared into the sky above them, and the spreading started. They were armed with a wheelbarrow and men more used to shovelling earth and coal were sifting the salt onto the ground. Not a gap was allowed and Cecily admired the painstaking care of the operation. One of the men went back to fix a line that was blurred by a gust of wind, then they continued, the white crystals falling like ice.

"This incantation will buy us a couple of days even when the circle starts to go. Tomorrow we're buying up every grain of salt in this lovely county of ours," Raf told them.

Then he began to speak the ancient words in that same, melodic way that Cecily always found so enchanting. On and on they walked and still the men shovelled, handing over to their shift mates even as Raf's recitation continued, lilting and tuneful. They climbed onto haycarts and even bicycles as the men shovelled on, slowly, laboriously encircling the little village and containing the monster that tormented them.

But would Aeshma choose to stay, or would the demon give up its hold on Ivy and leave to create chaos elsewhere?

Then what? They couldn't draw a salt circle around a county, let alone a whole island.

As they headed along the path at the foot of a row of gardens, Michael rested for a moment on a branch of one of the nearby trees. But he was alert, his eyes darting here and there, his ears twitching, as the shovelling went on. And Cecily was fairly sure she saw his tongue shoot out and catch a passing insect. Then he beat his wings and was spiralling up into the sky again, swooping overhead as he kept up his patrol.

Raf paused too, taking a quick swig of water from a bottle in his pocket, then he returned to the incantation. Birdsong seemed to follow them wherever they trod and the sun peeped out a little more boldly but of Aeshma there was still no sign.

And that in itself felt like a bad sign.

I know you're up there.

All of a sudden Cecily felt a sensation of dread so dense and cloying that she could almost put out her hand and touch it. She clutched the *cocosul* but when she glanced from Raf to the volunteers spreading the salt she saw nothing amiss. Since meeting Raf, Cecily had begun to accept that not being able to *see* a threat didn't mean that no threat existed. It was a skill that few people shared.

But there aren't even any flies, nor the smell or the shrieks.

Even so, her heart was pounding. But when she looked up, she saw only Michael flying beneath a cloud, looking down on them. Then the cloud seemed to split in two and from it burst Aeshma and a buzzing shroud of flies, the whole unholy legion coming straight at him.

"Read the words, Sis! I love you!" With that, Raf's clothes and charms fell to the path and the pipistrelle bat darted up into the sky like an arrow, aimed straight at Aeshma's body.

Cecily started to recite the words, written in Michael's clear and even handwriting. She had no idea what the incantation meant or whether she was saying it properly but still she went on because she knew that the village and little Ivy were counting on her, even as she kept half an eye on the battle in the sky above.

Raf slammed into the demon's wing and went straight through the stained glass like a stone hurled through a window. The hole he left was small but it was proof of one thing — Aeshma could be harmed, damaged, maybe. And if he could be harmed, then there was new hope that he could somehow be defeated.

As the demon let out one of those blood-freezing shrieks, Raf circled round and headed back towards earth with all the speed of a falling star. The howling creature hurtled after him, its glass tongue flicking out as though it might catch Raf with it, just as Michael had caught the insect before. Michael sailed through the air after them and with a mighty beat of his wings caught Aeshma a blow that sent it hurtling towards the ground ever faster.

As Raf thundered towards the wheelbarrow filled with salt, the men with shovels dropped to the ground and threw their hands up over their head. Yet Cecily kept reciting the words even as she watched the demon, its flight out of control thanks to Michael, spinning down towards him. At the last moment Raf darted sharply to the side and slammed with no grace or precision straight into Cecily's shoulder. Aeshma, however, was either too large and unwieldy or too out of control to change course and instead the demon clattered violently against the wheelbarrow with a screech of pain and frustration.

Aeshma seemed dazed and slumped onto the earth in a way that Cecily hadn't begun to hope was even possible. The ground was snowy with the freshly laid salt and as soon as Aeshma struck it, its glass carcass began to crack.

Still chanting, Cecily scooped up a handful of salt from the barrow and threw it over the demon. Aeshma shrieked as the sound of cracking glass filled Cecily's ears. Its reign was well and truly over. Cecily turned to pick up a spade, but the next sound she heard almost turned her flesh to stone.

Aeshma's wings were beating again, the shrieking replaced with a furious hiss, and before Cecily had a chance to run, razor-sharp talons sank into her shoulders. She screamed with pain and terror as she was lifted off her feet and up into the sky as though she weighed nothing.

Raf was a second behind them, darting up from the ground at a breathtaking pace, but they were climbing higher and higher and faster and faster, leaving the earth behind. The last thing she saw before the swarm of flies swallowed her was a talon of glass lashing out to flick the little pipistrelle away, then all she knew was darkness.

Chapter Sixteen

When Cecily opened her eyes, the sky above her was grey and lumpen with boiling cloud. And piercing the view, dull without sunlight, was a weathervane.

Where the heck am I?

Cecily put out her hand to push herself up and froze the moment she touched broken glass. Tentatively, she moved her hand along yet only came up against more shards of glass. And each movement sent jabbing pain into her shoulders where the demon had dug in its claws. Cecily lifted her head and her hair snagged, tangled in the glass. And when she tried to lift her feet, she heard the sickening scrape of glass against glass and carefully laid them down again. Her shoes were long gone. She wouldn't be able to stand, let alone run away, without shredding herself to pieces.

Cecily turned her head the little that she could, only to see on either side of her a heap of snapped, twisted stained glass as if she were in a nest made from the stuff. And now, staring straight at her, was the face of

Christ—the face of Beatrice de Chastelaine—from the shattered east window.

"Help me, Bea. Help me," Cecily whispered. "I can't move."

She couldn't give up, but what else could she do? She was trapped inside a glass nest, brought there by a demon. If she tried to get out, she would only succeed in slashing herself to ribbons. And if she stayed there— but how could she, when that damned demon would come back?

Maybe I'll pass out before anything too horrible happens to me.

But it was hardly a comforting thought.

Raf… Where is he? Is he looking for me?

But would he find her? Was she even in Acaster Garrow anymore?

She heard a scraping noise and flinched in fear, the glass grazing her arm where she had moved. And all that she saw above her was the weathervane slowly change, pointing to the north.

"Raf…" she whispered. "Raf… Find me. Please find me. I don't know where I am."

She focused her all on Raf and tried to ignore her fear. The aerial battle had been horrible to witness and she sincerely hoped he was all in one piece. And as she lay there, she felt what she thought must be his pain— his sore, bruised limbs.

Find me, Raf. Find me…

And he was worried, too. Of course he was. There was no surprise in that, but as Cecily lay there, she was sure she could see Raf, pacing back and forth. Somewhere…in a lane near their home.

And I have a home now, and I will see it again.

She stared at the weathervane. Would it give him a clue? She stared and stared at it until she had to blink and the afterimage burned and throbbed behind her eyes, green then purple then gone.

The wind whistled through the nest like a glass harmonica, sounding like the howling of ghosts. So Cecily started to sing to herself, the song Raf had sung to the children as they'd carried their cargo of salt.

The song was as calming as Raf had promised it would be, a balm against the rising tide of fear that threatened her. She focused her thoughts on Raf, picturing him in the lane again. He paced back and forth still, his face darkened with worry, his thoughts in turmoil as his eyes searched the sky above. He would find her, she was sure. Because if he didn't, she couldn't imagine what the future would hold for either of them.

Cecily blinked as a dark shadow fell over her, bringing with it what felt like a dart of ice that travelled through her blood and straight into her skull. She hardly dared look up because she already knew that Aeshma was above her and as the shadow grew darker, engulfing her, Cecily knew that the creature was getting closer.

She sang ever louder, even though, as she breathed, she felt the corners of the broken glass pierce her clothes. The demon was above her, its face so close that if it *did* breathe, Cecily would have felt its exhalation. She willed herself not to panic as Aeshma's monstrous mouth opened as wide as a snake swallowing its prey, the jaw detaching with a grating click, then the false god let out a high-pitched scream that felt like a blade fashioned from ice stabbing right through her heart.

Cecily resisted the instinct to cover her ears to avoid tearing her skin and the scream went through her, thrumming through every nerve. It was cold and burning all at once, searing and freezing Cecily's blood in her veins and filling her head with a sound like hell itself.

So this was it. She had survived through so much and now that she was free, her life would end in a horrible glass nest, at the hands of a malignant glass demon.

She tried her best to console herself, even though she didn't want to be dragged away from life. At least she'd met Raf. At least she'd known love, even though it had only been for such a little while. It was something, wasn't it? Such an intense, beautiful love. Enough love for several lifetimes. And maybe that was why she couldn't have anything more.

Cecily pictured Raf, his hair standing on end as he ran his hand through it again. She saw it so clearly she could almost have reached out and smoothed it down.

Raf, Aeshma's in the nest with me. If I never see you again, remember that I love you. I'll always love you, no matter what.

Because a love like theirs could pass through the grave and survive death itself.

Cecily tasted something metallic in the back of her throat just as a warm trickle of blood wound its way from her nostril and onto her top lip. She realised with a pang of despair that the creature was killing her. Without laying so much as a finger on her body, Aeshma would end her life with its torturous, loathsome scream.

That monstrous glass tongue emerged from the sharp jaw and in one painful sweep Aeshma lapped up the blood that was running from Cecily's nose. On and on went the scream, until Cecily felt as though her very skull would crack in two, splintered like the stained-glass window. She could see her own blood as it ran through the demon's body of glass, threading dark veins deep inside the creature in a map of cruel despair.

And as abruptly as it had started, the screaming stopped.

Aeshma's body lurched to one side with a fearsome crack, its head drawing back beyond any physical limits. Cecily wasn't sure exactly what had happened, but something fundamental had changed.

And in her mind's eye, she saw Raf stop his pacing. He turned on his heel and fixed his suddenly determined gaze on the distant church. Then, with a cry of *Sissy*, he set off running.

Nobody ever called me 'Sissy' but you.

Ignoring the sharp stabs of pain from the glass and the wounds in her shoulders, Cecily lifted her arm and wiped the blood from her face. She battled her urge to recoil as she smeared the warm, red wetness on the demon's cold, fracturing body. There was salt in her blood and it was enough to weaken Aeshma, to send hairline cracks across its grotesque form, just like the spidering veins its bite had left on Ivy's innocent hand.

And the church bells began to ring.

This time the howl of pain belonged not to Cecily but to Aeshma, the false god's body buckling and cracking further with every deafening peal of the church bells. The creature's vast, beating wings swept the sky with the by-now familiar clanking sound and it ascended towards the heavens at a lurching gait, no longer the attacker but the fleeing victim. With a last shriek of pain Aeshma disappeared into the darkness of the clouds that might be natural, but might be flies, leaving Cecily alone in the fearsome nest.

Cecily felt the bells vibrate through the nest, but they sounded oddly muffled. Tears rose in her eyes as she realised that the demon's screams had robbed her of her full hearing.

But she had her life, and she'd rather live to be eighty in a muffled world than die in a nest made of glass before she was thirty.

And as a tiny pipistrelle bat swept over the razor edges of the nest that she thought would be her last earthly bed and peered down at her, Cecily knew that she wasn't alone anymore. Somehow Raf had found her, just as she had willed him to.

"Raf!" Cecily smiled with relief. She wanted to reach up to him but couldn't. "You've found me! Thank heavens, you've found me!"

He dipped down and touched his face to her nose, then flitted safely clear of the nest and landed on the roof of the building beyond the broken glass. A few seconds later Cecily found herself looking at her fiancé, as naked as the day he was born, bruised and battered from his flight earlier but alive and at her side. His face was stricken with worry but then the fear transformed into a smile filled with love.

"Stay where you are!" she warned him. "It's sharp!"

"Don't worry about me," Raf said, his tone urgent with concern. "Are you all right, Sissy?"

She could only just make out his words over the hissing in her ears. "Almost. I'm bleeding. And I can't hear very well. The demon screamed and screamed so loudly, right in front of my face, but I can't move so I couldn't put my hands over my ears to make it stop."

"That demon *will* bloody scream, the bastard," was Raf's reply as the bells ceased. In the silence he raised his voice and shouted to someone unseen, "I need some clothes up here. And we've got a broken glass problem to deal with. But definitely bring up my clothes, Mike, or I could end up with a very disappointed Sissy!"

Typical Raf, making a joke of such a thing.

That's why I love him.

With the instructions relayed, Raf moved carefully around the nest, clearly looking for some point of weakness in the demon's trap. Cecily could sense his concern for her, the feeling of love so acute that it was stronger than even her fear had been. Raf had heard her. From a distance that no voice would ever be able to travel, her lover had heard her.

"You told me that you loved me and showed me the weathervane," he said as he sank to his knees on the far side of the fearsome cluster of glass. "And I smelt your perfume so clearly that I thought you were there beside me. You're the most amazing person I've ever known, Cecily Pincombe."

Raf looked up and smiled as Cecily heard the muffled sound of a door opening from deep within her razor-edged prison. "And here's Mike, trying to deliver clothes without seeing me without any!"

"Good Lord! Good *Lord!*" Michael gasped. "I thought we had pigeons up here! And, instead, there's —"

Cecily saw Michael over the edge of the nest. He had a ripening black eye and flecks of salt in his hair, which seemed odd when teamed with his dog collar. Michael held his hand to his brow as though shielding his eyes from the sun and passed Raf a small pile of clothes.

Raf dressed quickly, pulling the tangled charms over his head once he was clothed. He didn't put his shoes on his feet though, but instead on his hands. Then he knelt beside the nest and began very slowly and deliberately to stamp down the shards of glass so they laid flat. It was a painstaking operation but, bit by bit, it allowed Raf to make his way ever closer to Cecily. She wasn't alone anymore. She was going to see home again.

"Mike," Raf said. "Can you get everyone together and bring up blankets or anything like cushions and whatnot? We need to cover this glass or Sissy'll be cut to ribbons. And something to plug our ears, in case we need the bells again?"

"Yes, yes, of course!" He half-turned to go, then looked back at the nest. "Wait! I recognise some of this. Isn't it from the east window?"

Raf nodded. "It's Bea's work. I'm trying not to break it and make it any more dangerous but..." He blinked up at his brother, still carefully flattening down the glass as he continued to mark out a path to reach Cecily. "Could we use it again? Maybe patch up the broken bits of our old east window with it? Aeshma can stick that in his pipe and smoke it."

"I don't see why not." Michael smiled, then he seemed to recall himself. "Now I must get on. I'm terribly sorry this has happened at St Anastasia's, Cecily. It's usually a peaceful place of contemplation and fellowship."

And with that, Michael hurried off.

"Your lavender showed me where to find you," Raf told Cecily as he moved ever closer over the carpet of glass. "She'd turned towards the church and then I heard you calling me and —"

His voice caught and he pinched his fingers to the bridge of his nose.

"Sorry," Raf said, smiling again. "I just love you so bloody much."

"The lavender?" That little cutting, a grey twig with new green shoots—how could such a thing show the way? But it seemed that anything could in Raf's garden. "I love you, too. Oh, Raf…the demon is weakening. A little more, just a little more and it's over."

Raf reached out over the edge of the nest, his arm at full stretch for Cecily. For a moment his fingers strained, then they caught hers and he held onto her hand for all he was worth, just as he had when they faced the judge at Whitmore Hall. Just as she had held onto him through the weeks of his recovery after that battle to the death. Just as they would hold onto each other for the rest of their lives.

Help was coming, Cecily knew, and Raf's simple touch meant the world to her. There was so much good in the world, no matter what wickedness tried to destroy it, and she and Raf would always face it together.

And they wouldn't let go.

Chapter Seventeen

The steeple's staircase was tight and narrow, a stone screw set into a corner of the tower. Raf carried Cecily down, wrapped in a blanket, because she was so exhausted that she could barely stand. Cecily knew he must be as tired as she was but he silenced her protests with a kiss and they emerged to the cheers of the villagers who had been ringing the bells.

All Cecily heard was concern from her new friends, all she saw in their faces was worry for the woman who had already become a part of their community. It warmed her even through her exhaustion and she clung closer to Raf, feeling the reassuring thud of his heartbeat in his chest and the softness of his lips against her hair.

"I'm taking you to see Mim," he soothed as he carried her through the church, past the skeletal east window. "The sun's not far off setting. Better to get some rest and come back fighting in daylight."

Cecily remembered Mim at the pub, waiting in Ivy's bedroom to help the little girl and her stricken parents. All at once Cecily forgot about her scratches and thought only of the wounded child. "Ivy! What's happened to the girl? She was turning into glass. Is she all right?"

Raf shook his head as they stepped out into the sunset. He drew in a long breath and replied, "It's moving slowly but…it's moving. We have to beat him tomorrow, but we will."

"Mr de Chastelaine!" Mrs Hodge hurried out of the church in pursuit. "He doesn't much like the bells so we were thinking…we could keep them ringing all night? Take it in turns, ring a peal every half hour or so to ward him off?"

Raf nodded and told her with enthusiasm, "That's a brilliant plan, Mrs H, and nobody can run a ship like you can. I'm putting you in charge of the bell-ringers, all right? Let's raise the roof off Acaster Garrow."

Mrs Hodge nodded, businesslike and efficient. She smiled down at Cecily and promised, "You'll love it here when this is sorted, miss, truly you will."

As Mrs Hodge departed Raf said, "I was wondering…what if we bring Ivy's pals into her room? Get them talking, telling stories, jokes, all that sort of thing? If that beast thrives on hate, maybe we can ward it off with the opposite."

Cecily nodded. Every sound was so muffled but with effort she could make out the words. "Yes, bring her friends—bring everyone. If we're all together, if we're all happy, perhaps we'll be safe."

"I'll get Mike on that job," Raf told her, and once again without him saying a word or stumbling on his feet, Cecily felt his exhaustion every bit as acutely as her own.

As they made their way towards the pub, its shimmering shroud of flies swaying and humming, his step finally faltered for the first time. She felt his strong chest heave and wondered at what the stench must be like to her lover faced with so many of the creatures.

How can he even bear it?

Then Raf took a deep, steadying breath and nuzzled his face against Cecily's hair, breathing in and out with rhythmic determination as he strode across the road towards the de Chastelaine Arms.

Cecily wondered as Raf stumbled then gathered himself and continued when he had actually allowed *himself* to rest. Her heart was filled with love and concern for him. Then, as Raf's step faltered again, Cecily heard first one set of footsteps approaching, then another, then a third. Faces she recognised from her welcome party gathered round and buoyed off Raf as though they were pulling a drowning man from the ocean. Some of the villagers wrapped their arms around his waist, others around his shoulders and as one, they supported the exhausted dhampir as he carried Cecily into the pub.

The pump was still spraying water high into the air and on the threshold of the de Chastelaine Arms, Raf paused. He lifted his face from Cecily's hair and glanced back at the pump. When he smiled, she knew without a doubt that her lover wasn't beaten yet.

Not my Raf.

Never.

"Here's a project for you, Tommy," Raf told one of the men who was supporting him. He was young and robust, a farmer, Cecily guessed, from his ruddy face and broad shoulders. "Get your pals together and see if you can get a fire hose onto that pump somehow. There's all kinds of rubbish up in the outbuilding at my place, so have a dig around. If you *can*, let's use the water to wash these bloody flies off the pub."

"Count on us, Raf," Tommy told him. "I'll get the lads on it."

With that, Raf carried Cecily over the threshold into the pub. Finally alone, he crumpled down onto a padded bench beside the door and gathered her into his embrace.

"Love you, Sis," he murmured. "You're going to be all right, I promise."

Cecily clung to him. "You need to rest," she urged Raf. "You're exhausted. And am I...? I'm talking really loudly, aren't I?"

Raf grinned and replied, "Just a bit loudly, but I don't mind." He put his fingers beneath Cecily's chin and lifted her face to his. For a long moment they simply gazed at each other then, tenderly, he kissed her.

Outside there were raised voices, but not in anger now. There was hammering then the sound of a spray of water as it raked the front of the pub. The air inside was fresher almost at once and Cecily knew that Raf's plan to rid the outside of the pub of its shroud of flies was working.

One by one, Ivy's friends arrived and went up to her room. They might have been sombre as they entered but that didn't last long and soon, even with her damaged ears, Cecily could hear the children upstairs, their footsteps clattering over the floorboards.

Then she heard another sound. A sound that had been absent.

Someone was laughing.

The door to the pub opened and the woman who had growled at her in the post office entered the pub, jolly with flirtatious good humour, her hair and shoulders dotted with beads of water from the hose pipe. In her wake followed two equally chipper women, each of them carrying heavy pots of stew in their oven-gloved hands.

"We might not be burly farming boys, but if the WI can't feed the workers, what use are we?"

And feed the workers they did, with rich meaty stews and fresh-baked bread and cake. Where they had found fresh food Cecily couldn't guess, but this was a village where people pulled together. This was a village that no demon could conquer.

As she and Raf ate, washing down the feast with beer, Cecily felt their mutual exhaustion lift. The sky grew darker but, as the peal of bells rang out over Acaster Garrow and the children laughed and played around their ailing peer, her spirits were restored.

Mim dressed Cecily's scrapes and scratches, and cleansed and bandaged the wounds on her shoulders. It really wasn't so bad. When she remembered lying immobile in the nest, feeling her doom upon her, it seemed a miracle she had survived as unscathed as she was. Aeshma had tried to kill her but the very blood with which it had tormented its victim had proved the fiercest weapon of all. Aeshma might be able to spill blood, but that same blood had become a weapon against the demon.

Thanks to the ladies of the Women's Institute, the message that people should gather in the pub had spread across the village and soon it was full of blankets and cushions as the locals settled for the night.

When the pub reached capacity, people bedded down in the surrounding houses, banding close together as though that alone were enough to protect them. But for all they knew, perhaps it was.

"I'm going to look in on little Ivy," Raf told Cecily as the bells took one of their regular breaks. The fact that she was sure the bells were no longer ringing seemed like a good sign too, as though some of her hearing was on its way back. "Do you want to come up too or will you wait?"

"I'll come." Cecily winced as she got up, but the worst of the pain had gone. It wasn't only bandages Mim had used but an incantation too, she was sure.

Together she and Raf climbed the staircase towards the landing. From the open door of Ivy's room, she could hear the sounds of children at play, but the sadness of Pearl and Walter was so strong that it was like a physical blow. Raf seemed to sense Cecily's discomfort and he held her hand tight as they stepped into the bedroom, lit now by the soft glow of the bedside lamp.

"How's our soldier?" Raf asked gently. "And how's Mum and Dad?"

Pearl's eyes were rimmed with red. She dabbed at them as she said, "She opens her eyes now and then, but I don't know if she can see us. I don't know…"

Ivy had been so full of life, so determined, that she seemed like a different person now. It wasn't fair to leave one who had been so vibrant so low, weak and damaged here in her humble little bed. *This* was what they were fighting for. This little child and all the other children who Aeshma would see destroyed.

Cecily stroked Ivy's clammy forehead.

"You poor girl…"

She could see that the glassy sheen had travelled as far as Ivy's upper arm and the sash that had been used to tourniquet her limb and arrest the spread of the fearsome bite was tied around her shoulder now. Once the infection—what else *could* she call it?—breached that joint though, Cecily couldn't imagine how they would stop it from coursing through her whole, defenceless body. Ivy's skin was already the same shade of deep red as the image of Aeshma had been in the window. It was as brittle and hard and cold to the touch too.

It isn't fair.

As the children played at the foot of the bed, Raf took one of the charms from around his neck and clutched it in his fist. Then he knelt beside Ivy as though praying, murmuring to the charm in his hand. Cecily recognised what he was doing because she had seen him do something similar in a Devonshire churchyard once upon a time. He was asking his late mother to protect the child as she fought against Aeshma's bite.

But what would happen to a child made from glass? Would she even be Ivy anymore or a mindless servant of Aeshma?

Tomorrow they would fight—for Ivy, for Acaster Garrow and, if Aeshma somehow released the demons from the other windows, for humanity itself.

The bells were ringing again when Raf and Cecily descended the stairs once more. Rather than return to the crowded bar, they stepped out into the pub's darkened yard and breathed in the cool night air. It smelled different though, fresh with salt and alive with the sound of the church bells and the cry of gulls.

"'It's very peaceful here," Cecily said. "'I'm glad there's a change in the village. But if we banish Aeshma, will it go somewhere else and wreak havoc?"

"We're not going to banish it." Raf settled onto a wooden bench and drew Cecily to sit beside him. He wrapped his arm around her shoulders, holding her close. "It's trapped in a salt circle on one side with the ocean on the other. The air's filled with salt. It's cornered and it must know it. Tomorrow, whatever it takes, we're finishing it. I don't care if it can hear me, it knows there's nothing it can do to stop us now."

Until the incantation on the salt circle ran out. They couldn't salt the village *every* day for the rest of their days, after all.

They couldn't salt the world.

"If it gets out, what about all those other demons in all those other windows?" Cecily swallowed, the memories of Aeshma's scream and the scrape of that glass tongue against her cheek all too recent. "And was Kwaalveld the only place that imprisoned demons in its windows? What if there's thousands of them all over the world?"

"Mike says the other Kwaalveld windows are secure. It's had it from the top, apparently." Raf shook his head as though to say, *whatever that means*. "Sometimes...sometimes we have to stop the things we can stop and believe that it's enough. If it could summon the others, it'd have done it long ago. Demons don't usually hang around when it comes to things like that."

"That's something, at least!" Cecily said, relieved. She rested her head on his shoulder. "Goodbye, horrible demon! Good riddance!"

Raf kissed her hair and said, "They're probably all packed away in a warehouse somewhere. They didn't have the salt trap, though, only Aeshma. That tells me that it's the boss." There was another kiss then, reassuring her. "How're those ears feeling?"

"Better, I think. I don't feel like I've got my head under a pillow anymore!" Cecily tapped the side of her head. "And apart from a few scratches, I'm as fit as a flea."

"I wish I could've taken everybody up to the house." She heard the remorse in Raf's voice, though she knew that the idea would have been too risky. How could they possibly defend a whole village against whatever lurked above the clouds? Here they were as close together as they could be, packed into the pub and neighbouring houses, able to hear the protective peal of the bells. "I just didn't want to risk them on the road. And we couldn't chance moving Ivy or leaving her folks here to cope alone. Do you think I've made the right decision, Sis?"

"You have, darling," Cecily said, her tone gentle. "It'll keep away while the bells ring. And if it attacked on the road again, you and Mike fought it off last time but let's not risk it again."

He snuggled her closer still and admitted, "I wanted you to come to Acaster Garrow and fall in love with it. Instead, it's been— Just look what's happened. When this is all done, will you still want to call this little village home?" She heard a tease in his voice. "This doesn't happen every year. Usually it's just dhampirs knocking about looking after the gardens and *we're* all lovely blokes!"

"I'm here because *you're* here." Cecily kissed his cheek. "And when the locals aren't under the influence of a demon, they're the loveliest bunch of folk. Look how they've all pulled together!"

He nodded, then yawned. "If we could just force that thing out into the sea…" Raf rubbed his hand over his bruised face, then stretched one arm above his head, the other arm still wrapped around Cecily's shoulders. "All that salt, just waiting to turn him into sea foam."

As they sat together, Cecily glanced round at the sound of a tiny bell. A cat leapt onto the yard wall and peered down at them.

"My hearing is definitely coming back—I heard that cat!"

"Hello, puss." Raf patted his knee, inviting the cat to perch. "Come and say hello to Captain Sissy."

The black cat hopped down and trotted up to them. It purred as it rubbed its head against Raf's knee. He scratched behind the animal's ears as the sound of ringing bells fell silent again. Now the only bell to be heard was the gentle tinkle of that worn by their new feline companion.

"You ready for bed, little friend?" Raf asked the cat. Then he scratched Cecily's head and teased, "What about you? Are you as knackered as I am?"

"Almost," Cecily said. "I haven't turned into a bat today, though, so I suspect you're far more tired than I am!"

Together they stood, still wrapped in each other's embrace. The little cat snuggled into Raf's arms and let him carry it with them into the pub. The bustling taproom had been transformed into a dormitory during their absence and the atmosphere was one of tranquillity, albeit shot through with a sense of tension that felt like an approaching storm to Cecily. There was fear, of course, and worry for the little girl who languished in the power of Aeshma, but the fury of last night was gone, fled with the swarm of flies that the men had washed from the pub's walls.

Seeing the couple and their feline friend approach, a woman with her hair in curlers welcomed them with a smile. Cecily recognised her as one of the stalwarts who had prepared stew for the villagers that afternoon. No doubt conscious of those who already slept, she nodded them into a corner of the bar where a little makeshift bed had been created, tucked away just a little from the others. It was stacked with pillows and blankets and someone had left a sheet of paper atop the patchwork quilt on which was written, *Reserved*.

"Get your sleep," the woman whispered. "You've both earned it."

"And you, Maggie," Raf told the woman with a smile. He put the cat down and it hopped onto the bar, watching over the sleeping room like a sentry. Then he bowed and whispered, "After you, Captain Sissy."

Cecily got under the patchwork quilt and gratefully laid back against the pillows. "This might just be the best bed I've ever slept in. There's even enough room for my legs!"

"That's not a problem I've ever had," was Raf's cheeky reply. He snuggled beneath the quilt and cuddled against Cecily, resting his head on her shoulder. His hair tickled her cheek and she saw more grains of salt there, a memory of the fight earlier. "Little bats have little legs. What a day we've had, I was ready for bed."

Cecily was about to kiss him when she stopped. "Raf...they've put us in the same bed... Should we tell them we're not...? They know we're not, but have they forgotten?"

But Raf shrugged, as though those sorts of rules didn't apply just now. Or perhaps they didn't apply in Acaster Garrow. It seemed like a rather singular place, after all.

"I think" — he kissed her nose — "that they know we need each other. And we're almost married. You've got a lovely old ring, so that just about counts."

Cecily held out her hand. The ring was still there on her finger, even though she'd lost her shoes when the demon had carried her off. And she'd far rather have lost those than the ring. "I haven't had the chance to show it to everyone yet!"

"Lots of de Chastelaines have worn that ring, but none were as pretty as you. And even the bravest weren't anywhere near as brave as you've been." He lifted Cecily's hand and kissed it. "What does it feel like to be a sensitive? Sometimes the smells can overwhelm me, like the flies did or the fish turning rotten… Is it like that for you? How did I hear you and see the weathervane like I did?"

"I thought of you…" Cecily stroked Raf's back and rested her hand on his waist. "I thought of you and I spoke to you in my head. I could picture you pacing about." She rested the tip of her nose against his and gazed into his eyes. "It was so clear…and all I could hope was that you could hear me. And see what I could see."

"I could hear you and see what you could see," Raf whispered. "That's never happened to me before today. I knew you were alive and frightened and — I felt helpless. Then I heard your voice saying that you loved me. It sounded like you were saying goodbye. That's when I saw the weathervane and I *knew*. And I've never moved so fast as I did then."

Cecily held Raf tight. She sniffed back a tear. "I thought that was it, I really did. I couldn't see how I could escape. And it was shrieking—so loud my nose bled… I thought I was going to die up there in that horrible glass nest."

"It's nowhere near a threat to a girl like you. You just flicked it away with your brilliance." He kissed her, then lifted one hand and wiped her tears from her face with the pad of his thumb. "If I'd been a bit bigger, me and Mike might've been able to hold it down in the salt."

Perhaps that was true, perhaps not. But if Raf had been bigger and more unwieldy, he would have died in the rose garden at Whitmore Hall. There was a lot to be said for being a little pipistrelle, able to dive and weave in the sky.

"So today wasn't our day." He glanced upwards, towards the room where Ivy slept. "But we'll get it tomorrow instead."

Cecily kissed him, then heard the cat's bell jingle as the creature walked along the bar.

"If the cat knocks over that bell for drinking up, half of Acaster Garrow will be awake!" she said.

Raf gave a soft laugh. "When I was nineteen I was a bit worse for beer—I know, can you *imagine*—and decided to put on a little aerial show for the punters." He drew in a breath of air then admitted, "Mike said I was showing off and he put the bell on top of me and left it there until I'd had a chance to calm down. Cheeky bugger!"

"A drunk bat?" Cecily laughed. "Is that the same bell?"

He nodded. "It's old as anything. It came off a ship that beached in the village hundreds of years back. It's an Acaster Garrow bell, it's got to come with a story, hasn't it?"

Cecily chuckled. "So it didn't fall out of the belfry!"

"Not our belfry anyway." He blinked across at the polished bell on the bar. "Maybe somebody else's, though!"

Something was fidgeting at the back of Cecily's mind and slowly an idea began to push through her tiredness. "There must be all sorts of bells in Acaster Garrow…"

"Probably." Raf drew back a little to look at her, narrowing his eyes as he asked with affection, "What're you thinking?"

Cecily propped herself up. "*It* doesn't like bells, does it? Maybe… If we rang every bell in Acaster Garrow — the church bells, the bell on the bar, the bells on cat collars, bells from the fishing boats — we could drive it off the land and out over the sea."

She saw Raf running through the idea in his head, saw his blue eyes gleam as he considered it. Then he nodded and replied, "I like that idea. We'd really have it cornered then. Shame we don't have any bullets made of salt knocking around too!"

Cecily grinned. "I suppose you know someone in the Carpathians who could make some for us? And silver for troublesome werewolves?"

"Yeah, actually I do. Wish he was here right now!"

Cecily held her hand over her mouth, trying not to laugh.

"But it's the start of a bloody good plan." Raf cuddled Cecily, bringing them down into the pillows. "And tomorrow we'll get everybody on it. Because this is going to need every hand we can get."

Chapter Eighteen

The next morning there was toast for breakfast at the pub because the baker from the next village had brought in a delivery of fresh bread, the men of Acaster Garrow neatly closing the salt circle behind him. They were pulling together now as surely as they'd been divided before. Once everyone had eaten, Cecily got up onto the bar and sat on its edge, swinging her legs back and forth.

Everyone was still talking, until she rang the bell.

"Sorry, everyone!" Cecily hoped they wouldn't think she was rude, interrupting them like that. But she could hear footsteps up in Ivy's room and the thought of the illness the poor girl laboured under drove Cecily on with urgency. "We need to get cracking, don't we? So...Raf and I have a plan. More or less. The demon hates bells—and everyone who kept the church bell ringing all night have kept him away from the village. But we've got bells everywhere in Acaster Garrow!" She held up the one from the bar. "We need you to round up your bells—on cats, bicycles, you name it. We'll drive it into the sea with the biggest racket of bells that you ever heard in your life!"

Raf nodded. "Little Ivy's counting on all of us. She looked after the children, and now she needs us to return the favour and look after her." He glanced towards the window, where sunlight poured in through panes that had once been coated with foul-smelling insects. "And since you hosed off the windows, those rotten flies haven't come back. It's on the run! This devil's no match for Yorkshire!"

Everyone raised their cups of tea and cheered.

Cecily grinned at Raf, then said to the crowd, "So if you can go home and get back here in an hour with your bells—then we can defeat the demon once and for all."

Raf was gazing out of the window again, looking at the damaged pump, the length of hose coiled neatly off to one side. He seemed to be in another world, his face set with concentration.

"We live in a fishing village," he murmured, an idea clearly occurring to him. Then he slammed his hand down on the bar top and asked, "Have we got anything that would— On the harbour. Have we got anything we could use to pump water out of the sea? We could hit it with a makeshift cannon if we have!"

A man with rosy cheeks and thick knitted jumper raised his hand. "There's the bilge pump. We use it for sucking water out of the tanks on boats, but it's got a backwards setting on it. Reckon that'd do, Raf?"

"I reckon it might," Raf said, filled with enthusiasm. "And whoever owns the little cat with the bell…can I borrow his collar?"

A woman near the back raised her hand. "That's my Pyewacket, that is. You can borrow his collar if you like. It's got a bell on it, after all. I suppose you'll be wanting the bell on my budgie's mirror too?"

"Every bell we can get," Raf told them, the church bells chiming over the village as if on cue. "Bring them down to the beach and we'll see if we can get that pump working too. I'll see you all there!"

Cecily and Raf headed back home, striding with purpose along the lane where they had once fled the onslaught of Aeshma and the flies—Cecily in a pair of shoes borrowed from Walter because Pearl's feet were several sizes smaller than hers. They were still wary, on the lookout in case Aeshma should reappear, but the cold day was bright with sunshine and there was no sign of the demon anywhere.

Apart from in that little bedroom upstairs in the pub. The glass had spread even farther through Ivy's body. It had crept across her chest and up over her throat, its brittle cruelty beginning to show on her face. No tourniquet could stop it now, no drawn poison to awaken her from her enchanted slumber. All they had was the hope that Raf was right, and that bringing Aeshma down would save Ivy's life.

And Cecily wasn't willing to consider the alternative.

Once inside her new home, Cecily hurried from room to room, gathering every bell she could find. She was glad of Raf's mountains of clutter now. On a shelf in the hall she found a bell with an Indian elephant carved on it. Hanging around a door handle she discovered a string of bells on red thread that she hung around her neck and which jangled with her every step. And propping open the door to the scullery, a beautiful handbell with what looked like Greek letters set around its mouth.

She ran up to their bedroom where Raf was getting ready, chiming all the way.

"There must be some more bells but this is a good start, isn't it?" She held out the one with Greek writing on it to him. "I don't know why this one's being used as a doorstop—it's lovely!"

Raf was sitting on the edge of the bed, rubbing his homemade sun lotion into his naked chest, as businesslike now as he had been mischievous when they'd snuggled in the bar just last night. He looked up at her then held up his hand and said urgently, "Oh, no, no, no! Don't ring that, Sis. You haven't, have you?"

"Erm... I didn't ring it, no." She turned it upside down, revealing that it was stuffed with yellowing newspaper, silencing the clapper inside it. "Is it very old—would it break if we rang it?"

"If we ever want Moby Dick's even bigger brother to visit the harbour and say *how do*, we'll ring that bell." Raf grinned, showing off his canines. "But that moment hasn't come yet."

"Right... I'll just pop it down over here..." Cecily trod with painstaking care towards the corner of the room and set the bell down. Then she showed him the one with the elephant on it. "This won't summon a big fellow with the trunk, though, will it?"

Raf cocked his head to one side, his expression thoughtful. He chewed his lip, continuing to muse for a few more silent moments.

"What month are we in?" He rolled his eyes heavenwards as the answer came to him, then said, "Nope, it's his mating season. We'll be all right to ring that one. He's busy."

"And are these going to be all right?" She indicated the string of bells around her neck, accepting that they could very well not be. "They won't unleash pixies or a thunderstorm or a thousand angry wasps?"

"The only thing unleashed right now is one very cheeky dhampir." He laughed. "Will you do my back? I still need my lotion whether I'm a bat or a bloke."

Cecily set aside the bells and sat behind Raf on the bed. She half-closed her eyes as she breathed in the perfume of his lotion and began to rub his muscular back. As she massaged it into his skin, she wondered which of his tattoos were for guarding against beasts like Aeshma, and just how powerful they were. The inked symbols overlapped, jostling for space, and some were blurred blue with age. But still Raf had added to them — and would no doubt add several more.

"This is a bit of a silly question." Raf glanced back over his shoulder and met Cecily's gaze. "But when I'm busy batting, would you mind fastening that little cat collar around me? It's a bell, it's all I've got against his nibs."

"Of course." Cecily ran her hand up to the back of his neck under his necklaces and charms, smoothing the lotion on. "Just here, a little bell for a little bat. But, Raf — are you sure you want to do it? Isn't it dangerous?"

He shook his head. "Don't you worry about me. I'll only go up if I have to. If everything goes just like I hope it will I'll be able to keep my clothes on and my feet on the beach."

Cecily knelt up behind Raf and hugged him. She'd nearly lost him once, and the thought of risking it again was too devastating to countenance. "I adore you, Raf. Please be careful, darling!"

"With you waiting for me?" Raf tipped his head back and kissed her cheek. "I'm definitely coming home."

Cecily tightened her embrace. "Of course I'll wait for you. I'll always wait for you."

"If I do have to go up after him," Raf said, his lips resting against Cecily's cheek, "I need you to keep everybody focused. Use the song I taught them. It'll keep things calm. We can't afford it to start feeding on their fear again. Ivy might not get another chance if today doesn't come off."

Cecily nodded, even though her trepidation was returning. "I'll do it, don't worry. I'll do my best."

"Right-o." He let his lips linger against Cecily's skin. "And the next bells we hear will be chiming for our wedding. You can count on that, Sissy!"

Chapter Nineteen

As the bells tolled in the church tower, a procession wound from the de Chastelaine Arms towards the sea. A tinkling, jangling, ringing procession of bicycle bells, handbells, ornamental glass bells, cat-collar bells, budgie-mirror bells, shop-door bells, counter bells, every last bell in Acaster Garrow that could be carried and rung was heading down to the beach.

And at its head walked Cecily and Raf like generals leading an army, Cecily skipping along so that the string of bells around her neck would jingle all the more, the elephant bell swinging at her side.

On and on they walked, every one of them driven forwards by the thought of Ivy, the girl who had cared for and protected the children of the village when their own parents had forsaken them. The girl who now lay in a restless, senseless limbo, counting on everybody in the village to come to her aid just as she had come to theirs. And somehow, things seemed quietly in their favour. The clouds of flies had not returned and the horizon was clear and bright, the autumn sun glittering on the soft waves invitingly. Yet somewhere out in that fathomless sky, blue as a painter's canvas and just as perfect, the tormenting demon named Aeshma was watching.

And waiting.

Were a motley collection of bells and a bilge pump really a match for the creature that had terrorised Kwaalveld, for a devil that had taken the whole might of the church itself to contain it?

They have to be, because Ivy has no other hope.

They had left Mim at the pub with Ivy and the glass girl's fretful, exhausted parents, all of them chanting endless spells of health and vitality. And Michael was at the church, part of the bell-ringing relay that was keeping the skies above Acaster Garrow alive with a cacophony of sounds. Fishing boats bobbed along the shore in readiness, their crews poised to swing into action. Finally, the harbour master and a team of men brought the bilge pump down to the edge of the sea, trying to stop it from sinking into the sand as they worked to the sounds of the rest of the village ringing their bells as they crossed the beach.

On went the singing, on went the bells, on and on worked the men at the pump by the seashore and as they did Cecily followed Raf's gaze, scanning the skies above for any sign of danger. All was so peaceful that she began to wonder if, somehow, they had made a mistake, if the demon had left Acaster Garrow far behind and was even now tormenting some other unsuspecting little community as it embarked on a new campaign of wrath. As they waited, Pyewacket's owner came forward and handed the little cat collar to Raf, as sombre as if she were making an offering on pilgrimage. He took the collar with a whisper of thanks, then handed it carefully to Cecily, wordless now.

As Cecily took the collar a great splash erupted from the edge of the surf and the pump spluttered a jet of seawater down onto the sand. Cecily saw Raf's jaw tighten and knew that the moment had come. The battle was upon them.

"We're ready," Cecily whispered. "But how do we lure him down?"

Raf took a deep breath, readying himself to go to war. "We have to call it and it has to answer. It's bound by few rules, but that's one of them. And I want it to sound like a war cry."

Cecily nodded. Of course, they'd avoided saying its name as best they could, but how else could they lure it out? She turned slowly towards the crowd, all bravely ringing their bells and singing. They stood on the beach in fustian and corduroy, pinstripes and satin. Everyone from the broad-shouldered farm workers to the pin-curled secretary from the bank, from the aproned butcher to the retired schoolmistress. All of them ready to save Acaster Garrow and rescue Ivy from her unthinkable fate.

Together they could raise hell. But if they didn't stop Aeshma today, a child would die and the village might wither along with her. And what would follow for all the other villages, the other towns across the land? What if Aeshma escaped to release the other demons and call them to its destructive cause?

"Everybody—hello!" Cecily waved her arms until she'd caught their attention and the ringing bells ceased, the only sound the water sighing on the shore and the distant peal from the church tower. "We have to call the demon down. And we have to be loud. *Loud.* Like a war cry. Can you do that?"

The villagers cheered their agreement as one, ringing the bells they wielded and stamping their feet, making a deafening din as they did. Even those who still glanced nervously around in fear of ambush still raised their voice with their friends and family.

"And Cecily's in charge, you lot," Raf shouted, putting his arm around her shoulders and snuggling her against him. "If she says sing, you sing and you sing your hearts out for all you're worth. Whatever happens, I don't want to see any panic. Stay together, hold your ground and keep on singing! It's *one* worthless bastard. We're a whole community of friends!"

Everyone cheered again and Cecily tried to gather her courage. When she closed her eyes, she saw the glass nest again and Aeshma leering down at her. She had no wish to see it again, but to see it destroyed was another matter.

"Its name is…" Cecily took a deep breath then spoke louder. "Its name is Aeshma! Say it—go on! Aeshma! Aeshma! Out you come, you coward—*Aeshma!*"

"Aeshma!" Raf joined in, a gesture from his hand directing the harbour master and his team to ready themselves for action. "Aeshma!"

Unsure at first, the villagers chanted the name quietly, but they grew in confidence and soon their voices rose to a shout, the name *Aeshma* echoing from the cliffs that ringed the beach.

Cecily watched the skies, searching for the cloud of flies that had accompanied Aeshma before when she had unwittingly summoned it. But there was nothing. Ivy was lying unmoving in her bed, every moment teetering towards her last, and the demon who had caused it—where was it?

The answer came seconds later when screams rang through the crowd on the beach. Cecily jolted round and saw the sand stirring, shaking as if an earthquake were tearing the land apart. And as the shouts of *Aeshma* blended with the screams, the demon itself emerged from under the sand, its head jerking left and right as it seemed to take in its audience with an air of amusement. Then its spidery limbs unfolded as it took to the air and rose high above them.

But it wasn't only demons who could fly.

"Come on!" Raf bounded towards the villagers, clapping his hands. "Keep ringing the bells, keep singing. Don't let it frighten you—it's just an ugly bugger and there's only one of it! It'll feed on your fear—don't let it! We'll starve the bastard out if we don't let it scare us."

The villagers no longer shouted its name, instead singing just as Raf had instructed, singing and smiling and ringing their bells as the demon stared down at them, swishing its tongue as if tasting the air.

And you'll taste salt, Aeshma.

"Round it up," Raf instructed. "Walk it down towards the shore, keep it on a short lead with the bells. Lads, get ready with the hosepipe!"

The crowd shifted as one just as the flies once had, like a flock of sparrows heading for the safety of their nests, and Aeshma had no choice but to fly out over the sea to avoid the racket of the bells. Cecily saw cracks begin to web its glass body and one by one those thin fissures grew wider and more pronounced, but still the false god hung in the air, each beat of its wings a vicious snap.

Raf seized Cecily's hand, following Aeshma down to the surf. He held up his hand to the villagers, halting them, then said to the harbour master, "Hit it with the hose!"

The harbour master nodded to his team and together they let loose with the spray. A powerful jet of seawater that could have carried them off their feet burst from the hose and the harbour master shouted instructions as they tried to chase the demon towards the ocean.

"Up a bit — a bit more — to the left — the left!"

The water spray spattered across Aeshma's body and where it did it left pits and pockmarks in the glass like salt scattered across a drift of snow. The demon screeched and howled, lurching this way and that above them, limbs contorting and cracking even more. Its tongue whipped, snapping and cracking on the air, but Cecily had already learned that its kind could be treacherous. The demon may look as though it were suffering, but she wouldn't be convinced until it lay in pieces on the ocean.

The villagers' song grew louder, but they would soon be beginning to tire. Unlike Aeshma they were human, after all. Cecily paused ringing the bell, waiting for her arms to stop aching, and she noticed others in the crowd stopping, rubbing their arms before carrying on.

"How long will it take?" Cecily asked Raf. "It's still in the air!"

Before Raf had a chance to reply the demon flung its arms wide, its wings opening to their full span. The demon threw its head back and let out a scream, then with a glassy clank the wings snapped and Aeshma was flying at the harbour master and his men with the speed and precision of a torpedo. They threw themselves to the sand, their hands shielding their heads, as the demon caught the hosepipe in its clawed hand and wrenched it from the pump. It flung the pipe back onto the beach, sending the villagers scattering beneath its onslaught.

"Hold your ground!" Raf commanded. "Think of Ivy and hold your ground!"

The terrified villagers stopped on the spot, some having skidded to the sand. Then they carried on ringing again, their voices lifted in song even as they cowered from the demon that howled above them.

Cecily glanced at Raf. "We can't reattach it. What are we going to do?"

"I need to get up in its face, don't I?" Raf pressed a kiss to Cecily's lips. "Got my collar, Sissy? I'm going to need it."

Cecily nodded and held up the collar. But with all her heart, she couldn't bear the thought of Raf, as a tiny bat, going up against a vast glass demon. "Be careful. Don't take any risks. Please, Raf, promise me you won't!"

"Me take risks? *Never*." He took off his charms and put them around Cecily's neck. "Love you, gorgeous."

Cecily held his hand. "I love you, Raf." She smiled even though tears were rising in her eyes.

I don't want to lose you, darling. You're my everything.

"I'm going nowhere. We'll be back in our own bed tonight," Raf whispered, answering the words she hadn't spoken aloud. He kissed her again then, with a soft flutter, his clothes billowed down onto the beach. The pipistrelle bat performed a neat loop and landed on Cecily's palm, waiting for her to fasten the cat collar around him.

As the bells rang and the song was sung again, Cecily slipped Pyewacket's collar over Raf's neck and tightened it just enough so it wouldn't fall off. "Nod if that's all right. I don't want it to be too tight."

The bat gave a little nod of acknowledgement. As he did, Aeshma swooped down over the beach, first lunging at the villagers then retreating in the face of the bells. But they couldn't ring them forever. They couldn't sing forever either, but Aeshma had waited centuries to return. It had as much time as it wished. The likes of Aeshma weren't bound by their human frailties.

But that meant the likes of Aeshma didn't have their strengths either. It was a creature made of hate, and it was facing a community that was united against it. Surely togetherness had to be stronger than pure wrath.

Cecily kissed the top of Raf's head. Then she raised her arm, elevating the little bat for take-off.

"Good luck, darling!" she called. Then, still fighting back her tears, Cecily joined the villagers in their song.

Raf swept off into the sky but this time, rather than hurtle straight at Aeshma, he zigzagged and looped, making the best of his tiny form versus the demon's lumbering and unwieldy glass frame. Aeshma cracked its wings again and lunged down at the villagers, the fearsome talons extended like glass daggers, ready to rake and stab.

Ready to kill.

But Cecily had the bell with the elephant engraving and she rang it fearlessly at the face of the approaching demon. For a moment it seemed as though Aeshma would continue its advance but when the monster was only inches from her it drew back again, the wide ocean vast and deep beneath the devil.

Cecily walked from the beach into the shallows until the water washed and lapped at her ankles. Her tears had gone and she glared up at the demon who had tried to kill her.

"You won't win. You *can't!* You're pathetic!"

And it seemed as though Raf had taken a lesson from the tormenting flies and their unpredictable paths, because he didn't go straight for Aeshma. Instead he swarmed and darted, fluttering and jabbing around the creature's glass skull, first here then a moment later there, unswattable and uncatchable. Aeshma turned and twisted but Raf was nimble enough to stay behind it, on its shoulder or at its ear, the bell constantly tinkling against the demon's furious face.

Aeshma was so busy contending with the tiny bat that it seemed as if it didn't notice the people on the beach anymore — it made no more attempts to plunge down at them anyway. But how long could Raf keep flying, occupying the glass demon with his annoying flurries of activity?

The bells were flagging and Cecily marched across the beach, using her last scraps of energy to encourage the villagers on.

"Keep going! We're nearly there, we've nearly won!"

Even if she didn't entirely believe it.

Aeshma's tongue whipped and flailed, its razor edge trying to seek out Raf, but instead the glass tongue swept over Aeshma's own face with a sound that set Cecily's teeth on edge, a grinding, grating screech that tore through the air. She could see that Raf was clinging onto the back of Aeshma's neck and the demon swatted and batted with its claws, howling in frustration, twisting this way and that in an attempt to dislodge the bat.

We're going to need a boat.

Cecily wasn't sure where the thought came from or how she could be so certain, but it came to her with such clarity that she could almost hear Raf's voice against her ear saying it. But he couldn't have spoken, because he was a bat, latched onto the great glass demon as it rose higher and higher into the sky, twisting and flailing farther out over the sea.

"We're going to need a boat!" Cecily said aloud as she ran towards the harbour master. "Can we get them to come in, the ones out in the bay?"

"Of course!" The harbour master turned and stared out towards the boats, then with his arms outstretched and a handkerchief in each hand, he made a series of signs.

Semaphore, Cecily realised, though she'd never seen it done.

Yet the fishing boats must have understood because one by one their engines revved and they began to make their way to the shore, gathering beneath the battle as they waited.

Above the sound of the waves and the rumble of the engines there came another noise, this one high above them, filled with rage. From the sky there erupted a scream that silenced the singing and the bells and sent the villagers scurrying on instinct, not that Cecily could blame them. It sounded like a hole was tearing in the fabric of the heavens, loud and piercing and worse than any of the torturous howls that Aeshma had given atop the church. As the scream went on and the villagers tried to recover themselves, the bat on Aeshma's back disappeared, replaced by the unmistakable figure of Rafael de Chastelaine.

"Raf!" Cecily shouted. He'd said to her once before that he couldn't always turn into a bat at will, and as the unclothed figure of her fiancé tumbled out of the sky down to the sea, Cecily panicked. The glass demon fell with him, forced down towards the waves by the weight of Raf on its back, but that didn't offer Cecily any comfort. What had happened to her lover that had forced him to change from bat to man?

But whatever it was, it was working. What Michael couldn't do, what the pipistrelle *certainly* couldn't do, Raf could. He might be small in stature, but his weight was more than enough to drive Aeshma into the sea, the momentum of their plummeting descent dragging the dhampir down with it. The scream echoed for another second then there was nothing but silence and the sound of the rolling ocean.

The bells had fallen silent. The singing had stopped.

Cecily dropped her bell on the sand and wandered into the sea again, this time the water rising up past her ankles, to her knees. Her dress billowed out around her like the skirts of a jellyfish and she didn't go a step farther.

Floating on the waves were splinters of glass, each one torn from Aeshma's destroyed body. And as Cecily watched, one by one each piece dissolved on the water. A length from the tongue, a blade of its wing, all the many pieces of glass that had constructed the false god. And finally, melting into nothing, its hideous face, contorted in a last grimace of agony and defeat.

But where was Raf? There was no sign of him, no sign of anything now except the approaching boats.

There was something in her throat and Cecily coughed, helpless as a stream of seawater gushed from her mouth.

He's drowning.

Cecily waded out farther then swam towards the nearest boat, kicking against the cold water, ignoring the sting of the salt water against her wounds. Someone grabbed her arm and pulled her on board, shivering.

"Raf! We have to find Raf. Where is he? Did you see him land? Where *is* he?"

"We'll find him," was the reply of the man who had pulled her on board. His voice was stoic, certain. "Don't you fret."

Cecily coughed again, gripping the edge of the boat as she scanned the grey ocean for any sign of her lover. She clutched Raf's charms, which now hung around her neck. Perhaps she should have rung the bell that would have summoned the whale after all.

Then she heard another sound, one that she wasn't sure was even real. It was the delicate tinkling of a tiny bell, like the bell that Pyewacket had so generously allowed Raf to wear. He was out there somewhere, alive and desperate for help, and that humble little bell would bring him back to her. It rang again and again, the sound growing stronger with every passing moment.

"He's alive!" Cecily ran to the side of the boat and clung on as she peered into the water, listening for the bell.

The waves rolled on, rising and falling, revealing nothing but fresh waves beneath. She thought she saw Raf but a moment later she realised it was only a clump of seaweed, not his dark, wet hair. The ringing bell sounded nearer now, so near that Cecily glanced frantically back and forth across the surface of the water — he *had* to be close by.

Something held her gaze but she wasn't sure what, an indefinable, unguessable intuition that this must be the place. She focused all her energy on it and as she did, Raf's hand broke the surface of the water, the cat's collar clutched in his fist. Cecily saw his head emerge before he sank below again, pulled under by the current. Yet still his hand remained just above the waves, shaking the bell to summon them.

"There — he's there!" Cecily pointed and the fishermen sprang, throwing a life ring over the side that was attached to the boat with a length of rope. Their aim was perfect and the life ring slid over Raf's upraised arm, for all the world like a game at the fair.

Cecily's heart swelled with love as Raf's strong arm tightened around the life ring, clinging on for dear life. He hauled his head clear of the water and the men began to reel him in towards the safety of the boat, calling to him that he would soon be safe, that the danger was past. Coughs and splutters wracked his body and he spat out a mouthful of seawater but all that mattered to Cecily was that Raf was alive.

Raf was alive and Aeshma was defeated, but she could only pray that they had been fast enough to save the little girl who was turning to glass.

Cecily embraced Raf as soon as he was drawn over the side, unsteady on his feet and shaking from the cold. She barely noticed when the fishermen threw a blanket around them both. She was too busy holding Raf's cold body to her and covering his face with her kisses.

"Did we get the demon?" Raf asked through his spluttered breaths. "Did we?"

Then words deserted him and he clung to Cecily, shivering down to his very bones.

"Yes, *you* got it!" Cecily rubbed at Raf's skin, desperate to warm him. When she glanced up she saw the coastline moving by and she realised the boat was heading for the harbour. It was only then she remembered her ring, and she dared herself to check her finger for it. As if by some miracle the ring was still there, undimmed by its time in the sea. "We'll be onshore soon, we'll sit you by a lovely big fire!"

"*We* got the demon," Raf corrected through chattering teeth. When he spoke again Cecily knew that everything was going to be fine, that even the bitterly cold sea couldn't hold back her lover's mischief. "Sorry I had to flash half the village to do it."

"Needs must and all that," Cecily said. She untangled Raf's charms from around her neck and put them around his. "There, you're not all that naked now!"

He smiled, then took Cecily's face in his hands and kissed her, holding her to him as a chorus of birdsong sang out over Acaster Garrow.

Chapter Twenty

By the time they arrived at Acaster Garrow's little white harbour, Raf had been more or less dried off and put into a spare set of clothes gathered from the men on the boat. He looked warm and rugged in the outsized fisherman's jumper, the trousers turned up several times so he could walk in them without tripping. Cecily had borrowed an oilskin coat to put over her soaking dress and they headed down the gangplank to dry land.

They should have gone straight home, but an unspoken decision had passed between them and instead they went straight to the de Chastelaine Arms.

Straight to Ivy.

The building was still, silent and watchful in the autumn sunlight. There was no sign of life from within, no indication of what they might find and no sound of celebration from the little bedroom upstairs. Cecily uttered a silent prayer for Ivy as Raf opened the door and the couple went inside.

The bar was still untidy with makeshift beds from the night before, lending the place an abandoned atmosphere. Still there seemed to be no sound from upstairs, until Cecily caught the soft sobs of a woman crying.

No.

Cecily squeezed Raf's hand. "We were too late…"

"No," he whispered as the sound of Walter's sobs joined those of his wife. But Raf's answer wasn't a correction — it was a gasp of disbelief. His body sagged and his breath caught as he faced the truth that Ivy, so vibrant and brave, had been snatched away from them all as Aeshma's last terrible act. "I'm not having this."

As they headed up the stairs, Cecily's tears fell. She didn't care that she was wet through, that her shoes had been ruined in the salt or that her watch had stopped. None of that mattered when Cecily thought of the girl who had died.

"She was so young!" Cecily exclaimed. "And such a brave, resourceful girl. She should still be alive. Why couldn't Aeshma have taken *me* instead?"

At the top of the stairs Raf pulled Cecily gently into his arms and they held each other tight. Neither spoke and the sobbing went on from Ivy's bedroom as Cecily's tears fell, unchecked.

It seemed like minutes had passed when Raf broke the heavy silence and whispered, "We should go in. I wish — " He dashed the back of his hand across his eyes. "Do you want to wait here, or will you come in?"

Cecily tried to wipe away her tears. "I'll come in. I won't cry, it's all right." She offered Raf a small smile as she took his hand.

The curtains in Ivy's little bedroom were open and the room, still dotted with toys and games from her visiting friends, was bathed in a soft autumnal glow. There was such stillness that Cecily's and Raf's treads seemed suddenly too loud, as though they were invading on the private grief of the little girl's bedroom.

"It's just— she was stirring and…" Walter's words were stolen by a fresh wave of sobs. He was kneeling beside his daughter's bed, his hand laying over Ivy's glass fingers. No scrap of human flesh remained of Ivy now. It was almost as though she had never been real at all. "Then it just covered her all over. And — and — we can't even kiss her goodbye."

Pearl, who was sitting on a wooden chair beside the bed, didn't speak. At Walter's words she only sobbed anew, and Mim, who had been crying too, put her arm around her shoulders and held her tight.

"I'm so sorry." Cecily had no idea what else to say. *Sorry* was such an inadequate word when someone lay dead. A girl of glass, brittle and lifeless. Her hair had become a vitreous plait and the lashes of her closed eyes were painted on like a doll's.

Raf said nothing, but gazed at the figure on the bed with his customary closeness. He furrowed his brow, then he gave a twitch of his nose and whispered, "I don't— Mim, have you been using aniseed in your potions?"

Mim looked up at Raf, then shook her head. "No, why?"

"I can smell aniseed." He advanced towards the bed, drawing Cecily with him. "It smells like Dad's study — when he's been chewing on *liquorice!*"

Cecily sniffed too but couldn't detect anything aside from the sickroom smell of disinfectant and the brine on her own body. It didn't mean anything though, did it? It didn't bring Ivy back from whatever the demon's bite had plunged her into.

"It does?" But as Cecily looked down at the glass girl, she thought she saw something move. She couldn't, of course, but it looked for all the world as if the glass were trembling. She remembered Ivy kneeling on the bar, eating liquorice as she breathed on the mirror, drawing a castle in—

She breathed on the mirror.

She's breathing on the glass.

The sheet of glass that covered Ivy's mouth misted, then cleared, then misted again with the little girl's breath. Raf saw it too and he darted forwards, the movement carrying Cecily with him as he exclaimed in excitement, "Ivy's alive under there! She's breathing!"

Cecily glanced around, wondering what they could use to break Ivy free. "A toffee hammer? Would that do to get her out?"

"You're not taking a hammer to my child!" Pearl exclaimed. "She's breathing! It's a miracle, my Ivy's still alive!" But Pearl wasn't angry—her voice was filled with amazement.

Walter thrust his hand into his pockets then patted down his shirt, as though there might be something hiding there that they could use to break the shell of glass. He reached into his back pocket and withdrew a heavy-looking penknife, the blade hidden in a polished wooden handle. He held it out to Raf and asked, "How's this?"

"Perfect!" Raf replied, taking the knife. Pearl started a little but Raf didn't draw the blade. Instead, he perched on the edge of the bed beside Ivy and took a deep breath. Then he brought the wooden hilt of the knife down against Ivy's hand in a sharp blow, using it as a makeshift hammer. "Come on, Ivy, help me if you can!"

It reminded Cecily of cracking the shell of a boiled egg, but as Raf tapped at Ivy's carapace, more and more fractures broke the glassy surface until finally the child inside moved, like a newborn chick forcing its way out into the world for the very first time.

"Ivy, my girl!" Pearl sobbed with joy. "Come on, my little lass, out you come!"

Raf dropped the penknife then tucked his hands beneath the long sleeves of his borrowed pullover, the wool protecting his skin as he snapped shards of glass free and dropped them onto the floor. The cocoon came away in large pieces and from beneath the shell Ivy began to help him, pushing her hands against the glass and kicking her legs in an effort to free herself. There was no wound on her hand now either, the bite from the demon gone as if it had never been. There was just soft, undamaged skin.

"That's it, Ivy!" Walter added his strength to Raf's and together they snapped off an enormous shard of glass, as though they were prising open the lid of a tomb. As soon as it was set aside Ivy sat up as though waking from a good night's sleep, her eyes wide.

She looked around the room with a bright gaze, then asked, "Did we get it?"

"Yes!" Cecily replied. "Yes, we did! It's gone now, forever."

Pearl and Walter took Ivy in their arms and held her tight, and the girl seemed surprised by the fuss. If she had any memory of what had been happening for the past twenty-four hours, she showed no sign of it. Ivy sank into her parents' loving embrace, even as she told them, "This is a right to-do, is this."

"I'll look her over, but I think she's making an excellent recovery," Mim assured Raf and Cecily. "You're quite a duo, you know."

Cecily grinned at Raf, then she asked Mim, "And speaking of duos, where's Mike?"

"Supervising Mrs Hodge as she supervises the bell-ringers." She patted her hair unconsciously. "But I'm sure he'll be here soon!"

And the bells had changed, Cecily now realised, no longer the desperate, tuneless clang that had echoed through the night, but a beautiful peal of celebration which rang through the village.

And I can hear them so clearly!

"You're never paying for a pint in this pub again," Walter told the assembled little gathering through happy tears. "I won't hear of it. Not ever again!"

Raf laughed and promised, "Then you'll be seeing a lot of us in future, you can count on it." He slipped his arm around Cecily and whispered, "Home?"

"Yes—let's go home."

As they headed out into the village's main street, Cecily heard the toot of a car. The harbour master waved them over as he drove past.

"Can I drive you two anywhere? You both look like you couldn't walk another step!"

"Oh, that's a lovely sight, is that." Raf laughed as he opened the door and ushered Cecily inside. "Home, please, and don't spare the horses!"

"Beautiful day, isn't it?" the harbour master remarked as he pulled away from the kerb. He changed gears none too smoothly and Cecily bumped into Raf as he took a corner, but Cecily didn't care—she laughed instead. Raf laughed too, using their closeness as an excuse to kiss her cheek. It felt oddly like spring again, as though the village was thawing after a long, painful freeze.

The harbour master insisted on taking them all the way to the top of the driveway and hopped out of the car to open the door for them. He was an unorthodox chauffeur, but a welcome one all the same.

"Anytime you two need anything, anything at all, you let me know," he said, and patted Raf on the back as he climbed out of the car. "The two of you saved this village!"

"No." Raf smiled and corrected him. "Acaster Garrow saved itself. That's why I love this place. Now get back to the village and have a pint on me."

"Right you are, then!" The harbour master gave them a wave as he got back into the car, leaving a footprint of sand on the slab behind him. "You two have an easy night!"

Cecily waved as his car bounced away along the drive. A soft wind buffeted them and her salt-stiffened hair scraped against her face. "Oh, heavens, I need a bath—we both do!"

The huge reptilian eye on the door knocker blinked as they approached. This time Cecily didn't do a double take and Raf greeted his old friend with a happy nod. He slid the key into the lock and turned it before stepping back to tell Cecily, "After you, my gorgeous chatelaine!"

Cecily wandered inside. It was so wonderful to be home again. And it was so quiet, with only the sounds of the old house settling to disturb the peace. She peeled off the fisherman's oilskin coat and hung it on a peg before kneeling to prise off her sodden shoes. Beside her, Raf dragged the enormous borrowed sweater over his head and kicked off the trousers that had swamped him. Naked save for his tangled charms, he offered Cecily his hand and asked, "Ready, madam?"

Cecily took his hand and kissed it. He tasted of the sea.

"Of course!"

And together, hand in hand, they ascended the staircase that Beatrice de Chastelaine had built.

Chapter Twenty-One

A month later

Cecily had spent the night before the wedding at Mim's house. They had stayed up late and gossiped about their men and Cecily had roared with laughter to find out that Michael turned up for evening assignations in bat form before transforming into a man. It was one way to arrive unseen, perhaps, even if everyone in the village knew very well who the huge bat was.

The next morning Mim helped Cecily into her wedding gown. It was a long, elaborate dress of silk and lace, and on her head, Cecily wore a floral crown, just as brides wore in the Carpathians. And even though the first snows had fallen, the flowers from Raf's garden that bloomed in her crown and in her bouquet were as fresh and bright as if it were midsummer.

How her life had changed in twelve short months, and how glad she was for it. She was glad, too, to see Graham and Harriet Culpeck when they arrived from their stay in the village, her oldest and closest Devonshire friends returned to her once more.

Harriet was her matron of honour, and as a much-loved teacher, who was better to shepherd the bridesmaids and page boys than she?

And who better to lead those bridesmaids than Ivy? Just thinking of the little girl following her along the aisle made Cecily beam. The sure knowledge that Graham's arm would be linked with hers to give her away made her smile even wider.

"Here's the car!" Graham told them as Raf's little Austin 7 drew up outside. White ribbons had been tied on the bonnet and they fluttered in the breeze. Walter climbed out, dressed in his finest suit, his face proud. Turning from the window, Graham crossed the room and put his hands on Cecily's arms, looking at her with an expression that was more like a proud father's than an old friend's. "I watched you grow up at Whitmore Hall from a lovely little lass into a capable and beautiful woman and —"

He swallowed hard then blinked, his eyes glistening with gathering tears.

"Your mother would be proud to see you today, and your brother too." Graham pecked a kiss to her cheek. "I hope Rafael knows just how lucky he is, Cecily, because you're a picture of happiness together, you really are."

"I'm sure he does." Cecily glanced down at her ring, its stones catching the light and sparkling. "If it wasn't for your friendship and Harriet's — well, we're here today, aren't we? A happy old bunch if ever there was one!"

"Not so old as… Let's say maturing nicely instead," Graham replied. He offered her his elbow and asked, "Might I squire you to your carriage, Miss Pincombe?"

"Thank you, Headmaster, I would be very pleased…" She looped her arm through his and with an awkward laugh as Cecily tried to corral her bouquet and her long dress and train, they climbed into the car.

As they drove along the streets of Acaster Garrow, Cecily peered from the window at the village that had become her home. The villagers had welcomed her into their community and she had felt their welcome like an embrace, basking in its genuine and heartfelt warmth. Everything was restored now from the pump to the fresh produce in the shop windows, but most importantly of all, she had not heard so much as a single cross word since Aeshma's remains had crumbled to nothing on the tide. Now she knew Acaster Garrow for the happy community that it was, and she had never felt so much at home anywhere.

Cecily could hear the bells before she saw the church. And when it came into view, she gasped to see the flowers that had been tied to the lychgate and the little trees that lined the path up to the church's door.

"What a lovely surprise!" Cecily said as she wiped away a tear.

Clustered around the door to the church were the village children who would be her attendants and in pride of place were Harriet and Ivy. The little girl was holding Harriet's hand and at the sight of the car her face lit up and she turned to excitedly address the other children.

Still organising, Cecily realised happily.

As Cecily got out of the car, she could hear Mim on the church organ. Someone must have passed a message to her inside the church because as Cecily and Graham swept along the path and the children fell into place behind, each taking part of Cecily's train, Mim began to play the Wedding March.

Cecily glanced at Graham. "Is that a tear, Mr Culpeck?" she joked. Even as she dashed away her own.

An unwelcome memory of her first wedding returned to her—there had been no gown, no flowers, no music and no one to give Cecily away. There certainly hadn't been any love. How different today was going to be.

"It might be," he admitted with a smile. They were at the threshold now and Cecily could feel every eye on her, because everyone in Acaster Garrow had squeezed into St Anastasia's to mark the day.

The shade of the curate had returned to the baptistry, an unseen wedding guest as he polished the brass. The knight on his tomb sat up to watch, yawning as he stretched his ancient arms, with the dog at his feet now curled onto his lap. And only Cecily could see them.

And there at the top of the aisle was Raf, rumpled and—of course—barefoot, his shoes poking out from behind the front pew. Behind him the old east window had been returned to its former place, with Beatrice de Chastelaine's serene face, rescued from Aeshma's nest, patching the damaged pane.

And beside Raf was a man Cecily had only recently met—as little as her fiancé, crumpled, strapping and sunburnt, with a Father Christmas beard as white as snow. It was Raf's father, back in Acaster Garrow a week and serving as his son's best man.

Raf turned to look down the aisle, watching Cecily's approach. There was a sprig of the lavender she had brought with her all the way from Devon in his buttonhole, and in his bright blue eyes, tears of happiness glittered. Beatrice smiled down at them from the window but Raf's grin was the biggest of all, fangs or no fangs.

The walk towards Raf seemed to take forever, and once Cecily finally reached the top of the aisle, she took his hand and smiled at him. She turned, sensing that some extra guests had arrived, and when Cecily looked over her shoulder, she saw the quick flit of the shimmering phantom of a bat as it went up into the church rafters and —

— and at the back of the church, noticed by both the curate and the knight, there was the faint shade of her late brother Sandy, with their mother on his arm. They acknowledged Cecily with a wave before fading to a shimmer that stayed on the air like an echo.

They were still with her. They always were. And so was Raf's mum, it seemed, settling up in the rafters as she folded her silken wings.

Cecily smiled at Raf as Michael opened the service.

It passed like a dream, the voices of the choir raised in celebration, the voice of the reverend filled with pride and affection. And when Raf slipped a gold wedding band onto Cecily's finger and she slipped one onto his in turn, Cecily could sense that the tears in the church weren't from sadness, only joy. In her wildest dreams she couldn't have imagined a day like this would ever be hers.

But in her wildest dreams, she wouldn't have been able to even begin to imagine Rafael de Chastelaine.

Everyone was invited back to their home for the wedding breakfast, the fortress now a place of celebration, and the children who had once sheltered there from Aeshma played and ran through the rooms of the house as if the demon had never threatened their village at all.

There was laughter and speeches and dancing and the party spilled out into the garden despite the winter air. Raf's garden, after all, didn't succumb to such things and neither, it seemed, did the villagers of Acaster Garrow. Cecily and Raf were at each other's side constantly, their hands linked and their fingers entwined as they greeted their guests, and when they waved them off as the night drew in, they were beaming as broadly as they had been at the start of the day.

Cecily was still wearing her wedding dress and her floral crown, and her feet were sore from dancing. She was happily tipsy and kept kissing Raf.

And I always will.

"So now I'm Mrs de Chastelaine," she said. "I'll have to keep practicing that. *I'm Mrs de Chastelaine, enchanted to meet you!* Does this sound all right?"

"Sounds like heaven," was Raf's cheery response as he slipped his arm around her waist and snuggled her close. "I've got one last little gift for you before we retire to the marital bed, Mrs de Chastelaine. Close your eyes and hold out your hand and see what your dhampir gives you."

Cecily closed her eyes. "A gift? Are you turning into a bat, darling?" She held out her hand, giggling in anticipation. She heard the gentle sound of rattling jewellery and the tinkling of a bell. Then she felt cool metal on her palm.

"Open them," Raf whispered.

She did, and there on her palm was a silver bracelet with a little bell hanging from one of the links. From another dangled a smooth piece of bright blue glass. When she looked closely, she recognised the tiny bell — it had once been on the cat's collar that Raf had worn around his neck when he'd battled Aeshma over the ocean. The bell that had summoned his rescuers. She smiled at him — at her husband — then examined the little piece of glass.

"Is this from Beatrice's window?" she asked.

He nodded. "Edged in silver. With a couple of grains of salt thrown in." Raf shrugged, suddenly bashful. "Just in case."

"I love it!" Cecily gave him a kiss before trying to open the bracelet's catch. "Will you help me put it on?"

With great care, Raf took the bracelet and fastened it around Cecily's slender wrist. The bell gave a soft chime and he smiled.

"That looks lovely," was Raf's verdict. "But it's still not nearly as lovely as my wife."

"Your slightly drunk wife in her wonky crown," Cecily added. Then she remembered the trunk she had left open in the dressing room and the shoes scattered across the floor. Cecily had begun to inherit Raf's untidy ways. "Your slightly drunk wife who hasn't finished packing for Egypt yet!"

"There's plenty of time to pack." Raf swept Cecily into his arms, easily lifting her despite the difference in their heights. "I think it's time to go to bed, Mrs de Chastelaine. And let's make this another night to remember."

As Raf carried Cecily up the stairs, she glanced from her husband to the portraits of de Chastelaines past that lined the walls. She had become a twig on that eccentric family tree, a rather tall twig at that, and one with the ability to sense the dead. And when she turned to kiss her dhampir husband, she wondered where their lives would lead them. But as long as she had Raf de Chastelaine at her side, whatever happened — whatever ghoul or beast pursued them, whatever curse might plague them — Cecily knew she would never be unhappy.

Want to see more from these authors?
Here's a taster for you to enjoy!

The Man in Room 423
Catherine Curzon & Eleanor Harkstead

Excerpt

Lizzie saw him in the light of his uncurtained hotel window. He leant one hand casually against the pane, looking back at her across the dark December street.

She watched him over the rim of her glass. Office Christmas parties were loud in the bar around her, but she was barely aware of them. All she could see was the man at the window, immaculate in a dark-coloured suit, the white of his shirt as crisp as frost.

"Earth to Lizzie. Come in, Lizzie!" Long, coral pink acrylic nails snapped in front of her eyes and Donna set down two glasses of a bright red cocktail, a cherry bobbing on the surface like a drowning man. "You need a crowbar to get served in here tonight!"

She wasn't going to tell Donna about the man in the window. She wanted him for herself, so that she could pass through what remained of this evening with her sister in the knowledge that she and she alone had seen him.

And that he had seen her.

The interested glance of a stranger.

"What on earth sort of cocktail is that?" Lizzie attempted a grin. She put it to her mouth to taste it and exaggerated her recoil. "Gosh, that's strong!"

She allowed herself a quick look. He was still there. He was still watching.

He might even be smiling.

"Aaaand still nothing from Matt." Donna's frosted pink lips turned down into a frown as she stared at the phone she held. She sighed and threw it down on the table, sending it skidding into a puddle of someone else's spilled beer. "He finished training *hours* ago, where is he?"

"Maybe he's busy? You did insist on marrying a footballer."

"*You did insist*," Donna mimicked her sister, a petulant child once more. "And he's not playing tonight, he's not training tonight, he's not *here* tonight. So where is my Matt? There're some strange people out there, Lizzie, and he doesn't look out for himself sometimes!"

"I'm sure he's okay. Maybe he's drinking with the squad. Lads' night out. Or maybe he's at his mum's, eating beans on toast!"

"I hope so." Donna shook her head and swirled the cocktail glass by its stem. "We've had to get the police involved, you know. He's had some horrible messages sent to the club, really nasty stuff. They've said not to worry, but... Well, I love him. I don't like to think of someone being out to get him."

Lizzie reached across the table and gave her sister's hand a reassuring squeeze.

"That's terrible, Donna! But you've done the right thing, going to the police. It'll be okay."

Would it be? But her sister had chosen this existence, had sought it out, pursued it and embraced it.

"That's celebrity life, Don. I've heard similar from some of my clients. And you know what they say to me? *I knew I'd made it when I got my first stalker.*"

That seemed to please Donna, just a little reminder that she had won her premiership striker, that she was the closest Manchester came to royalty. Donna beamed a bright smile and patted her poker-straight blonde hair into place, though it was immaculate already. "I always said I'd be a WAG, didn't I? When you were stitching dresses for your dolls, I was dreaming about my footballers! A girl's got to have ambition, after all."

"Mine was to run my own business and be my own boss." Lizzie smiled. "And I am."

She took a sip of her cocktail, punctuating her comment, then pushed the glass away. It tasted like medicine.

Her sister just laughed in response and glanced around, her attention caught by a group of loud, tanned, gym-honed young men by the bar. As if by habit, her eyelids fluttered and she dropped her gaze, forming her lips into a perfect selfie-pout. Donna de Luca was confident in her glamour in a way that Lizzie had never quite been.

Lizzie propped her elbow on the table and peered outside again. He was still there. Had he watched her, even as she'd looked away at her sister?

Never breaking his glance, he slowly unbuttoned his jacket and flung it in one smooth movement onto a chair. His hands were at his throat, and seconds later, a tie went after the jacket. And now he was attending to the cuffs of his shirt. Although a street and several floors divided them, Lizzie was sure that he must have been wearing cufflinks. They went into his pocket.

She swallowed, her free hand toying with the beads of her wooden necklace.

He was unbuttoning his shirt, from the neck down. Then it was off. But on the floor this time, at his feet.

He pressed both palms to the glass, his toned, bare torso on show for her.

For someone. Had a complete stranger really just stripped for Lizzie Aspinall? Partially, that is.

His hands drifted to his belt. Then he turned his body away, his glance lingering for just a second longer before he strolled across the room and vanished from her sight.

"Matty!" Donna snatched up her mobile as a text buzzed across the screen. She swiped her thumb from left to right on the glass and immediately started to tap out a reply, her finger moving with confidence from key to key. "Oh my God, Lizkins. He was *tanning*!"

"A special coat of creosote for Christmas?" Lizzie laughed. "Is he going to come to our parents'? It would've been our turn at Neil's parents, but seeing as we've split up... I was thinking of going to our parents', but I'm tempted to lurk about the flat by myself. Just enjoy being on my own, in my PJs, even if — Donna, are you listening?"

"Just a mo, sweets." Donna didn't even look up from the screen, her finger moving swiftly from letter to letter. "I can't listen to you and text. I've had too many drinkies for that!"

Not for the first time, Lizzie wondered why she had agreed to come out. Because Donna had insisted, *'because you've got to go out and meet people'*. But Lizzie would've been content to stay at home. Even though home was makeshift, it was hers.

She looked again at the hotel room. It was empty.

Minutes passed, then from the corner of Lizzie's eye, there was movement. The man was back in the window.

Donna was still intent on her phone. Lizzie placed a hand to the side of her face, as if she were merely relaxing, but instead, she was staring.

The man was wearing nothing but a towel.

Neat and white, it was tucked in at his waist and hung to just below his knees. He ran a hand through his dark hair and slowly shook his head from side to side. Even from where she was, Lizzie could see the water droplets fly away. He resumed his pose, leaning with one hand on the glass. Leaning and looking across the street at Lizzie.

Who does he see when he looks at me?

Then he lifted his hand. The palm was still facing outward as though he was about to wave but instead, he folded his thumb down, to hold up four fingers. After a few seconds had passed, he folded down two of his fingers as though giving a victory salute then, finally, held up his ring finger alongside the others.

Lizzie held her breath. Had he just signalled to her? But what?

423.

She gestured with her hand, below the level of the tabletop so that Donna wouldn't see, but the man in the hotel room could. Her hand flicked back on her wrist.

What does that mean?

But even as he signalled again, Lizzie counted up the floors to his window. He was on the fourth floor.

He was in room 423.

And he wanted her.

A warm flush spread over her skin. A prickle of desire, of recklessness. *Why not. Why bloody not?*

"I'm — I'm off now, Don."

Donna still had her head in her phone. Lizzie knew she wouldn't be missed.

She took her coat from the back of the chair, tied on her scarf, shoved on her woollen beret, pulled on her gloves.

"I've literally *just* bought you a drink!" Donna looked up from her phone, her face set in a dark pout, but then she shrugged, glancing at the screen once more. "Matt wants to grab sushi, so I'll just tell him to head over here. He can have your cocktail since you're too boring to hang around and drink it!"

"Well, yes, I *am* an extremely boring person, as you have so often told me. Bye, sis."

"Hugs!" Donna pressed a kiss to her fingers and threw it to her sister. "And behave!"

"Yes, I shall behave in my slippers, with my cocoa… Night…"

Lizzie walked out of the bar, but once she was in the corridor outside, she ran. She jabbed her finger on the lift button, her reflection showing her the boring person her sister saw. The boring woman who was running to the bedroom of a stranger.

The lift was taking an age. Lizzie had to move, had to answer the thudding of her pulse. She pulled open the doors of the staircase and ran down, two steps at a time, jumping off each bottom step, propelling herself around each landing to the next flight, down…down…

Wrapped in her winter clothes, she barely felt the intense cold when she arrived in the street. She stopped and looked up at the window again. He was still there. And he saw her. She raised her hand slightly. A small wave. Just to be sure. Just to be certain that it was her, definitely her, that he had invited.

He turned from the window, almost disappearing, and for an awful, embarrassing moment, she thought there had been a mistake. He had been signalling to someone else, someone who even now was on their way over here too. But then he was at the window again and had in each hand a glass of what looked like champagne.

Waiting for her, for Lizzie Aspinall, with a glass of chilled champagne.

She hurried across the road, over the metal tramlines, and round the corner to the hotel's grand entrance. She couldn't run here. They'd find her out. She glided up the steps, nodding to the doorman who opened the door for her.

She tried not to stare at the opulence of the reception, of its leather armchairs and palms in brass pots. Up a flight of marble stairs and to the lifts. She pressed the button.

But nothing happened.

"Not got your room card, love?"

Lizzie shrugged at the other guest, a businessman in a pinstripe suit, his hair turned grey.

He waved his card over a brass panel and the lift doors opened at once. "What floor?"

"Fourth, please."

The doors closed. The businessman got out at the second floor, nodding an acknowledgment. The lift doors closed once more, the gears and cables clanking as Lizzie ascended through the building.

A robotic voice announced the floor and the doors smoothly opened. Lizzie paused.

Am I really going to do this? Sensible, boring Lizzie?

Yes. Yes, I am.

Out onto the plush carpet. A sign straight ahead. 423 indicated to her right. She tried to steady her breathing as she got nearer, counting down the numbers on each door she passed.

427, 425, 423.

She cleared her throat and knocked.

Seconds passed. Silent seconds, the moments ticking by as the world slowed to a crawl. Then the door opened and there he was, the man in the window, the man who had summoned her. His wet hair was slicked down, droplets of water glistening on his shoulders, smoothing down the light scatter of dark hair on his torso. The depths of his dark eyes sparkled. He stepped back into the room without saying a word, holding the door open for her.

Should she say hello? Tell him her name, comment on the coldness of the weather?

No.

Lizzie followed him into the room and shut the door behind them. She pressed her back against it, recovering her breath, gazing at him. His dark eyes... there was passion there, but something tentative too. Almost unsure. Did he think she would change her mind and run away?

She was aware of his clean, masculine scent, of the presence of him. Waiting. His soft, full lips fell slightly open. Did he still want her, now that they were face-to-face?

She reached one hand towards him, her palm up. Offering him her permission.

His palm met hers, their fingers entwining. She could feel the warmth of his skin through her glove, felt the strength in his hand and the fizz of electricity in the air between them. She drew him towards her and he came to her willingly.

She brushed her free hand against the side of his neck. He leant into her caress, lowering his eyelids, and she brought her mouth to his, not quite touching, but breathing the same air. His grip on her hand tightened, his eyes opened again, and Lizzie placed her lips on his.

Something tore itself free from the sensible inside of Lizzie Aspinall. Whatever had propelled her here demanded satiation, and with a hunger she hadn't even realised that she had, she was holding the nameless man against her, kissing him with an urgency she had never felt before.

Home of Erotic Romance

Sign up for our newsletter and find out about all our romance book releases, eBook sales and promotions, sneak peeks and FREE romance books!

About the Authors

Catherine Curzon

Catherine Curzon is a royal historian who writes on all matters of 18th century. Her work has been featured on many platforms and Catherine has also spoken at various venues including the Royal Pavilion, Brighton, and Dr Johnson's House.

Catherine holds a Master's degree in Film and when not dodging the furies of the guillotine, writes fiction set deep in the underbelly of Georgian London.

She lives in Yorkshire atop a ludicrously steep hill.

Eleanor Harkstead

Eleanor Harkstead often dashes about in nineteenth-century costume, in bonnet or cravat as the mood takes her. She can occasionally be found wandering old graveyards, and is especially fond of the ones in Edinburgh. Eleanor is very fond of chocolate, wine, tweed waistcoats and nice pens. She has a large collection of vintage hats, and once played guitar in a band. Originally from the south-east, Eleanor now lives somewhere in the Midlands with a large ginger cat who resembles a Viking.

Sign up to receive their newsletter at
https://curzonharkstead.co.uk/newsletter/

Catherine and Eleanor love to hear from readers. You can find their contact information, website and author biographies at https://www.totallybound.com.